# THE MAN FROM BOOT HILL: DEAD MAN'S PROMISE

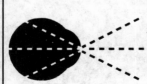

# THE MAN FROM BOOT HILL: DEAD MAN'S PROMISE

## MARCUS GALLOWAY

**THORNDIKE PRESS**
*A part of Gale, Cengage Learning*

GALE
CENGAGE Learning·

Farmington Hills, Mich • San Francisco • New York • Waterville, Maine
Meriden, Conn • Mason, Ohio • Chicago

LIBRARY OF CONGRESS CATALOGING-IN-PUBLICATION DATA

Names: Galloway, Marcus, author.
Title: The man from Boot Hill : dead man's promise / Marcus Galloway.
Description: Large print edition. | Waterville, Maine : Thorndike Press, 2016. | Series: Thorndike Press large print western
Identifiers: LCCN 2016040097| ISBN 9781410495495 (hardback) | ISBN 1410495493 (hardcover)
Subjects: LCSH: Large type books. | BISAC: FICTION / Action & Adventure. | FICTION / Westerns. | GSAFD: Western stories.
Classification: LCC PS3607.A4196 M363 2016 | DDC 813/.6—dc23
LC record available at https://lccn.loc.gov/2016040097

Published in 2016 by arrangement with Harper, an imprint of HarperCollins Publishers

Printed in the United States of America
1 2 3 4 5 6 7 20 19 18 17 16

*Many thanks to Ma & Stan,
for giving Nick his roots.*

# PROLOGUE

*Trader's Crossing, Missouri*
*1861*

It was a little place situated in a flat spot that didn't normally see much trouble from the rest of the world.

This, however, was not to be a normal day.

As far as towns went, it was little more than a bulge in the road where someone who didn't know any better decided to make their stand. The few buildings that made up Trader's Crossing were every bit as sturdy as a tent that had been pitched on a windy day.

Four buildings made up the settlement, two on each side of the road. There was a small stable that was sometimes used as a stopover for postal riders, a blacksmith who was open every other Tuesday, a restaurant, and a general store. The folks who worked those places lived on farms scattered nearby. The only other people to pay Trader's

Crossing any mind at all only did so because they were too lazy to take their business to a real town.

It was a quiet day and the air dripped with the thick, sweltering heat of a Missouri summer. When the wind was gracious enough to blow in the right direction, it cooled off those who got in its way. Other than that, folks just had to fan themselves and think of cooler times. The settlement looked all but dead on this particular day, except for the occasional creak of a door as someone poked their head out to try and catch one of those elusive breezes.

One such person was a girl with short brown hair tied back with a purple ribbon. She stood in the restaurant's doorway, lifting the hair off the back of her neck to dry up the sweat before it soiled the neckline of her dress. Just as she was about to head back inside to get back to sweeping the floors, she spotted something in the distance. The girl flattened out her hand, pressed it to her forehead to shield her eyes from the sun, and squinted to get a better look.

Sure enough, the town's population was about to increase by three.

"Betsy, get back in here," came a voice from inside the restaurant.

"Looks like someone's coming," she shouted without budging from her spot.

"Then get in here and clear off a table in case they want to eat something!"

Torn between the reflex to obey her mother and the desire to get a look at a face different from the five or six she saw every day, Betsy shuffled toward the door while keeping her eyes on the horizon.

"Betsy! NOW!"

That was enough to get the girl moving. She wasn't a child, but she was still young enough to snap to when she heard that certain tone in her mother's voice. In a swirl of light brown hair and cotton skirts, she turned her back to the rest of the world and grudgingly stomped inside.

The three riders were close enough to hear the door slam as their horses carried them down the widening trail. Of course, without much of anything around to get in the way, that slamming sound carried well past the anxious boys perched on top of those animals.

The tallest of the three boys rode in the middle with the other two flanking him and riding just a little behind. As with most fifteen-year-olds, size was still a big factor in deciding the pecking order. Nick Graves wasn't quite the tallest, but he outweighed the others by a good twenty pounds.

Nick's face was smooth and tanned to a rich, golden brown. His arms were lanky yet muscled and the scowl on his face had been put there after hours of diligent practice. He sat tall in the saddle with one hand resting on his knee while the other kept a tight hold upon the reins.

"I still say we should'a got guns for this," Nick said.

"Hey! Did you see that?" The boy who asked that had been slouched in his saddle for most of the ride. Now he sat bolt upright and raised an arm to point wildly toward the sorry excuse for a town. "That was Betsy Mills! Did you see her?"

"Shut the hell up, Joey. We got things to do and they got nothing to do with no Betsy Mills."

Joey Cooley had known the other two boys for long enough to be accepted into their inner circle. He was a lanky kid and tallest of the three. He had a narrow face and buckteeth with an unruly mess of hair on top of his head. It wasn't Nick who'd just tried to put him in his place, so Joey shifted in his saddle to get a good look at the third kid.

"I swear to God, Barrett, you wouldn't be saying that shit if'n we was off these horses."

Barrett Cobb was small enough to be the natural first choice when most other kids were looking to knock someone on his ass. It had always been that way and the only thing that had changed it was when he and Nick Graves had become close as brothers.

Leaning forward, Barrett tapped his chin and taunted, "Go ahead and swing. You couldn't hit your horse's ass with a shovel!"

As Joey leaned forward to take Barrett up on his offer, he was stopped by Nick's arm.

"Shut up, the both of you," Nick growled. "Where is this place?"

"Right there," Barrett said, pointing toward one of the small buildings. "The general store."

"You sure there's anyone there?"

"Yeah, but there ain't more than a few people in this whole place. That's what makes it so perfect. All we need to do is wait for the old man to turn his back so we can grab the money and skin out of there."

The squabbling from a few moments ago was ancient history. Joey Cooley nodded dutifully as he said, "And I'm the one who makes sure he turns his back."

"I'll hop the counter and grab the money," Nick recited.

"And I'll wait outside with the horses," Barrett finished. "Nice and easy."

11

"You always get the easy jobs, Barrett," Joey grunted.

"I'm also the one who scouted this place out. We're a gang, remember? We work together."

That caused all three of the boys to sit up straight and proud in their saddles.

"And this is gonna be worth the ride all the way over here?" Nick asked.

Barrett smiled and patted Nick on the shoulder. "I promise."

They were still sitting like kings on their thrones when they rode up to the front of the general store and came to a stop. A few faces peeked from the windows around them, but quickly lost interest when they saw the three new arrivals were barely old enough to be out on their own so far from home.

Nick swung down from his saddle and draped his reins over the post in front of the store. He strutted through the door and nodded at the old man sitting behind the counter.

Joey Cooley would have been right behind him if he hadn't taken the time to stop and stare into the restaurant. When he saw the girl with the purple ribbon in her hair peek through the door, he tipped his hat to her and gave her the best roguish smile he could muster. The sound of Barrett making loud kissing noises from atop his horse was enough to get Joey's mind back on track. He took a swing at the runt on his way into the store.

The owner of the general store was in his late fifties and had a bit of a paunch hanging over his belt. In the eyes of the three young boys, however, he was fat as a pig and older than the hills.

"Help you boys with something?" the old man asked.

"Just looking," Nick replied. When he didn't hear anything else, he turned to get a look at Joey.

Picking up on the urgency on Nick's face, Joey struggled to get the picture of Betsy Mills's face from his head so he could concentrate on the business at hand. Finally, he said, "Oh, I, uh, need some shoe polish."

"Shoe polish?"

Both Nick and Joey tensed. They'd had their doubts, but Barrett told them that shoe polish wouldn't be right up front.

The old man thought for a second before saying, "Right against the wall there on the last table."

Both boys looked around the store. Apart from the counter in front with the cash register and the old man himself, a bunch of tables filled up the space. Each table looked like it might have been made for a dining room, but was now holding anything from folded blankets and clothing to lanterns and boxes of candy.

Joey did as he was instructed and went to the table the old man had indicated. Although he'd looked pained at first, a bright smile jumped on to his face. Thankfully, it was gone by the time he'd turned around again. "Nope. It's not here."

Pulling in a deep breath, the old man got up from his stool and came around the counter. "Might've sold the last batch. Don't get much call for that sort of thing around here."

"My father needs it," Joey said like a bad actor reciting poorly written lines. "He is a preacher and will be conducting a wedding next Sunday. He needs to look his best so he can —"

"Yeah, yeah," the old man cut in as he pushed past Joey and Nick. "Let me take a look for myself."

Nick waited for the old man to bend down and start rummaging beneath the table before he ran to the front of the store and leapt over the counter. Joey stepped into the aisle to keep the old man from seeing what Nick was doing.

14

The counter was slightly lower than the fences surrounding the field where his father worked, so Nick cleared it as though it wasn't even there. His feet landed on the floor just behind the cash register and his fingers hovered shakily over the circular metal keys.

With all the planning Barrett had done, he'd never told Nick how to work a cash register.

He could hear Joey and the old man tossing words back and forth, but Nick didn't even try to figure out what they were saying. Instead, his mind was racing with what he could do to get to the riches that were supposed to be inside that damned metal contraption.

"Here it is!" the old man said victoriously. After a bit of shuffling and grunting, he was back on his feet and facing Joey with a small round tin in his hand. "I'll take this up front if you want to look around some more."

"Uhh, yeah."

"You're gonna have to get out of the way."

Nick heard that well enough, knowing it was only a matter of time before the old man got a look at what —

"Hey! What are you doing?" the old man shouted. "Get away from there!"

Aggravated to the point that his head

started to ache, Nick started jabbing at every button he could see.

The old man was trying to get to the front of the store, but was being held back by Joey Cooley's lanky arms.

"Goddamn little bastards," the old man growled.

Joey was about to toss back a few nasty words of his own, but quickly found himself being tossed to one side like a sack of flour. His feet didn't actually leave the ground when the old man pushed him. That is, they didn't leave the ground until the backs of his legs knocked into one of the other tables. Once that happened, Joey toppled over backward onto several stacks of linens and a short pile of bed warmers.

The old man was too busy to notice Joey's tumble into the next aisle. His feet slapped against the floorboards and his voice bellowed through the store like a thunderstorm. "Get away from that register! Goddamn you, get out of there!"

Nick's fingers finally found the right button, which rang a tinkling bell and shot a narrow drawer out from the bottom of the machine. The money in that drawer was more than he'd ever seen all in one place. Of course, being the son of a gravedigger, that wasn't saying a whole lot.

"Gotchya!" the old man grunted as he hustled around the counter and dropped a hand onto Nick's shoulder. His face split into a wide, victorious smile that lasted right up until Nick's fist slammed against his chin.

His fingers were still wrapped around a load of pennies and nickels when he'd balled up his fist and struck the old man. It wasn't the first time he'd hit anyone, but it was sure as hell the first time he'd punched someone who wasn't one of his peers.

The old man staggered back a step, more shocked than hurt by the punch. When he looked back up at Nick, he saw the kid staring back at him in disbelief.

Nick dropped the change into his pocket and helped himself to one of the thin stacks of bills in the drawer before the store owner came at him once again. With the sting of the first punch still working through his knuckles, Nick let out a low snarl and threw himself at the old man.

Both hands were balled up tightly and he followed up one punch with another and another. Every blow landed heavier than the first. When he saw blood trickling from the old man's nose, he let out a vicious holler. The old man staggered back until he bumped against the counter. His eyes were still open, but even Nick could see that there wasn't much of anything behind them.

Even so, Nick pulled his arm back and sent his strongest punch square into the man's face. He then used that same bloodied hand to snatch the last remaining cash from the register.

"Come on," Nick said to Joey, who was struggling to get a look behind the counter. "Let's get out of here."

When he stepped out of that store and felt the heat of the sun on his face, Nick lifted his chin and shouted as if he was baying at the moon. He was feeling too good to keep quiet and too excited to form any words. Once that howl was out of his system, he climbed into his saddle and snapped the reins.

Barrett waved anxiously toward the skinny kid rushing out of the store. "Come on, Joey, we need to skin out of here!"

Standing outside the store, Joey took the reins but didn't lift one foot toward a stirrup. Instead, he took a moment to look around at all the frightened, confused faces staring back at him through various windows and doorways. When he saw the girl with the purple ribbon in her hair, Joey tipped his hat and gave her a wink before finally jumping on to his horse's back.

"You little sons of bitches!" came a gruff voice from the general store. "Those bastards robbed me!"

Suddenly all the doors flew open and townspeople came running out of every last one. The two boys looked at the shop owners stomping out onto the street. Then they looked at each other before deciding to get the hell out of there.

The guns started going off a second later, filling Trader's Crossing with thunder and the sound of angry hornets whipping the air. By now, Barrett Cobb and Joey Cooley were in their saddles and whipping their horses like the animals had committed a crime. No matter how tired those horses were, the sting of leather and the ruckus of the gunshots caused them to blaze a trail down the street.

In a matter of seconds, they'd caught up to Nick. Once they were together, the boys found the courage that had brought them into that general store in the first place.

"Go on and scream all you want!" Nick shouted once he could tell that none of those shots were coming close to any of them. "To hell with you, old man!"

"Yeah," Joey chimed in. "I'll be back for Betsy too!"

As if an invisible line had just been

crossed, one of the shop owners managed to fire a round close enough for the boys to hear the hiss of lead somewhere near their heads. That was more than enough to encourage all three of them to put their backs to the town and keep riding until their horses were about to keel over.

When they steered off the trail at a familiar stream, they let their horses stagger over to the water and start lapping it up.

They couldn't stop laughing to save their lives. Once they'd caught their breath, Barrett asked Nick for an account of what had happened inside the general store. Nick gave him an exaggerated story, ending with an overly exciting account of how he'd beaten the old man mercilessly.

Victoriously, Nick held up his hand, which was still clenched in a tight fist. There were a few cuts on his swollen knuckles, but it was plain to see that most of the blood wasn't his. For the first time since he'd left the store, Nick uncurled his fist and held his hand out flat for the other two boys to see.

He was holding eight dollars and forty-two cents.

The three boys looked down in awe at the crumpled bills and dirty coins. It seemed like a pirate's treasure to them.

At that moment, Nick realized what he wanted to do with the rest of his life.

# ONE

*Keeler, Wyoming*
*1883*

It was easy to blend into the woodwork in a town as big as Keeler. Despite all the folks who came and went through that town, Nick Graves didn't pay much attention to the flow of people through the streets. He no longer listened to the rumors floating through town, even though he was in the best vantage point possible. He had enough weighing down upon him without taking on more weight from the rest of the world.

Nick was sitting at a table near the end of a long bar in a smoke-filled poker hall named Petunia's. At first, the name had seemed odd painted across the front of a festering hole like this one. He'd asked the curvaceous bartender about it on his first day there and she'd given him the same answer she gave to everyone else.

"Used to be flowers on every table," she'd

replied that first night. "That is, until folks started setting them on fire to light their cigars."

When it came down to it, the name didn't matter. Neither did the origin of the name. Most of the time, knowing one or the other didn't make a damn bit of difference. All that was important was that Nick could find the place because it served some of the best stew in three states and had home-brewed whiskey that he could actually stomach.

As Nick thought about his early years with Barrett Cobb, he still got a fond smile on his face. When he thought about burying that same friend not too long ago, he felt like he needed more whiskey than anyone could ever pour.

"Set you up with another round?" asked a woman with healthy curves and chestnut brown hair that flowed all the way down to the small of her back. When she leaned against the bar toward Nick, she displayed an ample bosom that was barely contained by a loosely tied peasant blouse.

"No thanks. I'm doing just fine."

"Isn't tonight Kaleb's game?"

"It is," Nick said. "As long as he shows, that is."

"After the pounding you gave him last week, I wouldn't be surprised if he's sitting at a table in Deadwood by now. Those boys would be merciful compared to you."

"A man's got to make a living, Belle."

"He sure does," Belle replied while tossing some stray hair from her face. "I heard you know an honest trade. Maybe you should practice it before you get cleaned out one way or another."

Coming from a woman like Belle, that suggestion was downright tender. Her skin was smooth and soft, but only if she was in the saloon itself. In the daylight all the creams and ointments she used were plain to see. Her rouge-tainted cheeks simply did not belong in the same light as respectable folks.

After all he'd been through, Nick figured he was in that same boat.

Belle's most recent words hung like bits of dust snagged on the cobwebs in his mind. Some of them, like "honest trade" hung heavier than others.

He did know an honest trade. It had been taught to him by his father and plied throughout different parts of the country. It was a specialized craft that was always in demand and it had earned him a place in more than one community. Unfortunately, there was even a time when he'd looked down on that trade as something so far

25

beneath him that he wouldn't even consider it.

That's how he used to think when he was younger. Actually, back then, it was only the "honest" part that had bothered Nick.

"About time for some dinner, isn't it?" Belle asked.

Glancing at the dented watch in his pocket, Nick nodded. "Fix me a steak, would you?"

"Sure thing, handsome. Maybe tonight you'll let me help you work off that meal back in my room. At least you might work off some of that liquor in your system one way or another."

"I might just take you up on that, Belle." Just then, the front door of the saloon swung open, allowing a spindly man to come in amid an unwanted torrent of sunlight. Spotting the figure instantly, Nick added, "That is, if you don't mind waiting until after my game."

Belle smiled as she caught sight of the man who'd just walked in. "He showed, huh? Try not to break him too badly, Nick. Remember, the man has a wife at home."

"Yeah," he grunted unconvincingly. "I'll try to remember that."

Nick had yet to move more than an inch or so from his spot. Even as he got a jittery wave from the man who'd just walked into Petunia's, Nick only responded with half a nod. That skinny man was the way Nick was forced to make money nowadays: off him and others like him who were just as bad at playing cards.

It was enough to earn a living, but not enough to sleep in a place better than one of the rental rooms across the street. Nick shook his head as he thought back over the course of his life. Things had gone from bad to worse, to better, to bad, to worse, to better, and now to worse again. It was an uneven chain of events that barely even made sense to the man who'd lived through it.

And that chain, much like the name of the filthy saloon where Nick was plying his new trade, didn't seem to make one damn bit of difference when everything was said and done. Nick barely even knew when night turned to day anymore. His eyes were blurred. His belly was full of cheap whiskey and his head was full of memories of the days when he'd ridden with friends who were close enough to be his brothers.

Those brothers were dead now. For the ones who Nick didn't actually kill, it had been his stupidity that had brought their lives to an end. That was some bitter medicine to swallow and sometimes the whiskey didn't even help.

"You ready for our game?" the scrawny man asked as he tried to dredge up some confidence.

Nick leaned forward so a stray bit of light fell onto his face. His eyes were sullen and his dark hair had been allowed to grow long enough to act as a stringy curtain when he was too tired to look at the world around him. Scars marked that face as well, but paled in comparison to the wounds that were his most distinguishing feature.

The hands protruding from Nick's stained sleeves looked as if they'd been chewed on by a hungry dog. Half of his left pinky was missing. The ring finger of his right hand was a gnarled nub about a quarter of its natural size. The tip of his right middle finger was gone and the parts that remained were callused and leathery.

The sight of Nick in the pale light was enough to push the scrawnier man back a step or so before he composed himself. It wasn't the first time he'd seen Nick up close, but the sight wasn't exactly easy to get used to. There were plenty of others with wounds far worse than his, but Nick's seemed to cut deeper than the scarred flesh.

"I'll be there in a little bit," Nick said, settling back into the darkness, which was one of his only real comforts these days. "Just let me finish my drink."

That cheap, nearly toxic whiskey was his other comfort.

Poker was no longer a game for Nick. It was his primary source of income. He'd always liked gambling and had gotten pretty good at it over the years. Once that hobby had become a job, the fun had leaked right out of it.

The cards fell his way because he played them all properly. There was hardly any risk involved, since the men sitting at his table were about as skilled as overeager ten-year-olds and could hide their emotions just as well. Reading everyone's faces was easier than reading a newspaper and Nick waited until just the right time to make his moves.

There was no excitement.

No adventure.

No risk.

Nothing but a bit of profit after a grueling night's work.

"Not a bad haul, huh?" Belle asked when Nick approached the table closest to the bar and slumped into his normal seat when his work was done.

There was light coming in through the

windows, but it was the light of early morning. The game had lasted throughout the entire night and the other players had already scuttled out to face the sunlight as well as the wrath of the wives waiting for them at home.

Settling behind him, Belle rested her arms over Nick's shoulders and leaned in so her breasts pressed against the back of his neck. Her hands slid down the front of his shirt and she started tussling the hair she found there. "You should be set up for a while after that game," she said, once again trying to get a reaction from him.

All she got was a half-hearted grunt.

Resting her chin on his shoulder, Belle stayed there for a moment with her hands wandering aimlessly over his chest. Finally, she spoke in a heartfelt whisper that drifted straight into his ear. "What are you doing here?" she asked.

That question caused a twitch to work through Nick's head that ended with a single word coming from his mouth. "What?"

"What are you doing here? If you were a professional gambler, you'd be a hell of a lot richer. If you were a drunk, you wouldn't be able to watch that door so intently every minute you're in here. If you were a gunfighter, you would have started some trouble by now. So what's your story? Who are you hiding from?"

Nick shifted and turned in his chair. Once he was able to look straight into her eyes, he studied her carefully.

"Why do you think I'm hiding from someone?" he asked.

"There isn't much left. In case you haven't noticed, I've been watching you pretty closely since you got here. You know why that is?"

Nick shook his head.

"Because you're not like the others who come through here. You act like you're staying, but you're ready to leave at any moment." As she spoke, Belle tapped Nick's chest as though she was sending a telegram. "You act like you're stuck here sometimes, but there's nothing tying you to this place more than any other. I give a lot of advice to folks who drink here, but the one who needs it the most doesn't ever seem to want it."

Nick relaxed and settled back into his chair. He knew that Belle's intentions were good, even if she was treading on some dangerous ground. "All right, then. I'm listening."

"Well, the first thing you need to do is

have some coffee. Too much liquor will sour your brain."

"So far, so good. I'll take a cup."

Belle stepped to one side and grabbed Nick by the wrist. She pulled him from the chair with surprisingly little effort and dragged him to the door.

"Hey," Nick grumbled. "I thought you said you'd get me some coffee."

"I am. We're just not drinking it here."

"Aw Jesus, I've had a long night and all I want is some rest."

"If you wanted rest, you would have crawled off to bed. Looks to me like you want to sit in the dark some more and I can't allow that."

"What about this place? Who's watching the bar?"

"Day shift's been here for almost an hour."

Nick looked over at the bar in disbelief. Sure enough, the fresh workers of the next shift were already in their spots and straightening up the mess from the night before. Suddenly Nick felt the weight of the last forty-eight hours land squarely upon his shoulders.

"Good Lord," he muttered. "My head's starting to hurt."

"See what I mean about too much liquor? Come on. There's a place not too far from here that serves a mean breakfast."

"I know. You mention it after every long game I play."

"And have you ever gone?"

Sighing, Nick replied, "No."

"Then I say it's high time we try it out." And without waiting for another word from Nick, she wrapped her arm around his and walked him through the door.

Nick didn't exactly feel like following her, but he was too tired to put up much of a fight. When he stepped outside, the daylight hit him like a fist in the face and he recoiled from it instinctively. After a few more steps, the warmth began to seep into his skin and he was able to open his eyes a little more.

Although he'd been in Keeler for a while, Nick felt like he was looking at the place for the first time. The folks on the street were going about their lives without a care in the world, occasionally shooting a troubled glance in his direction. When Nick glanced down at himself, he could see why.

His clothes were grungy and clinging to him like moss to the underside of a fallen log. His hair stirred a bit in the breeze, but most of it was plastered to his scalp. Suddenly he became aware of the stubble on his chin. When he reached up to rub the back of his hand along his cheek, he was surprised to find the growth to be even longer than he'd expected.

"Things tend to slip past you when you lock yourself away, don't they?" Belle pointed out. "I take a shine to a rugged-looking man, but you struck me as someone who needed to get out and get some fresh air."

"I get plenty of fresh air."

"Walking to and from a boardinghouse doesn't count. Besides," she added while tapping Nick's temple playfully, "the air isn't too fresh when you pull it in through all the smoke and whiskey that've been filling your head lately."

They made it to the front of a little restaurant when Nick stopped and began fussing with his shirt and jacket. "Maybe I should clean up first," he said.

Belle smiled and moved around so she was standing directly in front of him. "That's the spirit, but I think you need to have something in your belly first. Besides, I'm worried that you might slink away somewhere before I get a chance to have a word with you."

Pausing before walking into the restaurant, she straightened Nick up and pushed his hair into place. Although Nick was rolling his eyes at her, she smiled approvingly.

The restaurant was a little place with less than a dozen tables. Nick didn't even catch the name on the front window before he sat down and positioned himself toward the door. Absently, he shifted the holster around his waist and then settled the rest of the way into his seat.

"That's another way I knew you were running from someone," she said quietly.

"What's that?"

Nodding toward the gun, she replied, "The way you check that pistol when you sit down, just to make sure it's still there."

Most folks didn't think much about the gun at Nick's side. It wasn't much to look at since the handle was chipped and broken off to a nub of what it should have been. The hammer, barrel, and cylinder all seemed to have been pieced together from other weapons like a quilt stitched together from rags. Most of those pieces came from Schofield pistols, but a few of the bits were custom-made. The leather of the holster was stretched and worn in odd places, holding itself together out of sheer loyalty to the man wearing it.

The pistol looked more like junk than anything dangerous and Belle was in the small percentage of those who regarded it for more than an instant. Seeing that weapon around Nick's waist was the only thing to take the smile from her face.

When she looked up again, she pulled in a breath and said, "I have something to confess. I know who you are and I've got a pretty good idea of why you're here."

Those were the words that Nick had been hoping not to hear. The fact that they came from Belle made things even worse.

# Two

*Ellis Station, Missouri*

The town hadn't always been called Ellis Station. When it had been founded three decades ago, it was known as Saunders Pass. It had only been a few years since the railroad had pushed through the area. Ever since then, things started changing on a daily basis. Once the workers had moved on and the tracks were laid, the dust settled and folks were allowed to try and get back to the way things had been before there was a steel path cutting through their land.

Of course, like plenty of other towns before it, Saunders Pass quickly realized that there was no going back. The wheels of progress had left their mark and there would be plenty more wheels rolling through in the years to come. Some folks had moved on, only to be replaced by the workers who'd decided to stay. After all was said and done, the town had a new building alongside the new tracks as well as a new gateway to the rest of the country.

Quiet mornings and tranquil nights became filled with the rattle of wheels against iron bars and the shrill cry of train whistles. The freshly cut boards of the new platform were beaten into the ground by new boots every few days. It was a time when Ellis Station was setting its sights on truly blossoming from the damp Missouri soil. It was a time when the cosmopolitan set began making bold predictions about the town's future.

Those hopes and a whole lot more were blown to bits when a gang of outlaws got the bright idea of robbing the train ten miles outside of town. They planted a bit of dynamite on Parker Bridge, hoping to bust the tracks and stop the train so getting on and off the locomotive would be no problem. Instead, they had to sift through what was left from the twisted steel and smoking remains of the train and its passengers at the bottom of a gorge.

The outlaws' dynamite had taken out Parker Bridge altogether, turning the train into a junk pile, the folks aboard it into ghosts, and the town of Ellis Station back to the old days before the constant clatter of wheels and the shrill cry of whistles. In fact, since the railroad wasn't interested in rebuilding a bridge when there was another spot to cross a bit farther along, the town was quieter than ever.

Some folks missed the prosperity and promise of the railroad. Others liked the old days better. All of them agreed on one point, however.

There was no turning back now.

The two-eleven stage from St. Louis was more or less on time, since it was always ten minutes late. The tardiness was so absolute that it was almost like clockwork.

Coming to a stop at the old train platform, the stagecoach creaked and wobbled until the doors finally opened and its passengers were allowed outside of the bouncing wooden box. One of the less agitated souls to step onto the platform was a man in his late thirties who was dressed in a manner that put him somewhere between the suited businessman who'd practically fallen out of the stage and the more rumpled couple who seemed perfectly comfortable throughout even the roughest spots of the ride.

The man in his thirties tugged at his dark brown jacket while clearing the way for the other passengers to claim the bags being tossed from the top of the stage. He looked up at the sign welcoming him to Ellis Station and pulled in a lungful of air that smelled of horseflesh and rotten timber.

Two other men exited the stagecoach, causing the springs beneath the carriage to groan appreciatively. One was a tall man with dark skin and the other had stringy blond hair that stuck out like dry straw from under his hat. Although these two wore their guns in plain sight around their waists, the man in his thirties wore his jacket so it covered all but the bottom tip of his holster. The businessman and younger couple who'd shared the stage with them quickly gathered up their things and didn't breathe easier until they were well away from the armed men.

"Well, this isn't quite what I expected," the man in his thirties said. When he spoke, the waxed mustache on his upper lip wavered slightly and the patch of hair running down the middle of his chin twitched like an anxious spider.

"You sure this is the place, Warren?" asked the bigger of the two other men. His clothes hung on his dark-skinned frame the way a blanket hung over a horse. They covered him, but with no extra frills. A plain cotton shirt stretched across his chest and sleeves were rolled up to reveal thick, muscular forearms and beefy hands. His face was covered with thick, dark stubble.

The man in his thirties nodded. "Yeah. This is it."

The blond looked around and grimaced. His skin was burned to a reddish hue, which showed that he wasn't predisposed to spending too much time in the sun. Flakes crusted along the edges of his forehead and blisters marred the back of his neck. Judging by the expression he wore, he was feeling every bit of the punishment the sun had given to him. "Then let's get to work. I'm already sick of this shit hole."

The days were getting longer and warmer. After weathering the biting cold of a harsh winter, every extra minute of sunlight was appreciated by every warm-blooded soul living under it. Some folks felt such differences right down to their bones and one such man was walking along the main street of Ellis Station with a smile on his face.

He walked the familiar path, knowing the texture of every battered board beneath his feet before his heels even touched them. He'd walked that same route so many times that he could do so blindfolded. As he made his rounds, he nodded to the locals along the way who were so entrenched in their own routines that they would have nodded back even if he wasn't there.

On instinct, the man broke his stride, stepped through a doorway, and entered the Saunders Hotel. The door was propped open with a set of books that had been stuck together after being left out in the rain too many times. The man stepped over the leather-bound doorstop and placed both hands flat on the chipped edge of the front desk.

"Why the long face, Nate?" the man asked the portly fellow on the other side of the desk.

Nate's face was naturally long. Although he wasn't an old man by any means, the hotel's owner wore his years badly and they tended to pull his cheeks down as though something was trying to drag him to the floor by his chin. When he shook his head, the loose skin around his neck waggled. "Nothing, Sheriff. Nothing for you to worry about."

Still wearing a bit of the smile that he'd had during his walk, Sheriff Bristow kept one hand on the desk as he shifted on his feet to lean with his hip against the dented wood. "Come on now. I could tell something was bothering you from outside. What's the matter? Did some troublemakers come in from St. Louis on the last stage?"

Nate's head snapped back as though he'd

been rapped on the nose. His eyes reflexively darted toward the stairs leading to the upper rooms and he shifted nervously upon his feet. "How'd you know?"

"Jesus, Nate, I was only kidding. Did I hit close to the mark?"

"More like dead center."

The sheriff reached out for the register, which was still open, on the desk. He pulled the book close enough to read it and glanced over the most recent entries. "Did they sign in?"

"They sure did."

"None of these names ring a bell. What's the trouble?"

"They were wearing guns."

"I've been trying to get folks to stop wearing guns in town, but that'll take some time."

"No no. Not just that. They looked like the sort who knew how to use them. Plus they were asking about old Stan."

After a moment of thinking, Bristow asked, "The gravedigger?"

Nate nodded, causing his face to wiggle in another direction. "I just didn't like the looks of them."

The sheriff had no trouble noticing the way Nate kept glancing toward the stairs. Right about then, he heard the sound of heavy footsteps coming from that same direction. Sheriff Bristow kept a casual look on his face as he shifted his weight so he could lean with his backside against the edge of the desk. Although his hands were placed upon the desk behind him, they weren't too far from the guns at his side.

When he set his eyes on the men coming down the stairs, Bristow smiled just enough to lift the edges of his bushy salt-and-pepper mustache. He reached up with one finger to tip the edge of his hat, showing a hint of gray mixed in with his otherwise coal-black hair.

The three men filed down the stairs. Warren returned Bristow's gesture with a tip of his own hat. The other two glanced at the sheriff's badge first and by the time they managed to look at his face, they seemed ready to spit in it.

Once the three walked through the front door, Bristow took half a step outside so he could watch where they went. He pulled his head back into the hotel just when the biggest of the other men was starting to glance back at him.

"Those the men you were talking about?" Bristow asked.

Nate nodded while nervously glancing at the door. "That'd be them."

"It couldn't hurt to watch them for a bit. Would that put your mind to rest?"

Already, Nate was starting to act more like his normal self. His smile was as ugly as it was genuine and he nodded enthusiastically. "They're probably just on their way to the saloon. Guess I'm getting a little fidgety after those rustlers came through here last spring."

"Well, don't get too worked up," Bristow said as he tapped the desk and headed for the door. "I'll make sure they don't try to shoot out those new windows you just put in."

The teasing tone in Bristow's voice was enough to put the hotel owner's mind at ease. Catching a glimpse of the lawman's crooked smile allowed Nate to let out the breath he'd been holding for the last several minutes.

Sheriff Bristow stepped onto the board-walk and fell into an easy stride. The good mood that had been working its way through his system had now managed to find its way out again. The Missouri air would soon be thick with heat that wrapped around the locals like a familiar, albeit soggy, blanket. For now, though, the sun was bright without being brutal and the nights still took on a pleasant chill.

Springtime was a time for stepping out and enjoying the warmth. It worked that way for the good and lawless alike. All kinds enjoyed a pleasant night, just as all kinds sought shelter in the dead of winter. Now it seemed that wickedness knew no season and was just as happy to intrude on his good day as it was to shatter a quiet night.

All of this went through his mind in a rush. He hadn't taken more than a dozen steps along the boardwalk when he caught sight of that big fellow up ahead turning to check over his shoulder. He spotted the sheriff instantly and muttered something to the other two.

In a matter of seconds, the man at the front of the group stopped in his tracks and listened to what the bigger one had to say. As they conversed among themselves, all three of them started looking back to where Sheriff Bristow was standing.

This didn't look good to the lawman. Not good at all.

But the sheriff wasn't about to break his stride and was soon coming up behind the other three. Just as he was getting close enough to hear what they were saying to each other, all three of them turned around and looked him straight in the eyes.

"Afternoon, Sheriff," Warren said. "Fine

day, isn't it?"

"Sure is," Bristow replied with an easy grin. "I don't think I've seen you boys around here before. You just get in?"

"We sure did."

"The name's Bristow. I'm sheriff around here."

"Yeah," grunted the smallest of the three. "We could tell by the badge on yer chest."

After giving the other man a subtle shake of his head, the leader shifted his focus back onto the lawman. "I'm Warren Wheatley. These are my associates, Deacon and Bo."

The bigger man nodded to the first of those names and the blond acknowledged the second.

Deacon was a big enough fellow in his own right, but carried himself in a way that seemed to add several pounds to his frame and a few inches to his posture. His skin was a dark mix that made it next to impossible to guess his lineage and the cruel glint in his eyes discouraged anyone in their right mind from asking him about it.

"Pleased to meet you fellas," Bristow said in a friendly drawl. "Care to mention what brings you to Ellis Station?"

Warren put on a neighborly façade. "We're here to pay someone a visit, Sheriff. Nothing too interesting."

"Really? Who is it you're after? Maybe I could point you in the right direction."

"No need to point," Warren said. "We know our way." With that, he tipped his hat and put his back to the sheriff.

The other three followed suit and turned the next corner.

Sheriff Bristow waited a few seconds before going after them. It didn't take long to spot them again, especially since they were headed for a less busy part of town. He followed them all the way down Mercantile Avenue to a storefront wedged in between the town's newspaper office and a candle maker.

It was the undertaker's parlor.

# THREE

"Can I help you fellows?" asked a stout man in his late forties. Although his face was devoid of the lines that would betray anyone else's age, the wariness in his eyes hinted at the weight on his shoulders. A ring of thinning gray hair wrapped from behind one ear to the other and a few stray wisps crawled up over the top.

Warren stepped into the parlor just enough for his other two partners to come in behind him. Even after he'd planted his feet on the wood floor, his eyes were still darting around to take in his surroundings.

The room was fairly large and mostly open. Several rows of empty chairs filled the front portion of the room just beyond the entrance. In the back of the room, there was a large oval table in one corner and the other corner was sectioned off from the rest by a dark velvet curtain. In between them was a table just big enough to hold an open casket that was currently empty.

As with most others who came into the parlor for the first time, Warren and his men found themselves focusing more on the casket than anything else.

The stout man was dressed in a simple black suit. The only accessory on him was the silver watch chain that crossed his belly. After waiting for an acceptable amount of time in silence, he cleared his throat and spoke a little louder. "Excuse me. Is there something I can do for you gentlemen?"

Shaking himself away from the pall that was creeping over him, Warren centered his gaze upon the stout man in front of him. "I'm looking for someone."

"If this person is among the dearly departed, I don't have a service scheduled for another —"

"No," Warren interrupted. "He's still alive. At least, for now. Who are you?"

Snapping to attention and putting on a friendly smile, the stout man extended his hand. "Harold Abernathy. I'm . . ." Harold's words were cut off as Warren took his hand and gripped it as though he was going to pull off his arm. "I'm the undertaker for Ellis Station," he continued in a slightly wavering voice. "Have been for quite a while."

Warren's eyes narrowed as he took a good, long look at Harold's face. Leaning in, Warren pulled Harold closer as if he meant to peer into his eyes and take a glimpse at his soul. Finally, he shook his head and all but pushed Harold away. "You got anyone working for you, Harold?"

Now the undertaker was starting to look nervous. "If you're looking for work, I really can't help you. I hear there's jobs to be found at the —"

"I told you already," Warren interrupted. "We're looking for someone. That someone should be working here and if he ain't you, then he's got to be someone who works for you. Does that make sense or do we need to start looking around for ourselves?"

Hearing that, the other two men who'd come in with Warren stepped forward. A light shone in their eyes as their hands flexed in anticipation of all the possibilities for damage they could inflict upon the well-maintained parlor.

Even though it was plain to see that Harold rarely ventured from the tidy confines of his business, he picked up on the threat in Warren's voice easily enough. "No need for that. I'm sure this is a misunderstanding."

Bo had had enough. He stepped around

Warren and made sure to knock against Harold's shoulder as he walked past him. The impact was sharp and strong enough to knock the undertaker back half a step. "You got anyone working for you or not?"

"Y . . . yes. I do," replied the flustered undertaker. "But he can't be the man you're after. He's a good fellow and a hard worker. I'd vouch for him against anything you think he might have done."

Leaning over to place himself between Harold and Warren, Bo put himself nose to nose with the undertaker. "Where is he?"

Harold's eyes flitted like butterflies trapped in his skull. They darted around to all three of the new arrivals, the door through which they'd come, and every other possible spot in between. Nervous breaths came into his throat just so he could swallow them down again like a man who hadn't seen a drop of water in weeks.

Finally, Harold's eyes fixed upon a point behind Warren and Deacon. Only then did he let out the breath he'd been about to choke on. "Good afternoon, Sheriff," he said with the relief of a man whose prayers had just been answered. "What can I do for you?"

Standing just outside the doorway to the funeral parlor, Sheriff Bristow straightened up so that he nearly filled the entire space. His guns were still in the double-rig holster, but his hand was close enough to it to send a message that he could be heeled at a moment's notice.

"Afternoon, Harold," Bristow said. "I see you've got some visitors."

"Yes, they were just . . . well . . . they said they're looking for someone."

"So I hear." Shifting his eyes to Warren, the sheriff looked at him expectantly.

"I told you we've got our own business to conduct," Warren said in a voice that was close to a snarl.

"So do I," Bristow replied. "And so long as your business stays nice and proper, there's no reason for me to step in. Until then, I'll just stand here and wait for my turn to have a word with Mr. Abernathy."

Quiet until this very moment, Deacon wheeled around on the balls of his feet. The movement was quicker than anyone might have expected coming from a man of his size. As sudden as it had started, the movement was over just as quick once Deacon was glaring straight into the sheriff's eyes. "You're following us and there's no reason for it."

Sheriff Bristow didn't back down from the other man's glare. Instead, he took a step forward until he was close enough to feel the hate pouring from Deacon's eyes. When he spoke, all the civility had drained from the lawman's voice. "You're damn right I followed you. Conduct your business like gentlemen and I'll apologize. Step out of line too far and you'll wind up on Harold's table over there."

Putting on a smile that would have been more comfortable on a snake, Warren said, "We'd just like to meet this man who works for you, Mr. Abernathy. No need for all of us to —"

But nobody else in the room seemed to hear any of that. Deacon was squaring off with the sheriff and Bo was moving around to do the same. Before Warren could say another word, Deacon had already reached out with both arms to knock Sheriff Bristow a few feet back.

The shove felt like two posts being jabbed into the lawman's shoulders. Even though he resisted the impact, Bristow was still forced out of the doorway and on to the boardwalk outside.

That brought an angry snarl to Bristow's lips as his hand slapped down upon the grip of his pistol. "You touch me again and it'll be the last time."

Deacon flashed a challenging smirk and

took a step outside as well. "Do your worst, old man."

"Deacon! Bo!" Warren shouted. "Don't make another move! You hear me?"

The other men weren't listening. They were too distracted by the fight that was brewing outside the parlor. It was like a scent that drifted through the air and teased the most primitive part of every man's soul. It was the scent that formed crowds around angry drunks and turned standoffs into bloodbaths.

Already, the normally quiet stretch of street was attracting curious folks who'd caught a hint of that scent for themselves. People stopped on the boardwalk. Faces started poking out from nearby windows.

After patting Deacon on the shoulder, Bo moved past the bigger man so he could step outside. The expression on his face showed that he was anxious for the confrontation to hit the next plateau. An insult was on his lips and ready to be spit out when it was stopped by the *clang* of steel against wood.

Sheriff Bristow's eyes snapped toward the source of the sound, which was inside the parlor. The other four men turned to get a look at what had caused this interruption. All they found was a grizzled man in dusty work clothes holding a dirty shovel in his hands. That shovel slid off the edge of the table it had just been smacked against to tap against the floor.

"There," the man said in a voice that was quiet yet solid. "Maybe they can hear you now."

For a second, Warren didn't catch the other man's meaning. Then he turned to look back to where his other two partners were standing. "Don't make another move," he repeated. Although Bo and Deacon hardly even budged, their muscles relaxed under their skin and the violence in the air seemed to recede.

"Get in here," Warren said when he felt the storm pass.

Neither of the other two was eager to respond to the scolding tone in Warren's voice, but they did as they were told.

Sheriff Bristow could read those other two well enough to know the threat was still hanging ominously overhead.

"And who might you be?" Warren asked in an overly polite manner that fooled no one.

The man with the shovel wore a plain cotton shirt that had once been white. Now it was yellowed by a mixture of sweat and dirt. The sleeves were rolled up to expose a set of thick arms covered with coarse gray hair. Those arms were relaxed for the moment, although the dust and splinters were still flying from the blow he'd delivered to the edge of the casket display table. "I work for Mr. Abernathy," the grizzled man said. "And if you want trouble, you can go somewhere else."

Shifting on his feet as though everyone else in the room had disappeared, Warren walked up to the older man. "What's your name, gravedigger?"

The lines in the older man's face deepened as he watched Warren approach. His grip tightened around the chipped handle of his shovel. "I am Stasys."

"You got a last name?"

"I do."

"You want to tell me what it is?"

After a moment of looking at the men who were now all staring at him, Stasys straightened his back and said, "No."

Now that he had a new target in his sights, Bo practically tripped over himself to get back into the parlor and head toward Stasys. "We tried to do this the polite way and nobody wants to help. If'n we need to bust some heads, that's fine by me."

Stasys's knuckles whitened around the shovel's handle. In the next instant, his arms were swinging the tool with expert precision. Rather than smack against the table one more time, the rusted metal blade cut through the air and chewed into the floor in the exact spot where Bo's foot was going to land.

Surprised by the older man's quickness, Bo had to struggle to maintain his balance while finding another spot to place his next step. That was done easily enough, but he didn't look too happy about it.

"Stan has been working for me for years," Harold said, mutilating the other man's name. Reaching out to place his hand upon Bo's shoulder, he said, "Please, let's just —"

In a swift motion, Bo reached up and grabbed Harold's hand, clamping it in place. His other hand reached for his gun, but was stopped by the unmistakable *click* of another pistol's hammer being thumbed back.

"You boys have worn out your welcome," Sheriff Bristow said.

Warren, Bo, and Deacon all looked back at the lawman with venom in their stares. The latter two shot a quick glance toward Warren and got a subtle shake of the head for a reply.

"We don't want any trouble," Warren said. "And we don't want to stay where we're not wanted. Come on, fellas. I could use a drink." To Stasys and Harold, he added, "You two can join us if you like. Just to prove that there's no hard feelings." Then Warren walked toward the door as though there wasn't a single gun drawn or a harsh word in the air.

Keeping their eyes on the lawman and Stasys, Bo and Deacon followed Warren. Before stepping outside, Bo fixed his eyes on Stasys and kept them there.

Stasys held his ground — and his shovel — without so much as acknowledging the lethal promise in Bo's eyes.

And in the next moment, all of the strangers were gone.

Only after he watched Warren and the other two cross the street and turn a corner did Sheriff Bristow ease the hammer of his pistol back into place and fit the gun into its holster. "Do you know those men?" Bristow asked the undertaker.

Harold shook his head. "I've never seen them before. What on earth would possess them to come in here like that? Who are they after?"

The sheriff's face was a stony mask. Still on edge from having to draw his gun, he ignored the undertaker's continuing rambling. "What about you, Stan?"

"Why would I know such men? I dig graves and fill them up again."

"I know, but they said they were after someone who works for Harold here and you're the only one who fits that description."

Stasys's hands had relaxed and he now leaned on the shovel as though he needed it to stay upright. "I dig graves," he repeated with a sigh. His voice was like gnarled wood, textured further by a thick European accent that curled his syllables noticeably. "Anything else and I would tell you. I follow the law, Sheriff."

"All right, Stan."

Looking to Harold, Stasys asked, "Can I go back to work now, Mr. Abernathy?"

The undertaker ran his fingers through the wisps of hair plastered to his head by a thick layer of sweat. "Sure, sure," he said with exasperation. "And after all these years, why do I need to keep asking you to call me by my first name?"

Stasys opened his mouth slightly, but stopped short as though the words he meant to say had sprouted hooks and latched onto his tongue. Lowering his head, he pulled in a breath before looking up again with a strained expression.

"Just a suggestion," Harold said, knowing

that trying to correct Stasys's ways was like trying to gently nudge a wagon out of a set of deep tar-filled ruts. "Can you think of any reason why men like that would come looking for you?"

"They don't want me," Stasys said without a doubt in his mind.

"What about your boy?" Bristow asked.

"They make a mistake. That's all."

Bristow nodded. Seeing that, along with the nod from Harold, was enough to get Stasys moving. He picked up the shovel, swung it over his shoulder, and walked out through the back door from which he'd entered. The narrow door shut on well-oiled hinges to blend in almost perfectly with the rest of the wall.

Harold was already walking over to look at the spots where Stasys's shovel had knocked against the floor and table. Shaking his head, he fussed with the nicked portions of wood as though they were the biggest of his worries. "Those men will come back. I can feel it in my bones."

"The best way to get rid of 'em is to know what they want," Bristow pointed out. "You sure you can't help me?"

Still concerned with the nicks to his floor and furniture, Harold shook his head. "If I knew, I'd tell you, Sheriff. So would Stan."

"Yeah. I know." Even though he said that, Sheriff Bristow didn't seem to put much feeling into those words. But when he saw that he wasn't going to get much else from either man, he shook his head and declared, "I'll keep an eye on those three, but I can't promise they won't be back. If there's any trouble, you be sure to let me know."

"Will you be checking back here from time to time?" Harold asked hopefully.

"Sure thing. And tell Stan I didn't mean to cast any dispersions. He's always been a good sort."

"I'll tell him."

Before leaving the parlor, Bristow walked to the back door. Opening it, he looked outside to find a small shack less than twenty paces from the parlor's back steps. Stasys's shovel was leaning against the shack and the older man was hard at work arranging clean cross-shaped stones into a row.

Bristow knew there wasn't anything else left for him to do. "I'll send one of my deputies by later," the lawman said.

"All right. Thank you, Sheriff."

Bristow left the parlor and walked down the street. There were still plenty of folks milling about outside, whispering back and forth about the bit of excitement they'd seen. He headed for the first local he saw whom he knew had been standing there for a good while. With a tip of his hat, he flashed a friendly grin to the young woman that was immediately returned.

"Afternoon, Maddy," Bristow said.

The young woman was the type whose natural instinct was to cringe a bit when someone spoke to her directly. Even so, she warmed up quickly to the lawman. "Afternoon, Sheriff."

"Did you see what was going on out here earlier?"

"You mean with those three strangers? I sure did. I hope nobody got hurt."

"Just some bruised pride, is all."

Maddy smiled at that and started to go about her own business.

Bristow stopped her with a quick, yet gentle, "One more thing, Maddy."

She stopped and turned.

"Did you see those three men leave here?" Bristow asked.

Maddy nodded while reflexively looking down the street. "They headed off that way," she said while nodding toward the busier section of town. "All three of them stomped down there and turned onto Third Street."

With a tip of his hat, Sheriff Bristow started walking in that direction himself.

"Thanks, Maddy. Tell your brothers I said hello."

"I will, Sheriff. Be careful."

With a little steam on his stride, Sheriff Bristow was able to catch up to the men in the space of a minute. Even in a crowd, however, the wiry blond man would have been hard to miss. He was leaning against the front of the post office, watching the street with slowly roving eyes.

Sheriff Bristow made no attempt to keep out of Bo's sight as he walked down the street. On the contrary, he made a point to tip his hat to the blond before taking up a spot on the opposite side of the street. From there, Bristow was not only able to watch the blond, but was also able to get a good look through the large front window of the post office.

The other two were in there, all right. By the looks of it, they were conducting their business without kicking up as much dust as they had earlier. Since he wasn't anxious to start trouble, Bristow stayed where he was.

Bo lifted one hand, curled his fingers into the shape of a gun, and took an imaginary shot at the lawman.

Inside the post office, Warren and Deacon

stood at the tall counter that stretched across the entire front of the room. Behind the counter, a young man with spectacles and tussled brown hair was rummaging through a pile of papers.

"When do you want to head back to that undertaker's place?" Deacon asked.

"No need for that," Warren replied in a voice that was just loud enough to reach the other man. "We got what we needed the first time around."

"You mean that old-timer with the shovel? He's probably just some gravedigger. There's other towns around. Maybe we should check them before sending word."

This time there was an edge to Warren's voice that even caught the attention of the bespectacled man behind the counter. "I told you there was no need for that. We found who we were after."

Deacon glanced at the young man, who'd found what he'd been looking for and was now slowly approaching the counter. "You sure that was him?"

Warren nodded. "I'm sure." His arm snapped out like a whip and he plucked the paper from the young man's hand. "And when Red gets here, there'll be plenty more graves being dug around this place."

# FOUR

A pot of hot coffee and a basket of biscuits were brought to Nick and Belle's table by a young girl in her early teens. She looked at them both with mild disinterest after taking their order. She then walked off and found something else to do in another part of the room.

Once the young girl was gone, Nick leaned forward and spoke in a harsh whisper. "So, why the sudden interest?"

"From what I know about you, you're an interesting fellow."

"What do you know about me?"

"First of all, I know your name is Nicolai Graves."

Hearing that name, even though it was his own, made Nick's eyes narrow and his hand wander an inch or so closer to his gun.

Belle went on nevertheless. If she noticed the movement of Nick's hand, she didn't give a sign. "I also know that you're wanted by some men who belong at the end of a noose."

"And how did you come by this information?"

"I've kept my eyes open and I pay attention to everything that goes on in my place." Glancing up at the waitress as she walked by, Belle stirred some sugar into her coffee before adding, "I'm also real good at guessing."

Nick let out the breath he'd been holding and took a sip of coffee for himself. The hot liquid washed away the taste of stale whiskey and cigarette smoke that had become as much a part of him as the dirt on his face. Already, his eyesight was starting to clear up.

"You act differently around me, Nick. You let your guard down just enough to show me a few pieces until I've got enough to put together a picture. My guess is that part of the reason you never leave Petunia's is because most folks in there don't give a damn one way or another about anyone else."

Noticing the look on Nick's face, Belle raised her coffee cup in victory.

"How do you know so much?" Nick asked.

"Because that's the same reason I started working there. I got so comfortable that I just bought a share of the place until I became the one running it. I'm also one of the only ones in there who doesn't drink themselves into a stupor every night, so I see every little thing that happens. Even the best of them tend to get sloppy when they've been drunk for days on end."

Shaking his head, Nick wondered if he was actually slipping or if he'd meant for this moment to come without even knowing it. "And what about those men looking for me? How'd you come to that conclusion?"

"Well," Belle said, shifting in her seat as though she was playing a well-played hand of cards one by one. "Your hand moves to that gun when strangers come in or look at you for too long. You've twitched like that a few times when the law walked by, but not too much. Mostly it's toward the unsavory types."

"Good guess," Nick said in a resigned grumble. "What now?"

"Now is the part where I do something that goes against every fiber of my being."

Nick's eyes focused on Belle even harder.

"I think you should pull your head out of the hole you've buried for yourself and try to face up to whatever it is that you're running from," Belle said without flinching under Nick's hard stare. "Since that means waking up from the whiskey haze that's been around you, I might just be running off one of my favorite customers."

The laugh came from the back of Nick's throat like a cough. It scratched and burned for a moment, but only because it had been a long time since he'd made that particular noise.

Belle smiled when she saw the awkward way that Nick tried to regain his composure. In no time at all, she was laughing right along with him. "You see?" she said after catching her breath. "You look like a new man already. What in God's green earth could turn you into the lump that's been growing at one of my tables over the last few weeks?"

Nick's mind drifted back to his old friend Barrett Cobb. Like two pictures melted together, he saw the kid who'd raised hell with him back in Trader's Crossing along with the bloody face that was now wrapped in a box six feet under the ground. "It's a long story."

"I don't mind listening."

Slowly, the smile faded from Nick's face. It was replaced by a haunted, faraway look in his eyes that made it seem as though he wasn't even looking at anything that anyone else could see. Catching himself drifting off,

Nick forced himself back into the present and took another sip of coffee.

"Well, maybe I mind telling it," he said.

Belle reached out for one of Nick's hands. He twitched back reflexively, but not because of the wounds that had turned his fingers into gnarled stumps. When she finally did take hold of his hand, Belle looked at him with a softness that Nick hadn't seen in all the time he'd spent haunting that saloon.

"Whatever you did," she told him, "it can't be as bad as you think it is. And even if it's more horrible than I could imagine, you still need to face up to it."

"I used to think that too," Nick said, turning his hand so he could wrap his remaining fingers around Belle's. "I thought I needed to hunt down my demons, look them square in the eye, and tell them to go straight back to hell. But sometimes a man's demons are stronger than he is. When I found one of mine, it turned out to be one of my best friends."

"What happened?"

"I killed him."

Nick closed his eyes for a moment and drifted back to the last time he'd spoken with the friend in question. "It was a mess," Nick said with a weary shake of his head.

"But most things turned into a mess where Barrett was concerned. Things got out of hand." Nick's mouth was open, but the rest of his words refused to come out.

"Are you talking about Barrett Cobb?" Belle asked, saving him from whatever he was struggling to say.

Nick's eyes snapped open and his grip tightened around Belle's hand. "What the hell do you know about it?"

"Only that some men came through town a while back asking about you. I heard them talking and they mentioned Barrett Cobb's name. I've heard of him, Nick. He was a killer and a thief."

"Yeah. He was."

"I'm sure you didn't have a choice. Whatever happened, I'm sure that you did your best for things to turn out better."

Nick winced a bit. Without meeting her gaze, he said, "I don't think you'd care so much if you knew what kind of man I was."

Her hand tightened around his elbow and then slipped down to his forearm. "You're not that man anymore. Whatever you might have done, you're not a wicked soul. Otherwise, you wouldn't be stewing over all those things from the past. You need to put your demons to rest."

It wasn't the first time someone had said

that to Nick Graves. It wasn't even the first time he'd thought it for himself. At that moment, however, it felt like the first time that he'd actually heard it. "I've been trying," he said. "Believe me, I've been trying. Maybe I just don't deserve the salvation set aside for most folks."

"Or maybe you've just buried that part of you so deep that it's going to take someone else to dig it out again."

"I suppose that'd be you?" Nick asked suspiciously.

Belle shook her head. "As much as I'd like to try, I don't think I'd get too far."

"Why?"

Leaning forward, Belle took hold of Nick's other hand. "You can't tell me that, in all the time you've been around and all the places you've been, there wasn't someone who got to you like nobody else. There's got to be someone you think about when you're staring at the bottom of a bottle who keeps you from drowning yourself in it. I've got to tell you, Nick, that I've seen too many men walk into my place and drink themselves into their graves. They're too far gone to listen to me or anyone else and you're getting real close to joining them."

Once again Nick let out a laugh. It was the dry, humorless kind. "Most folks would just tell me I drink too much."

"That's not the problem, Nick. Some folks drink, some crawl into an opium pipe, and others put guns to their heads. All of them are just looking for a quick way to forget about the messes they made. You need to fix those messes rather than make them worse. That's the only way you'll see clearly again."

Belle's voice lingered in Nick's mind for a few seconds. It lasted right until the young girl came back to drop two plates unceremoniously on to the table. She walked away just as Nick pulled his hands free and switched the plates so they were in front of the person who'd ordered them.

"So, how long have you been preparing this little conversation?" Nick asked.

"Right about the time when you stopped bugging me to get my hands on some of that vodka you insist on drinking and started tossing back the cheap bar whiskey I serve to everyone else. It just seemed like you stopped caring and that's never good."

Taking a bite of her fried eggs and bacon, she smirked and added, "Clean yourself up and stop acting like a lump on a chair. Things will look better to you when you do, but I'm not about to hunt down a bottle of that stuff you insist on drinking."

"Fair enough."

With that, Nick and Belle ate their breakfast like two normal folks enjoying a meal together. Belle did most of the talking and that was perfectly fine with Nick. It was the first time he'd actually tasted his breakfast in well over four months.

They finished their meal, paid the damages, and left the restaurant. Nick still didn't know the name of the place, but his belly was full and he was feeling more human than he had in quite a while. Walking outside, Nick stood on the edge of the boardwalk and gazed out at the street in front of him.

It wasn't a particularly inspirational sight, but all the little details were jumping out to catch Nick's eye. The faces, the horses, the shops — they all offered him a range of sights and smells that were so easy to overlook. At that moment, he didn't feel like overlooking a single one of them.

"Did anything I said back there make it through that thick skull of yours?" Belle asked while standing beside him.

"At least a word or two."

She reached out to rub his forearm before squeezing his hand. There was something different about the way Belle took his hand that time that set it apart from the others. After years of experience in his more respectable line of work, Nick knew that touch very well. It was the touch of someone saying good-bye for the last time.

Belle threaded her fingers around what was left of his hand and held on as if she was the only thing that kept Nick from falling off a cliff. "You won't get what you're after by using that gun of yours."

"Really? Then I suppose you know what I should do instead?"

"No," she replied with a gentle shake of her head, "but you do. Everyone knows what's best for themselves. All it takes is the courage to follow up on it. But if you wait too long, your chances will dry up and blow away."

Now it was Belle's turn to look away from Nick. Although she'd spoken to him from the bottom of her heart, her last sentence seemed to come from the deepest part within her. It came from so deep that pulling it up into the light stole the breath right out of her.

When she looked up again, the smile she wore was still genuine, but also very tired. Belle let go of his hand so she could walk away. "You're welcome to visit me, but I'm not serving you any more liquor."

"I can't tell if I'm being run out of Petunia's or out of Keeler."

"Since you haven't had the gumption to get out of your hole, then I'll be the one to kick you out. Just don't forget to come see me the next time you're in town." And with that, Belle turned her back to him and walked down the street. There wasn't a bit of malice in her words, but there was a finality that nobody could have missed.

An hour later, Nick could still hear Belle's voice, just as he could still feel her hand on his shoulder. What kept her there was something that he knew to be truer than any gospel.

She was right.

Once he admitted to that, Nick felt everything else shift into focus.

He was walking down a street shared by plenty of shops, places to eat, and a few bakeries. The air smelled like horses, turned soil, and baked bread. A wind carried the scent of straw from a stable on the corner.

Folks on either side of the street talked, laughed, and quarreled among themselves. Their voices mingled with the slapping of hooves against the dirt, doors slamming, windows rattling, and boots knocking against the boardwalk.

Earlier that day the town had been nothing but a wash of browns and blacks, but in Nick's tired eyes everything was now coming alive. He could even see the patterns of the grain on wooden planks. Women's dresses were showing up like bright flowers in a field. Even the faces that turned toward him were a whole new sight to behold.

Nick had only taken notice of bits and pieces of those faces when he'd first arrived. Back then, which seemed so long ago, he'd just been looking for a threatening gaze turned in his direction or a scowl that contained a world of meaning between two armed men.

Eventually, Nick had taken to looking at people the way a carpenter might look at a house. He didn't see individual differences, but rather the component parts that pointed to significant flaws. Twitches or sniffles meant plenty in a card game. A narrowing of the eyes could mean life or death if someone's hand was too close to his gun. Once people around him were reduced to those basic pieces, it was all too easy for Nick to become nothing but a fragment himself.

As he walked the streets of Keeler and filled his lungs with fresh air, Nick felt as if he was awakening from a deep sleep. Along with the sights, smells, and sounds that he'd been blocking out, there also came a rush of memories that hit him with renewed force.

There had been a reason for coming to Keeler and there had even been a reason for him burying himself inside a hole. Now that he was thinking a little clearer, those reasons came into sharp focus. Some other things came into focus as well. When they did, they stopped Nick dead in his tracks.

In a flickering moment, Nick went through everything Belle had said to him over breakfast.

She knew who he was.

She'd heard something about him from someone who'd come looking for him.

Someone had been looking for him.

More than that, someone had found him. Unfortunately, most of the men on Nick's trail weren't exactly the kind to just give up and go away when they were told to do so. If they'd gotten that close, odds were that they were still that close . . . or closer.

"Jesus," Nick snarled as he turned and headed back to Petunia's. "How the hell could I have missed that?"

# FIVE

Nick stepped through the front door of the saloon that had become his home over the last few weeks and took a good look around. His arms were straight out to hold the door open, but he also looked as if he meant to catch anyone who tried to get past him. The holster normally strapped around his waist had been shifted a bit since the last time he'd been in the saloon. Now the gun was resting over his belly with the handle angled toward Nick's right arm.

Nobody in Petunia's moved more than what was required to get a look at who was making the commotion. Once they got a look at Nick, most of them shifted back to what they were doing.

At this time of day, the only people inside the saloon either worked there or were there so much that they had roots connecting them to their spots. Nick recognized every last one of them. Until a few minutes ago,

79

he'd been one of them.

Belle was nowhere to be seen, so Nick went to the only other person in the place that wasn't three sheets to the wind.

"Can I have a word with you, Robbie?" Nick asked the bright-eyed man behind the bar.

Robbie nodded, stepped up to the bar, and leaned over to meet Nick halfway. He had clean clothes and steady hands, which separated him from the patrons like day and night and kept him from being fully accepted by the drunks who haunted the saloon during the earliest hours of the day.

"What can I do for you, Nick?"

"I was talking to Belle and she said that someone was asking around about me a while back."

Hearing that, Robbie winced and suddenly looked as though he didn't want any part of the conversation.

"It's all right," Nick assured the younger man. "Belle said I should know about it."

At first, it didn't look as though Robbie was going to talk. But when he studied Nick's face a bit more, he saw something there that caused him to reconsider. Finally, he nodded toward the end of the bar closest to the door. "The fella usually sits right over there."

"You mean he still comes here?"

"Sure. He came to town a while ago, which was when he asked about you. He talked to me because I was the only one here, but he seemed to know more about you than I did, so I told him to have a word with Belle. She didn't tell him anything," Robbie said with assurance. "After that, the fella lost interest."

"But he still comes here to drink?"

Robbie nodded. "Sits in on a few card games, but mostly keeps to himself. I wouldn't worry about him. Truth is, I forgot about him until you brought him up just now."

Nick was done forgetting. "Where does he stay?"

The nervousness that Robbie felt was coming back in a rush. "I don't know for certain."

"What's his name?"

Nick's hand snapped out before he had a chance to think otherwise. His fist closed around the front part of Robbie's shirt and he nearly pulled the young man over the bar. "You've got to know something about him," Nick snarled. "It's important."

"Let the kid go," came a voice from no more than six feet down the bar.

The one who'd spoken was a grizzled old

man with hair that sat on top of his head like a silver rat's nest. A greasy beard coated the bottom part of his face and his breath reeked so heavily of liquor that the smell practically rolled in a cloud from his mouth. "It ain't the kid's fault you're too damn drunk to know when someone's after ya."

Letting out a breath, Nick eased up on his grip and set Robbie down. "Sorry," he said to the barkeep. "I just don't have a lot of time here."

"You had plenty of time to sit and watch that door," the old-timer pointed out. "And enough time to pour so much whiskey down yer throat that you didn't even see who walked through it."

"Yeah, well, that's changed now."

The old-timer had already gone back to his bottle. When he spoke, his words were slurred and echoed within the glass. "We'll see about that."

"I just need to know where to find that man, Robbie," Nick said.

"You might not want to go after him. That man doesn't seem like a very charitable sort."

"Where is he?"

"Across the street at the Sharps Hotel. I've seen him go there practically every night after you leave. I can see it right from here."

Nick glanced over his shoulder. The door was still swinging a bit on its hinges and he was able to see half of a dirty sign across the way with SHARPS written on it. Looking back to the barkeep, Nick asked, "How come nobody told me about this?"

"Why would we?" the old-timer replied. "So we could get a shooting fight started? This place is nice and quiet, which is just the way we like it."

Pulling himself out of Nick's grasp, the barkeep straightened his shirt and said, "Look for a fella with long hair and rough skin. That's how I recognize him. That and the limp."

"Thanks," Nick said as he walked for the door. Despite the fact that his gut was telling him to hurry, Nick took one more look at the saloon.

The place seemed a lot smaller this time. Petunia's had been his whole world the night before, but now it was just a dirty hole of a saloon filled with crooked tables and broken chairs. Even the familiar faces turned away from him like he was a stranger.

"Nick," Robbie called out. "All the man wanted to know was when you got here and where you came from. That's it."

"That's plenty," Nick grumbled as he stepped outside and put his back to Petunia's for good.

All this time, he'd been certain that his eyes had been open and he'd been watching everything like a hawk. It turned out that he only saw what he needed to see. The rest, like the Sharps Hotel, fell into the fog that had rolled in to claim the inside of his head.

But his brain was getting clearer by the moment. By the time Nick had dashed across the street, walked past the tobacconist's shop, and entered the Sharps Hotel, he felt more sober than he had in months. The narrow-faced man behind the front desk looked at him as if he hadn't seen Nick stumble from Petunia's practically every morning.

"Oh," the clerk said with a start once he put his finger on who Nick was. "If you need a place to lay down, I'm afraid I can't —"

"I'm looking for a man who's staying here," Nick interrupted. "Long-haired fellow with a limp."

"I really don't know about —"

"I know he's here. Just tell me which room he's in and I won't have to go looking for him. Less trouble that way."

Nick stared straight into the clerk's eyes.

His hands were flat upon the desk and his feet remained planted as if he'd sprouted roots from each limb. "I just need to have a word with him."

The clerk shifted uncomfortably behind his desk. "No trouble, you say?"

# Six

The door to the hotel room crashed in under one swift kick from Nick's boot. Nick's Schofield was already in hand and his finger was on the trigger before the door smacked against the wall. With the loud *bang* of wood against wall still echoing through the room, Nick stepped inside the room to face the man who'd rented it.

Nobody was in there. There was hardly any furniture in there, which left no place for someone to hide. A rickety chair sat next to the window. A table that was too small to hold a washbasin sat against the rear wall and a cot bearing a mattress stuffed with newspapers squatted in the middle of the room. The sheets weren't even long enough to reach to the floor, making it simple for Nick to get a look at the dusty floor underneath.

The folded piece of yellowed paper was covered with so much dirt and grit that

Nick almost missed it. His gun slid back into its holster, freeing Nick's hands to steady himself as he got down to one knee and reached out for the paper. When he picked it up, he found that it was the kind used by telegraph offices. Unfolding the paper revealed that it wasn't a telegram, but rather a receipt for a message sent from the local office. The receipt was marked with the time and date of the message.

The telegram had been sent that very day, less than an hour ago.

The creak of a floorboard drew Nick's eyes to the door to find a man already standing there. Even through the long hair drifting down in front of his face, the man's pockmarked cheeks stood out like a long stretch of rough road. Nick's presence in the room must have been a surprise to the other man because his gun was still nestled in its holster.

"Thought you'd finally crawled into that bottle for good, kid," the man said.

Nick hadn't been a kid since he'd left home. Even so, he did look like a boy compared to the weathered man standing in the doorway. A long brown coat covered most of the older man's frame and his skin resembled leather that had been tacked to the side of a barn and forgotten for about twenty years.

"Are you the one who's been asking about me?" Nick asked, even though he didn't really need to.

The older man grunted once. It wasn't so much of a reply, but more of a noise that accompanied the effort of stepping into the room. After planting one foot, he winced and pulled the other one behind it. "Been looking in on you for a while now. Me and some of the others."

"What others?"

"Here," the man said as he reached up with one hand. "Maybe this'll help."

Nick's hand twitched toward his gun, but stopped short of clearing leather.

Instead of going for a weapon of his own, the older man reached up to slide his fingers through the hair that fell down like a curtain over his face. He slid his hand straight back, taking the hair right along with it until the thick strands caught behind his ears.

Now that he was given a clearer look, Nick could see one of the many faces that he'd spent a lifetime trying to forget.

"Shad?" Nick asked, blinking to make sure that he wasn't seeing things.

The older man nodded and let his hand drop to his side. Some of his hair drooped back over his face and stuck to the wet corner of his scowling mouth. "You don't know how hard it was to keep away from you all this time. Especially after all the trouble I got to suffer from the bad leg you gave me."

Nick's eyes darted down to Shad's bad leg. Under the flap of the older man's coat, the glint of metal could be seen around his leg. Iron braces were held tightly by leather straps to frame a knee that was either swollen out of proportion or wrapped with layers of bandages.

"You did a hell of a number to me back in that barn."

Shad's voice, along with the mention of the barn, sent enough memories through Nick's head to take him right back to Virginia City all those years ago. He could still smell the mix of horses and gunpowder in the air. The scent of hay drifted into his mind, soon to be followed by the muffled gunshot that had blasted through Shad's kneecap.

"I thought I'd killed you," Nick said.

"Almost, but not quite. Plenty better than you have tried to put me down and failed. With the hurting you put on me, I would've liked to catch that bullet you shot at my skull. That was one hell of a night."

As Nick went through his recollections of

89

that night in his head, he remembered feeling the stab of pain as a glancing shot tore through his skin. He recalled seeing the masked shotgunner on the floor in front of the hay bale that had been Nick's only refuge. He recalled the Committee hunting him down like an animal and running him out of Virginia City. Indeed, it had been a hell of a night.

"Red sent you," Nick said.

Shad's face didn't flinch. He gave nothing away, apart from the fact that every move he made was still hampered by the wound he'd taken in that barn. "Skinner already caught up to Red somewhere in Nebraska."

Shaking his head, Nick said, "That business in Nebraska is over."

"You sure about that?"

"Yeah." A shadow came over Nick's face that chilled him down to the bone. It was that same chill that had driven him into the bottom of a whiskey bottle. "I'm sure. Since you've been watching me instead of taking a shot at me, I'd say that means someone's reining you in."

"Plenty of time for shooting right now. I sure as hell can't run too far."

Nick wanted to tell Shad that he didn't have a problem with him. At least that might keep the older man at ease long enough for him to say what he was doing there or who was on the other end of the telegram he'd sent. But no matter how much sense it made, Nick couldn't get himself to form the words.

He did have a problem with Shad and it had festered just like the ugly wound beneath the older man's knee brace.

"You can walk out of here if you tell me who you sent this to," Nick forced himself to say as he held up the telegram receipt. "After that, you'd be wise to head somewhere far from where I'll be."

Shad's laugh was half-snort and half-cough. "After you kneecapped me and killed my friends, you think all I want is a head start? Kid, I've dreamed about this more'n I'd ever dreamt about fucking a woman. Looking into your eyes while I burn you down is what I've been waiting for since Virginia City. I don't give a shit what Red's got planned for you."

"Red deserved what he got," Nick said. "His only problem was not knowing when to let sleeping dogs lie."

Shad's face twisted into a smile that looked perverse on his haggard face. "After what you did to him, you expected him to let dogs lie?"

"If he was so upset about that," Nick

replied in a voice that was as cold as the grave, "then maybe he should come talk to me himself."

Shad shook his head. "You don't need to worry about that and you don't need to worry about Red. Not no more."

Nick looked into Shad's eyes, waiting for the moment to reach for his gun. The closer that moment got, the heavier the Schofield felt at his side. Seconds dragged by as the rest of the world seemed to hold its breath and wait for one more soul to join the ranks of the dead.

The whiskey in Nick's system was like poison at the bottom of a well. His mind was sharp enough, but his body was still sluggish after stewing for too long in a dark saloon.

Shad's eyes narrowed a bit as the smirk grew upon his face. He knew well enough that Nick wasn't at the top of his game because it had been his job to sit and watch the younger man slip deeper and deeper toward the bottom of a bottle.

Suddenly Nick knew for certain that he wouldn't be able to outdraw the older man. The realization hit him with a jarring finality and settled into the bottom of his stomach like a lead weight. Lifting anything more than a glass to his mouth would be expecting a worn-out nag to outrun a racing horse.

Nick's arms stretched out and slowly lifted. Once his hands were over his head, he said, "This has gone on long enough, Shad. I'm tired of it."

Letting out a chuckle, Shad shook his head. "I been watching you for a while, kid, and I always thought you were on to me. Guess Red was giving you too much credit. When he hears about the sorry piece of shit you've become, maybe Red won't mind that I got to you first."

Before the older man went for his pistol, Nick crouched down low and took a lunging step forward.

Shad cleared leather, but his target was already too close to get into his sights. Before he could adjust his aim, Shad felt a solid impact in the middle of his chest.

Nick's shoulder made contact and shoved the older man back an inch or so. He snapped his right fist in a quick hooking punch that caught Shad in the ribs. Most other men would be wheezing painfully right about then, but most other men also hadn't been forced to live with a shattered kneecap for years on end.

The pain in Shad's leg easily overshadowed everything else. Nick's punches were strong, but they were only a mild discomfort to the older man. What concerned Shad more was twisting his gun around to blast a hole into Nick.

One more punch bounced off of Shad's ribs, cracking a few in the process. The older man didn't even react to that, however, since he'd felt much worse when he'd made his way up the stairs a few minutes ago. Just as Shad was able to turn the gun toward his target, Nick swung his leg back. Throwing that same leg forward like a catapult, Nick finally delivered some pain that Shad could feel.

Most of Nick's foot smacked against the metal knee brace, but his heel managed to pound against the kneecap that had never fully healed after being shattered by hot lead all those years ago in Virginia City.

The sound of his foot slamming into that steel-encased weak spot was like a choir of angels to Nick's ears.

Shad crumpled forward slightly and the pistol slipped from his fingers. His face twisted into a mix of surprise and shock as his eyes started to fill with tears. Although his mouth gaped open, no sound came out for a few seconds. After that, the room was filled with a sobbing groan.

Nick didn't allow himself to pity the other man until he'd picked up the gun that Shad

94

had dropped. Patting down the other man's pockets was easy enough, since Shad was using up all he had just to keep from falling over. In moments, he slumped down over Nick's arm so that was the only thing holding him up.

The older man's weight was almost enough to bring Nick down as well, driving home just how far Nick had let himself go. With a great amount of effort, Nick guided Shad toward the cot and let him drop onto the mattress.

"You son . . . son of . . . son of a bitch," Shad wheezed. "I s . . . swear. I'll . . ."

"You had your chance," Nick said, trying not to look as winded as he felt. "Now tell me what you know about Red. Skinner said he killed him."

Shad let out a hacking cough, tried to sit up, and dropped right back down again. His hands reached for the brace strapped to his knee. The clothing underneath the leather straps and metal rods was darkening with blood. "You'll never . . . know . . . until it's . . . too late."

With that, Shad gnashed his teeth together and forced himself to sit up so he could reach toward the little holdout pistol strapped inside his boot.

Nick hadn't even seen the gun there until

Shad started moving toward it. Running on pure instinct, Nick's hand closed around the gnarled grip of his pistol. Although the gun's handle looked as though it had been chipped and broken down to a twisted nub, the wood had actually been crafted to fit perfectly into his wounded hand. Shortened fingers closed around the handle and when he brought the gun up, similar modifications to the barrel and holster twisted the pistol even more securely into his grasp.

Nick brought the gun out and fired, watching Shad roll back on to the cot as hot lead tore a path through his chest. The Schofield barked once more, drilling a tunnel that went straight through the older man's heart.

Shad let out a gasp that was more relieved than anything else before slumping into a lifeless heap.

With the smoke still hanging in the air, Nick dropped his gun into its holster and launched himself into a flurry of motion. He overturned the table, emptied every one of Shad's pockets, and generally searched every inch of the room from top to bottom. In the end, the only answer he found was in the dead man's shirt pocket. It was a business card with RP COLLECTIONS printed across it.

Hearing the sound of feet scraping against the floor, Nick spun around and drew his gun. His speed had already improved, although the fire in his eyes was aimed at the wrong target.

"No need for that, mister," said a slender man in his thirties. He was dressed in a plain brown suit and was carrying an over-stuffed carpetbag. "Just trying to get by."

Nick holstered the gun and watched the man in the hall trip over himself to get to the stairs. Following him out, Nick walked to the same steps he'd used to get into the hotel and took them two at a time until his boots touched the ground. He didn't stop moving when he stepped onto the street.

Several people milled about nervously in front of the hotel and anxious faces peeked out of nearby windows. They whispered back and forth among themselves, but Nick stopped paying attention once he realized they were just talking about the shots they'd heard from Shad's room.

One man in the street took off running the moment he got a look at Nick. Just as Nick was about to chase him down, he saw it was the same man in the brown suit that he'd met in the hall. Now the fellow dropped his carpetbag completely and bolted for the corner.

"I just want to leave!" the man shouted. "Stop following me!"

Shaking his head, Nick saw that more and more people in the vicinity were starting to look in his direction. It wouldn't be long before the law would arrive and Nick decided not to waste any more time in answering the batch of questions that would surely follow.

The telegraph office was empty at that time of day. Actually, there weren't many times when the office wasn't empty. Nick strode into the cramped little room that was filled with stacks of paper, boxes of worn-down pencils, and one desk holding a contraption connected to the outside by a set of wires that came in through a hole in the wall.

Just then, the office was also filled with the smell of frying eggs as a small man wearing spectacles worked over a small stove.

"Excuse me," Nick said, trying not to look like he was in such a hurry.

After a while, the man glanced over and peered at Nick over his spectacles. "Fill out one of them forms and bring it to me when you're done."

"I'm not here to send a telegram. I want to know about one that was sent here."

The clerk got back to his eggs. "Can't tell

you much."

"I have a receipt."

Letting out a sigh, the clerk set his frying pan down and turned to face Nick. "We don't keep records of what was sent."

Nick held up the receipt he'd found under Shad's bed. He flipped the receipt over to show the folded dollar behind the receipt and said, "Then just tell me what you can."

The clerk took the receipt and the dollar, stuffing the latter into his pocket before so much as glancing at the former. After a few grunts and nods, he went over to a cluttered rolltop desk and examined the top page of his logbook. "This came today from the office in Ellis Station, Missouri. Ever hear of it?"

"No."

"That's all I got," the clerk said while handing back the receipt. With that, the bespectacled man was done talking. He was now more concerned with the smell of burning eggs drifting through the office.

Ten minutes later, Nick was in his rented room, stuffing his belongings into saddlebags. He left enough money to pay what he owed and left the place through a back door. From there, Nick collected his horses, hitched them to his wagon, and asked directions to Ellis Station. Apparently, the place wasn't in unfamiliar territory after all. By his estimations, the town wasn't more than a day's ride from the place where his father had been working for the last several years.

Nick thought he might pay the old man a visit. Then again, he'd probably be less welcome there than a case of the pox.

The heat was getting worse as the streets bustled with lawmen and others looking for whoever had shot up the room at the Sharps Hotel. Rather than think about the look on his father's face if he decided to pay him a visit, Nick snapped his reins and got the hell out of town before anyone decided to ask him any questions.

But before he headed back into Missouri, there was one important stop he needed to make.

# SEVEN

The last time Nick had been to Jessup was two years ago. More than just twenty-four months had passed since then. Although the scenery looked familiar and the trail was well-known to him, Nick felt like he was returning after living through a few more lifetimes. It could have been the throbbing pains that pummeled his head after giving up liquor, but Nick had suffered through those pains before.

What Nick felt this time was a weariness that washed right down to the bottom of his soul. It was a special kind of tired that came from taking several long journeys at once. He was no longer the man that he'd been the last time he'd seen that same stretch of prairie or been jostled by the same bumps in the road.

Then again, the closer he got to Jessup,

101

the more he felt some familiar things stirring inside of him. Not all of them were bad, but the ones that were had enough venom in them to set the hairs on the back of his neck on end. There was unfinished business that needed to be put to rest. In order for that to happen, it was necessary to trace his steps back a little ways. Nick just hoped that he had the strength to follow through when he got to where he was going.

The road from Keeler had taken a few days' ride, but that was only because Nick's horses weren't up to the task of going much faster than a quick walk. They too had their heads down and were breathing hard. It had been a long time since any of the souls connected to that wagon had seen so many hours of daylight in a row.

Whatever amount of fatigue that Nick was feeling began to flow out of him when he got his first glimpse at a familiar set of chimneys in the distance. Those chimneys belonged to the farmers' houses situated outside of Jessup. It looked like there were a few more of them since the last time he'd been there.

Rather than ride straight into Jessup, Nick steered his wagon off the path completely. He was headed for a field on the outskirts of town. Soon his wheels fell into a set of shallow ruts. He followed those ruts all the way to a shabby, poorly tended plot of ground with only the few wooden crosses sticking up from the dirt to set it apart from any other patch of undesirable land.

This was one part of Jessup that hadn't changed a bit since the last time Nick had seen it. Some folks would call it a cemetery, but that would be a stretch from anyone's perspective. Other folks would have called it a dumping ground for men who deserved to be a few feet beneath it. Others would call it by a more colorful name: boot hill.

Plenty of the wilder towns across the country would claim to be the first one to have a boot hill, but just about every town wound up with one. It was a burial ground for those who'd lived their whole lives flirting with death. When the outlaws died, they were dropped into a hole that was sometimes so shallow that the tips of their boots stuck up from the dirt.

Nick Graves had filled places like those for most of his life. In his youth, he'd been the one to supply the bodies. Later on, he saw to it that those bodies at least had a good box and a deep hole in which to rest. Now he was doing a little bit of both. Today, however, would be something new for him.

Today Nick was here to pull one of those

boxes out of boot hill so he could get a look inside.

After pulling back on the reins, Nick set the brake for his wagon and climbed down. Both horses, Rasa and Kazys, let out grateful breaths and nudged Nick's hand as he passed them by.

Nick walked straight for the short row of crosses stuck in the dirt and protruding from an overgrown patch of weeds. One of them had been there when Nick had arrived the first time a few years ago. The other cross belonged to an animal that had gone by the name of Skinner. Both of them had once been Nick's friends.

Now he hoped to God that they both stayed dead.

A few moments passed as Nick stood and looked down at those two graves. Time seemed to add to the heat in the air until it felt like the familiar humidity of his boyhood home in Missouri. Thoughts of Missouri often went hand in hand with graveyards in Nick's mind. After all, both places represented where he'd been taught the trade he now plied for a living.

After a while, the simple wooden crosses blended into the scenery until they seemed to have sprouted out of the ground like a pair of morbid trees. Nick wasn't exactly the squeamish sort, but he found himself unable to move from where he stood.

He remembered riding into this very town years ago so he could stand on that very spot. He'd been after a man named Red Parks, but had found Skinner instead.

In some respects, Skinner was more bloodthirsty than Red had ever been. It was Skinner who'd put Red into the ground. At least, that was what Skinner had claimed at the time. Nick had no reason to think Skinner was lying, since there was plenty of bad blood flowing between all three men to go around.

But things had changed in the years that had followed. After meeting up with his old friend Barrett Cobb, Nick had learned that Red Parks might very well be alive and kicking. The revelation had come from Barrett himself. The words had been pushed out of his mouth by some of the last breaths his old friend would take.

Seeing Barrett die still weighed heavily upon Nick's soul.

Killing Barrett had nearly driven Nick into the dirt.

Nick's breath was forced out of him so quickly that he made a grunting sound as if he'd been jostled out of a dream. When he refocused on where he was, all he could see was a job that needed to be done. Standing around and fussing about it wouldn't get that job done any faster.

As he walked back to his wagon, Nick peeled off the duster he'd been wearing and draped it over one of the wide wooden wheels. He kept walking around to the back of the wagon, rolling up his sleeves along the way. When he reached into the back to the spot where some of his tools were roped in place, Nick selected a shovel with a handle that was almost petrified after so much use. He took off his hat, rubbed some of the sweat from his brow, and headed back to where those two lonely crosses were waiting.

The blade of the shovel made it in less than two inches before it was stopped by a rock in the ground. Nick's hands twisted around the handle, settling into a familiar set of movements. Despite the loss of some fingers, Nick still dug into the earth with practiced ease. One foot remained planted while the other stepped onto the back of the shovel's blade to push it in a little deeper.

All around him, the prairie wheezed with the songs of crickets and the rustle of wind through tall grass. Trees rattled their leaves as dust was picked up and swirled from one spot to another as if the entire place was embracing Nick as part of the natural order of things.

Nick was shaken from the meditation of his movements when his shovel cracked against a flat piece of wood. He tapped the planks just to make sure, but already knew that he'd found what he'd been looking for. A smile came to Nick's face as the memory of his young fist opening up to reveal that stolen money came to mind. It had taken a hell of a long time, but he'd finally gotten around to digging up a box marked with something close to an X.

He uncovered the edges of the coffin and soon had the entire thing revealed. Looking down on the shoddy lumber, Nick was reminded of why he'd been content to leave this box in the ground the last time he'd been there.

It was very appealing to think of Red Parks as dead.

Facing up to the truth was like finding out that there was a worse place than hell. Some things were just better off left alone.

"I didn't think you'd come back."

The words startled Nick, but he didn't jump. His hand snapped to the holster around his waist as his boots shifted upon the dusty planks beneath them. In one fluid motion, he turned to get a look at who was behind him while bringing his specially modified pistol halfway out of its resting place. When he saw who was standing there, Nick let the gun slip back into its leather home.

He'd stared into those light brown eyes in every one of the few *good* dreams he'd had. The owner of those eyes walked into the clearing with her hands hanging at her sides. She wore a simple blue and white dress, tied at the waist to accentuate her already impressive figure. Most of her long black hair had been tied back, but some disobedient strands danced around the sides of her face.

She came to a stop a few paces past Nick's wagon. Once there, the brunette clasped her hands behind her back and looked around while rocking on her heels. Judging by the expression on her face, it seemed more like hours rather than years since the last time she'd seen him.

"Hello, Catherine," Nick said as he climbed out of the shallow hole he'd dug, using the shovel for support. "I was hoping to see you again, but . . ." Trailing off, Nick held out his dirty hands and motioned at the serene yet morbid surroundings. "Well, this wasn't exactly what I had in mind."

She walked up to him without saying a word. All the while, she kept her hands behind her back and her head tilted downward just a little bit. Her steps were slow, but not uncertain. And no matter how hard she tried, she couldn't hide the smile that was struggling to explode onto her face.

Having waited years for this moment, Nick wasn't willing to put it off one more second. He took the few steps needed to close the distance between them and wrapped his arms around her waist. She melted into his embrace with a long, relieved sigh.

Nick picked her up with ease and swung her around so he could feel her hair wrap around his face. She smelled like fresh air and roses. Her breath was hotter than the sun against his neck and the curves of her body pressed against him to send a rush through his blood that Nick thought he might never feel again.

In those few moments, Nick forgot about where he was and everything else that had happened. The only thing in his life that mattered right then was Catherine. Compared to that moment, everything else was a dark shadow that he'd been forced to endure when she hadn't been close enough to satisfy at least one of his senses.

As much as he hated to do it, Nick put her down and let the rest of the world back into his sight.

"What are you doing here?" Nick asked, looking around as if seeing the shoddy cemetery for the first time.

Catherine stepped back, but made sure to keep Nick within arm's reach. "I saw your wagon approaching town."

"You could recognize me from that far away?"

"Actually, I bought one of the old farm-houses and some land that borders Jessup. It's not a lot, but it's better than the place I had before. The road's pretty much right outside my window."

Nick was surprised Catherine still lived anywhere near Jessup. After what had happened the last time he'd been through there, he wouldn't have blamed her for wanting to forget all about him as well. But with Catherine close enough for him to smell the scent of her skin, it was hard to think about things like that.

"Still, I turned off the trail pretty quickly," Nick said. When he saw her look down a bit, Nick placed a finger under her chin and gently lifted until he could see into her eyes once more.

"I was watching the road," she said as a

110

sort of guilty confession. "I've watched that road a lot since you left. This time I guess I got lucky. When I saw you turn off and head this way, I thought you'd changed your mind or that maybe I was seeing things, so I followed you here.

"I'm so glad you're back, Nick," she said with renewed passion in her voice. "After the things I'd heard about you over the last couple years, I was thinking you would have found someplace to hide and not be seen for a while."

"I tried that already," Nick said. "Didn't work out too well."

"So you decided to come back here?"

"Yeah, but not to stay. I just needed to check up on some things. Tie up some loose ends."

Catherine reached out to place her hands upon Nick's arms. She stared at his elbows and moved up to feel the muscles that were still warm beneath his skin after the exertion of digging. From there, she slid her hands down along his bare forearms and then to his hands. She traced her fingers over them and even smiled when she felt the oddly shaped remnants of his fingers.

"You're really back," she whispered with her eyes closed. When she opened them, tears welled up in the corner of each eye.

"Please say you'll stay. For a little while, at least."

Nick nodded before he even knew it. "Of course. You're one of the loose ends I was talking about."

"You never were one for sweet talk, but it's still great to hear you try." Then Catherine looked down at the disturbed grave that was further marked by Nick's shovel sticking up from the dirt. "Do I even want to know about any of the other loose ends you mean to tie up?"

"It's not as bad as it looks."

"Really? Because it looks pretty bad. I thought you were more suited to digging those graves instead of . . . well . . ."

"Robbing them?" Nick asked, completing the question that Catherine hadn't.

Shrugging, Catherine nodded.

"It's not like that," Nick assured her. "I just need to get a look inside. If you want to leave me to this, you don't have to stay here."

Now Catherine's expression was more curious than anything else. She leaned to one side so she could look around Nick and at the shallow hole behind him. "No, you can do what you need to do. At least this way you've got a witness in case Rich hauls you in for stealing a gold tooth or some nonsense."

Nick turned around and picked up the shovel so he could continue uncovering the coffin. Some of the dirt he'd removed had been replaced by another layer when he'd scrambled out to meet Catherine. The planks were still visible, but the outline of the casket had been swallowed up. "Rich is still the law around here?"

"He's been sheriff since you left and has been doing a whole lot better job than the bastard who wore that badge before him."

The late Sheriff Manes had lorded over Jessup like it was his own. He'd supplemented his salary by giving refuge to outlaws and killers of all sorts. Two such customers were now resting in the dirt at Nick's feet.

"Things have been real quiet since you left," Catherine said while working her way closer to the grave so she could see more of what Nick was doing. "But folks around here can't stop talking about what happened. You know how that is. Rumors get started and then passed around the saloons until they're stories I don't even recognize."

Catherine was rambling and even she knew it. Still, the sound of her voice did a good job of filling the silence that normally covered spots like these. Her words were almost enough to chase the ghosts away.

By now, enough dirt had been cleared off the top of the coffin to make the box almost look clean. Nick had dragged his feet long enough to allow Catherine to find somewhere else to be. Although she seemed content to stay put, he gave her one last chance. "You sure you want to see this?" he asked. "It might not be pretty."

"I've seen worse," she replied.

Nodding, Nick once again climbed out of the grave and stood perched on the edge. After a bit of scraping against the edge of the wooden box, he had the tip of the shovel's blade wedged under the lid. Letting out his breath, he pulled on the shovel and levered the coffin open.

A few pebbles and some loose ground trickled into the coffin, pattering against the bottom of the box, which was empty apart from a few startled bugs.

The wince on Catherine's face quickly faded. "Well, that wasn't too bad."

Nick stared into the empty coffin before slapping the lid back down with his shovel. "Trust me," he said. "It's plenty bad."

# EIGHT

Nick didn't say a word as he tossed his shovel into the back of his wagon and pulled on his coat. After climbing into the driver's seat, he reached down and offered a hand to Catherine. She accepted his help and climbed into the seat beside him. While she could feel the tension coming from him, she knew well enough that it wasn't meant for her.

She could also tell that Nick didn't want to take part in any small talk on the way back to her house. He snapped the reins and got the horses moving. The wagon shuddered a bit, but started rolling all the same.

Holding on for dear life was enough to keep Catherine busy as the wagon bounced and rocked over the uneven ground. When they finally did pull onto the road, only a few more minutes of silence needed to be endured before she pointed to a good-sized house just ahead.

Compared to the dirty streets of Keeler and the even dirtier saloons that had become Nick's home there, Catherine's little house was a fresh slice of heaven. It wasn't the biggest place in town or even the fanciest, but it was clean and inviting, even though it was currently empty. Even without her presence inside, the house still seemed to be welcoming them with a light all its own.

"You'll have to excuse the place," Catherine said as the wagon came to a stop and she climbed down. "I wasn't expecting company."

Nick shook his head and smiled.

"You're thinking the place looks like a train wreck, aren't you?" she asked.

"Actually, the phrase 'sight for sore eyes' came to mind."

Catherine returned Nick's smile and hurried to the door. "I'll straighten up while you tie up your horses." Before Nick had a chance to say anything else, Catherine had opened the door, rushed inside, and slammed it shut again.

As he took off the bridles and unhitched both horses from the wagon, Nick patted their muzzles and got appreciative nudges in return. He whispered some meaningless chatter to them as he went about the task of showing the tired animals to a hitching post next to an inviting water trough. When he heard the creak of hinges, Nick turned to find Catherine watching him from the front stoop.

"What language was that?" she asked.

"Excuse me?"

"When you were talking to your horses, it was in some other language. Was it German?"

Nick had to think for a moment before he realized that she was right. He'd slipped into a different language. "It's not German," he told her.

Catherine moved in closer to him. "Then what is it?"

"My father's native language. It still goes through my mind, even though I haven't carried a conversation in it for years."

"Come on inside," she said while taking his hand and dragging Nick toward the house. "Have a rest and some food."

"I hope I'm not imposing."

"Don't be silly. None of this is for free." Placing her hands upon her hips, she squared off with him and declared, "I intend on hearing about everything you've been doing since you left."

"That might take a while."

"Well, it's either that or I'll just have to believe all the rumors that've been floating around here. Trust me, they're not all good ones either."

"Then I guess you'll have your story." Although the tone in Nick's voice was vaguely resigned, he didn't put up any fuss as she dragged him into her home.

The house was even more comforting on the inside than it was on the outside. A large room took up most of the space, consisting of a kitchen and potbellied stove in one corner with a dining table and a few chairs nearby. On the opposite side of the room was a fireplace and two larger chairs. Only one of them looked as though it had been used any time in the last few months.

Two doors led into smaller rooms. One of them opened into a large pantry and the other was closed.

"It's not much," she said. "But it's home."

The room was already starting to smell like coffee and Nick saw a kettle brewing on the stove. Settling into one of the chairs around the dining table, Nick let out a breath along with the words, "This is plenty good enough for me."

Catherine smiled and sat down across from him. "So, what happened after you left here?"

"I spent some time in the Dakotas. Got a job and made some good friends."

"Are you still in the same line of work? Are you still a Mourner?"

Nick smirked at that. It wasn't meant to be a slight against Catherine. It was just that most folks who didn't know him as a gunfighter or the thief he'd been in his youth only knew him as an undertaker. Nick Graves had learned the trade from his father. Stasys had taught his son to carve headstones, build coffins, and any number of other skills relating to that profession.

Eventually, Nick had gone on to become a Mourner. It was the Mourner's job to arrange wakes, send invitations to funeral services, and console the grieving relatives left behind. Sometimes Mourners would attend the services themselves and add theirs to the prayers and wishes for the dead. It did a family good to see one more seat filled at the funeral of their loved ones.

Mourners also arranged for the festivities centered around a hanging. There were plenty of other details that needed attending and a Mourner had to know every last one. At that moment, Nick was just impressed that Catherine truly paid attention to what he did and cared enough to ask him about it. "Yeah," he said with a nod. "I'm still a Mourner."

"People still remember the work you did here."

"How's Dan Callum?"

"He's still the undertaker around here and he asks about you every time I see him. You know, he's never hired anyone to fill your job. He'll be so happy to finally see you again!"

That caused Nick to turn his eyes downward. "That might not be a good idea, Catherine."

For a moment, Catherine looked confused. Then she understood what he meant. It was the very subject she'd been hoping to avoid. "It's about those men who came after you, isn't it? That killer who forced you to leave here."

She was talking about Skinner. Nick could see that the subject was still an open wound in Catherine's heart, body, and soul.

"He's gone," Nick assured her while reaching out to place his hand upon hers. "That's not the one I was here to check up on."

Although he'd only added that last sentence as an afterthought, Nick could see the relief that washed over Catherine's entire body after he'd said it. Her shoulders came down from around her ears and she let out a breath that she must have been holding ever since she'd found him at the open grave.

"Well, that's good news," she said. "I was glad not to see a dead body in that coffin you opened, but then I thought about who was supposed to be in there and I started to feel more frightened than I've —"

"Forget about him," Nick said. "That's over."

Nodding, Catherine took a breath and let it out. The scent of brewing coffee was starting to shift into burning coffee, so she got up and hurried to the stove. "Then what brings you here?" she asked while filling two cups. "And what made you . . ."

"Dig up a grave?" Nick asked to complete the already awkward question.

"Well . . . yes."

"I met up with another friend of mine a while ago."

"Is he a friend from when you were young?"

"Yeah. Barrett was one of the best friends I ever had, but it was from the days that I'd rather put behind me. Let's just say that he hadn't changed too much and things didn't turn out too good."

"What happened?"

"He wasn't as good a friend as I thought

he was," Nick replied. "And he forced me into a tough spot."

Catherine had taken her seat again and was stirring sugar into her coffee. Nick hadn't touched his own cup just yet.

"How tough?" she asked before lifting her cup to her lips to take a sip.

Nick wrapped his hands around the cup and let the warmth seep into him. Just thinking about what had happened with Barrett was enough to make him feel cold despite the heat in the air. It was the kind of cold that no fire could do a damn thing about. "I had to kill him," he finally said.

"That's terrible."

Nick barely seemed to hear her. "It made me feel like the murderer everyone said I was. Maybe even worse."

"That's not true."

"At least a killer or thief is up front about what he does. I was spouting on about helping and taking a higher road and I wind up killing my best friend." He took a sip of coffee and felt as if the hot liquid was trickling into an empty pail. "Some high road." After a moment, he said, "Before he died, Barrett straightened out some things for me regarding some men from our past."

"There's more of them?"

"Yeah," Nick answered, reflexively flexing

the gnarled remains of his fingers. "There's more of them. One in particular was the one I was after the first time I was here. His name is Red Parks and Skinner told me he'd already killed him. At the time, that wasn't too hard to believe. Seeing the grave marker was enough to put that to rest in my head.

"But Barrett told me differently and . . . considering the circumstances . . . I don't think Barrett had any reason to lie. So I came back here to see who was right and there was a real easy way to get that done."

"Now that you explain it, checking that grave doesn't seem so strange."

"Guess not, but seeing as how the coffin was empty, that means Red is still out there. And ever since what happened here the last time, word's been getting out about a man who looks an awful lot like me shooting the hell out of some known killers. From then on, like you said, rumors start to spread. Sometimes that's a real dangerous thing."

Catherine leaned back in her chair and sipped her coffee. "Well, I'll have you know that plenty of folks come through here asking about what happened to you and I don't tell them a damn thing."

"Thanks," Nick said, even though he figured that one woman's silence didn't make much difference in a world full of more willing souls. "Wait a minute. What folks have been looking for me?"

She shrugged. "They weren't as bad as Skinner, but they wore guns. Dan Callum said some of the men looked like Pinkertons, but they weren't."

"They went to see Dan Callum too?" Nick asked as the tension built up in his voice.

"Of course," Catherine replied with a nod. "You did work for him and he talks you up any chance he gets."

"And how do you know they weren't Pinkertons?"

"Because they left cards. I still have the one they left at the Porter House. Did I mention I'm part owner of that old restaurant now? Would you like to see the card?"

Nick was about to jump out of his skin. Instead, he stayed as calm as he could and let out a measured breath. "Yes, Catherine. I'd like to see it."

She got up and moseyed over to the door that was shut on the other side of the room. When she opened it, a bed and wardrobe could be seen inside the smaller room. Catherine went right over to the wardrobe, pulled open a top drawer, and removed a small envelope.

"Here it is," she said. By the time she got

out of the bedroom, Nick was already on his feet and waiting for her.

Nick did his best to keep from snatching the envelope from her hand. Inside the envelope was the small business card Catherine had promised. Even though he already had a suspicion of what that card would say, he still felt his stomach clench when he saw the words RP COLLECTIONS printed across the front. When he looked up again, he could feel the color draining from his face.

"What's the matter, Nick? What's wrong?"

"I need to go," he said quietly. "Right now."

"What's in that card?" Catherine asked in a more insistent tone. "Tell me."

"I'll handle this on my own, Catherine. Stay here and I'll come back for you once this is all over."

Nick started to walk for the front door, but was stopped before he could make it halfway there. Catherine all but jumped in his way, planting her feet and holding out her arms sternly to show that she wasn't about to let him take another step.

"No, you don't," she said. "Not again. I'm coming with you."

Nick considered that for all of three-quarters of a second before placing both hands around her waist, lifting her off the floor, and setting her down a few feet to one side. "Sorry," he said without convincing anyone that he meant it, "but I can't have you along for the ride on this. It might get dangerous."

Catherine hopped back into Nick's path. This time she stood in the middle of the doorframe and took hold of it with both hands. "Dangerous? You mean like the last time when I was held at gunpoint and nearly killed by the bastards who were after you?"

"Yeah. Something like that."

Catherine's hands moved quickly enough to catch Nick off-guard. They smacked against his wrists and forced him to drop her. "I didn't wait around two years for you to come back just so I could share a cup of coffee and watch you dig a hole! The only reason I stayed in this town was because I wanted you to be able to find me when you were ready."

"What?"

For a second, Catherine looked surprised by what had just come out of her mouth. Then she straightened up and owned up to it with a firm nod. "That's right. And I'm not going to let you get away again so easily."

Nick studied her for a moment, but pulled his eyes in another direction. "I won't put you in harm's way."

"The best way for you to watch over me is to stay close. Besides, if you leave me behind, I'll just come looking for you. How safe do you think I'll be out there all by myself?"

Catherine was plenty of things, but helpless certainly wasn't one of them. Of course, stubborn was getting mighty high on the list.

"All right," Nick said. "You need to listen to me and trust what I'm telling you."

"I will," she said with an anxious nod.

"Good. Then stay here. I'll be right back. I promise."

Catherine was just about to protest when she saw Nick adjusting the holster around his waist so the modified pistol was laying across his belly. She'd seen the gun there before. It meant that he expected trouble to be coming along real soon.

# NINE

Nick headed out the door. Although Rasa and Kazys were tied in front, he took a path around the house and ducked onto another familiar stretch of road. Finding shortcuts had been a talent ever since he was a boy. As an outlaw, remembering those shortcuts was a real good way to stay alive when things got hot.

Jessup wasn't a big place, but farmers tended to keep to their own affairs when it came to strangers. They weren't the ones gossiping as much as the drunks and gun hands in the saloon. When Catherine had mentioned that the only way to keep an eye on someone was to keep them close, it reminded Nick of his run-in with Shad back in Wyoming.

It was obvious that Shad wasn't just trailing Nick for his own amusement. If that had been the case, the older man would have called him out long before being discovered.

Nick had been ripe for the picking the entire time he'd been perched on his chair in that saloon. Instead, Shad had been content to keep an eye on him from afar.

If there was one scout watching for Nick, there had to be others. Even as he did his best to keep from meeting any of the glances that came his way, Nick could feel more and more locals trying to get a look at him. His arrival wasn't common knowledge just yet, but that couldn't last very much longer. Nick intended to stretch out what little time he had before it ran out.

This time he meant to get the drop on the scout waiting for him instead of it being the other way around.

Nick let his instincts guide his steps as he worked his way through the farmers' houses on the edge of town and into Jessup itself. Once in town, it was a simple matter of finding an alley and slipping from one dark corridor into another. Even the sunlight had a hard time making it between the buildings leaning in on each other like sagging oaks.

The first place he went was the undertaker's parlor down on Eighth Street. It was still at the end of the street without much else on either side. Nick could hear the sounds of a hammer pounding against a nail and could picture Dan Callum putting together one of the wooden boxes that would be used in an upcoming service. Nobody else was around the place, so Nick moved along.

There were a few saloons in town and Nick had to stop before simply making his way to the closest one. The saloons were the places where Nick had been built into either a demon or a legend. When he was seen at any one of those, word that he was in town would spread like wildfire and there was no way to go back from there.

He had to be careful and pick his spot just right. If he made one slip, his best bet would be to just stay put and let the scout come to him. Nick had made it through the last such encounter, but he knew well enough that luck had been a real big part of that. The last several days had gone a long way in burning the whiskey from his system, but he was tired and frayed at the edges.

Suddenly Nick's face brightened with a wide grin. Everything fit into place in that very instant, making his choice perfectly obvious.

When he blinked, he could still see the words that had been written on that letter Catherine saved for him. When he thought about that letter, he knew there could very well have been others that she didn't catch.

And no matter how many others there had been, they all had to go through the same spot.

Nick worked his way down a few more streets and stepped into the open for the first time. He kept his head tilted down so the brim of his hat covered a good portion of his face. Although some folks were passing by, they weren't paying him any mind just yet.

Doing his best to look casual, Nick glanced up and down the street until he found the post office down the street with telegraph wires connecting it to a nearby post. He walked into the modest building, which had the sights and smells of just about every other post office. At least, this one didn't smell like fried eggs.

"I'm looking for a friend of mine," Nick said to the middle-aged woman sorting letters behind a set of windows resembling those found in a bank.

The woman sifted through a few more letters, dropped them into a pile, and then got up to walk over to the window where Nick was waiting. "How can I help you?"

"I'm looking for a friend of mine. He was supposed to pick up some correspondence for me. It would have been from Missouri."

"A letter or telegram?"

"Probably a telegram." Nick smiled and shrugged. "I've been away for a while and this is an important matter."

"Where are the telegrams from?"

"Ellis Station, Missouri."

She didn't even have to go to the logbook. When she heard that, her expression turned sour and she pointed toward the street as if she was waving off a drunkard's advance. "Try the saloon on the corner. The only telegrams we've gotten from Ellis Station were sent straight over there. And when you see your friend, tell him we're a post office and not his personal delivery service."

Since the woman had already turned her back to him, Nick made his exit and glanced down the street. The saloon was half a block down and was close enough to keep watch on Dan Callum's parlor. Now all Nick had to do was find out who was waiting for him. It would be a shame to disappoint such a patient fellow.

The saloon wasn't the biggest in town and it surely wasn't the cleanest, but it was most definitely the darkest. That fact wasn't so much by design as it was a bad choice of locations. What did work in the place's favor was the bountiful supply of men who wanted to stay out of the sunlight.

There were drunks who couldn't bear the feel of warmth on their faces any longer.

There were some souls who'd simply lost their way.

Some had just visited a loved one in the undertaker's place just down the road.

And some just didn't want to be seen.

With this combination to pull from, the dirty little saloon on Seventh Street was always full of customers. The men filled the dreary space like ghosts haunting an attic, each one of them stinking of whiskey and glaring out at the world through narrow bloodshot eyes.

"Who needs another?" called out the barkeep, who was so skinny he seemed to have been lashed together using nothing but twigs and twine.

He got a few grunts and knocks on tables as a reply, which was enough to start him hobbling about the place on his clubbed foot, carrying a bottle in each hand. Making his way to those who'd answered him before, the barkeep topped off glasses and mugs with either whiskey or beer. The contents of both the bottles he carried were equally bad. In fact, the only way he told the two brown liquids apart was whether or not there was foam at the top.

"What about you, mister?" he asked the

man who was leaning against the bar.

The man didn't reply.

"Ain't you drinking?"

Still no reply.

Letting out an aggravated breath, the painfully skinny man hobbled to his normal spot behind the sorry excuse of a bar he kept. He slapped his hands flat down upon the surface he'd just wiped down so he could catch the silent man's attention.

"Yer either drinking or leaving, mister," the barkeep said. "Pick one."

"Fine" came the scratchy reply. "I'll leave."

Although the barkeep had started reaching for the stout club that was rarely out of arm's reach, he quickly decided that he didn't need it. The silent man was making his way toward the front door with his hands hanging at his sides.

Just when it seemed the man was going to leave peacefully, he stopped and looked halfway over his shoulder. "But I'm taking this one with me." With that, the man reached out and slapped his hand around the back of another man's neck.

That other man had been a regular for some time, but didn't exactly hold a warm spot in anyone's heart. He was simply a familiar stranger who'd occupied the same spot for long enough that he didn't attract any more glances. Nobody made a move to keep him from being dragged out by the scruff of his neck.

Nobody, that is, apart from the neck's owner.

"What the hell is this?" the man grunted as he felt himself get pulled away from the bar. In the next instant, he found himself heading straight for the front door. "Who the hell do you think you are?"

"I'm just the man you've been looking for," was the answer. And after he'd given it, Nick tightened his grip on the other man's neck and twisted just enough to look into the other man's eyes.

The man in Nick's grasp jolted as if he'd caught a spark from a piece of metal. After that initial reaction, his hand darted for the gun strapped around his waist. Before he could get a hold of the pistol, the man was given a painful reminder of where he was and what was happening. His feet stumbled against some uneven boards and then his face knocked against a battered doorframe.

Once outside, Nick jabbed an arm out that caught the man's shoulder. The impact sent the man stumbling against the front of the saloon, landing with a jarring rattle as his shoulders slammed against lumber.

Taking a moment to glance about, the

man saw that he was standing outside with his back against a wall, a few steps away from the saloon's front window. Standing in front of him, just as advertised, was the person he'd been waiting to see.

"Howdy," Nick said with a wink.

There was a moment where every sound in the world seemed to have been sucked away. Once that moment passed, the man against the wall reached for his gun. His hand made it to the weapon in his holster without being stopped. That good luck ran out, however, once Nick reached out to keep the man's hand in place.

Unable to draw or even take his arm back, the man let out his breath and stared Nick in the eyes. "What happens now, asshole?"

"I suppose that's up to you," Nick replied.

"You're the one who started this. I don't even know where the hell you came from."

"I've gotten good at sneaking around. Guess you could say it's sort of a necessity." When he said that last part, Nick grabbed the other man's shirt front with both hands so he could slam him against the wall one more time.

Once he realized his hand was now free, the other man went for his gun a third time.

There was the sound of iron brushing against leather, followed by the distinct *click* of a hammer being pulled back into firing position.

"But I'm still pretty good at other things too," Nick said as he pushed the barrel of his modified pistol into the other man's gut.

The man against the wall hadn't even cleared leather.

"You through trying to draw that pistol?" Nick asked. "Or do you want to give it another go?"

The man shook his head.

"Good. Use one finger and your thumb to pull the gun out and then let it drop."

Following Nick's commands to the letter, the man removed his gun from its holster and then let it fall to the ground. It hit the boardwalk with a noisy clatter before Nick kicked it into the closest alley.

Nodding, Nick backed off a step. He kept the gun aimed at the man's stomach.

"You got the wrong idea," the man against the wall said. "I don't know what you want with me."

"Let's start with why you're keeping watch on that undertaker's parlor down the street."

"I don't know what you're talking about."

Nick shook his head slowly. It was like the Grim Reaper coming to a decision on whether or not a man would live through the day. "You're not a good enough liar,"

Nick said. "Especially not after trying to draw your gun and shoot me down so many times already."

"Just defending myself."

"You were sitting in a spot so you could watch the street as well as that undertaker's parlor. You're not a drunk or a gambler and there were better places to sit if you were hiding. So, that only leaves one more thing for you to be."

"And what's that?" the man grunted.

"One of the men who's been hired to keep an eye on all the places I might be so they can report back to their master once they spot me."

The other man's face twitched so slightly that it could have easily been missed by an inexperienced eye. But there were no inexperienced eyes in front of that saloon. Nick spotted that twitch the moment it had started. After that, the bluster that was being forced into the other man's voice was as effective as cotton balls in a shotgun.

"I don't know who the hell you are or what you're talking about. But if you don't unhand me right quick, getting dragged in by the law is gonna be the least of your worries."

Nick weathered that storm with ease. When the other man stopped talking, he asked, "What law are you talking about? Maybe the likes of Red Parks?"

There was another twitch. Compared to the last one, this was an eruption under the man's face.

Nodding as though he could hear the thoughts flooding through the man's brain, Nick explained, "I may not know your name, but I know who you are. I sure as hell know what you're doing. Now I know who you're doing it for. You see, Red taught me the same things he taught you. That's how I know what to look for. And that's what made you stand out like a sore thumb."

The other man's first reaction was to put up another fight. But he could see well enough that it wouldn't have done any good. "You shouldn't have sent Skinner to do your dirty work," the man said with a new edge in his voice. "That son of a bitch was never good enough to bring Red down."

"The only place I sent Skinner was to his grave," Nick said. "And that was only because I thought Red was waiting on the other side to meet him."

"You're wrong about that."

"So it seems. Why don't you tell me where to go so I can set that straight once and for all?"

"I'll tell you where to go. You can go

139

straight to h—"

The man's threat was cut short by the touch of iron under his chin. When he heard the sudden burst of sound, the man nearly jumped out of his boots.

It turned out to be a nearby door rattling open, followed by the sound of heavy feet stomping outside.

Nick looked over to the pair of men walking onto the boardwalk with mild interest. The other two looked at him, then at the man against the wall, and kept walking.

"You see?" Nick asked. "That's the problem with thinking you're above everyone else. It tends to make people not give a damn about what happens to you."

"You gonna shoot me? Go ahead and do it."

"I just want to know where Red's at."

The other man shook his head. "He ain't here."

"All right, then. Where are the others Red sent?" Nick asked.

The other man squirmed a bit, but didn't respond.

Pressing the gun harder against the bottom of the man's jaw, Nick leaned in and repeated himself. "Where are the rest? I know you're not the only one here. When Red scouts a place, he never just sends one to do the job. Tell me where the others are or I'll kill you right here. Save me some time and I'll let you walk away."

Taking a moment to weigh his options, the man started sucking in his breaths as if each one was his last.

"Fine," Nick said while tightening his grip around the pistol. "Looks like I'll need to waste a few extra minutes."

"Wait, wait, wait! Hold on!" the man pleaded. "You're right, there's others in town."

"Where?"

"One's in the hotel down by the Porter House."

That was the restaurant where Catherine had been working the last time Nick had been through Jessup. It only made sense for Red to post a pair of eyes on that place awaiting his return.

"There's another watching some woman's house at the edge of —"

That was all Nick needed to hear. With a sharp snap of his wrist, the Schofield's handle cracked against jawbone. The light in the other man's eyes flickered out and he slumped sideways against the wall.

# TEN

Catherine's hands were wrapped around a rifle that was almost as long as a broomstick. Although she knew better than to stand around in the open when Nick had told her to keep inside, she wasn't about to hide herself away and just wait quietly. She'd been through too much already to allow anything to happen without putting up a fight.

At the moment, she was sitting in her kitchen with the rifle across her lap. Looking out through the house's back window, she could see anyone coming from the direction of town or the neighboring houses and could hear any horses approaching from the road out front. She had no trouble at all spotting the man who broke from the shadows to head straight to her and started to lift the rifle to give him a proper greeting. Catherine stopped short when she got a look at who that man actually was.

"Nick?" she said to the glass separating her from the rest of the world. "Is that you?"

She hurried toward the door and opened it so he could come into the house without breaking stride. Despite the fact that she hadn't been doing the running, she felt her own breaths coming in quick bursts right along with his. Catherine's heart bucked inside of her as though it was trying to break free from her rib cage. She'd only seen Nick move that fast once before and it was a night that lived on in her nightmares.

"Nick? What's wrong?" she asked once she was able to form the words.

"We need to get out of here," was his winded reply.

"What? Slow down and take a breath."

Nick hadn't stopped moving yet. Although he wasn't running, he was still darting from one spot to another as he made his way to every room in her home and glanced through every one of its windows. "Pack some clothes and whatever else you may need, Catherine."

"Why? What's going on?"

He wheeled around and fixed his eyes upon her. The full force of his gaze was almost a physical thing that pushed her back half a step. His hands reached out to take hold of her by the shoulders. His grip was insistent and strong enough to keep her from getting away.

"I can't stay here," he said. "They know I'm here. They know you're here. I need to leave town and you need to come with me. It's the only way for me to make sure you're safe."

For a few moments, Catherine couldn't take her eyes away from him. Nick's eyes were normally the color of a cool overcast sky. The color hadn't changed, but it seemed that the sun was trying to burn through the clouds in that sky. That intensity held her transfixed for a moment, rooting her to the spot.

His hands tightened around her shoulders before sliding up to land gently upon her face. "You just need to trust me on this," he said. "Please."

When she heard those words come from him, Catherine forgot about everything else around her. She forgot about the rifle in her hands and the reason she'd even picked it up. She forgot about the months of waiting and the months she'd tried to convince herself that she no longer cared about seeing Nick's face again.

All that mattered anymore was that instant. Thinking along those lines, the next words she said were really the only ones that she could ever imagine saying.

"I'll come with you, Nick."

With those words, she found herself being pulled out of the house and toward Nick's wagon. As Nick started to prepare the horses, Catherine stepped back and shook her head as if she was trying to wake up from a dream.

"Wait a minute," she said. "Where are we going? How long will we be gone?"

"I'm not sure," Nick replied. "It might be a while."

"Let me grab some clothes."

Nick watched as she propped the rifle against the wagon's wheel so she could run back into the little house. He wanted to go inside with her — if only to keep an eye on her while she packed. Then again, there was always the possibility that the men that had come into town to wait for him would close in around the house the moment Nick went inside. For every possibility or plan that Nick devised, a catastrophe took shape in his mind to match it. Rather than give in to any of the fears that were gaining momentum in his imagination, Nick stuck to what he could see and hear at that moment.

And, at that moment, he could see nothing but the rifle Catherine had left behind and could hear nothing but the sound of

145

her rummaging around inside her house. After a few minutes, she emerged carrying an overstuffed bag in each hand.

"I didn't know what to bring," she said while lugging the bags toward the wagon, "so I just brought it all."

Nick hopped down from the seat and took the bags from her. The smile on his face quickly vanished when his arm was nearly yanked from its socket and the rest of him was brought down as if he'd just grabbed an anchor. "You weren't kidding, were you?"

"I've seen you deal with worse things than a few heavy bags," Catherine scolded. "Now toss those up into that wagon before I change my mind."

Nick did as he was told and by the time he spotted Catherine again, she was already sitting in the seat at the front of the wagon. Before he could join her there, Nick looked around one more time. Those fears were still nipping at the back of his mind like persistent rodents.

"Stay right here," he said. "I'll be back."

Catherine twisted around in the seat to try and get a look at what Nick was doing. With the bulk of the wagon between herself and him, all she could make out was a broad shape covered in a battered set of clothes moving across the back of the vehicle.

"Here," came Nick's voice. "Catch."

Before she could ask any of the questions that popped into her mind, Catherine saw something almost as big as a broomstick flying through the air toward her. Reflexively, her hands snapped out and managed to catch the rifle before it hit her. The familiar weight of the rifle was little consolation now that she could no longer even see where Nick was.

Catherine sat in the wagon's seat with the rifle resting across her lap for a few minutes.

After a few more minutes had passed, she started to get mad that Nick had left her there alone.

One more minute after that, she started to get worried. But that wasn't because she was alone. It was because she could see she was about to be joined by at least two strangers making their way toward the wagon from a nearby cluster of trees.

One of the men was tall and broad-shouldered. There was plenty of girth on his frame, but more of that seemed to have come from eating too many pies instead of doing too much hard work. Then again, the shotgun he carried was more than enough bulk to make up for his flabby middle.

"Well, well," the stranger said. "Looks like the bitch is going hunting."

Before Catherine even had a chance to get offended by that, she saw more men stepping out from the surrounding area. She counted four of them before her eyes made it back to the one holding the shotgun.

Looking at that first stranger once more, Catherine saw yet another shape emerging from the surrounding cover.

"You know how long we been waiting in this piss bucket of a town?" the shotgunner asked. "So long I almost been ready to burn it down myself more'n once. But that waiting's all done now."

"Sure is," said the last man to step out from where he'd been hiding.

Glancing over his shoulder, the shotgunner only caught a glimpse of something moving toward him before he felt Nick's fist slam into his face.

Now the others who'd started to surround the wagon all turned to get a look at the last man Catherine had spotted. Nick wasn't about to let them get too good of a look before moving in to knock the next closest one off his feet.

Nick's knuckles were bloody by the time he made it to the second one in line, but that didn't stop him from punching that man in the mouth. The others who'd descended upon the wagon were bringing their guns up to fire, but were unable to get their sights on Nick before their target had moved on.

After a flurry of punches, Nick was close enough to the wagon to climb up on the side where Catherine was sitting. Rather than move aside to let him on, she brought up her rifle and pointed it at the side of his head.

"Better move," she said.

Nick didn't need to hear any more than that to do just what he'd been told. As soon as he ducked, the rifle let out a smoky belch over his head that set his ears to ringing bad enough to shake his brain. While he was hanging off the side of the wagon, Nick took a look behind him to see Catherine's target.

The man with the shotgun was still holding his weapon. In fact, he was pointing it at Nick's back and might have done some real damage if Catherine hadn't put a load of buckshot into his left shoulder.

A gaping wound yawned open like a toothless mouth in the shotgunner's flesh. A blank stare remained frozen on his face for a few moments before the shotgunner dropped over like a tin silhouette in a shooting gallery.

Climbing over Catherine's lap, Nick didn't waste time getting himself situated before taking hold of the reins and giving them a strong snap. The horses may not have been in their prime, but they were already rattled by the gunfire and more than ready to get moving. Feeling the crack of leather against their backs was exactly what Rasa and Kazys had been waiting for.

The wagon lurched into motion and Nick somehow managed to keep his footing. A shot cracked through the air and took a bite out of the wagon's backside. That gave the horses even more incentive.

"Nick? Are you all right?" Catherine shouted over the gunfire as well as the ringing in her ears.

But Nick was still on the move and jumping over the back of the driver's seat. "Don't worry about me," he shouted back at her. "Just take the reins and head out of town. I'll be right back."

"Back? Back from where?!"

When he was younger, Nick could have moved over the back of that wagon, even if it had been going twice as fast. In fact, when he was younger, he'd pulled even dumber stunts just to pass the time. But Nick wasn't exactly that man anymore. He was given a reminder of that when he tried to grab hold of the side of the wagon and swing himself down from the bouncing, creaking box on wheels.

A stabbing pain shot through his elbow as the joint was twisted a bit too much in the wrong direction. Gritting his teeth and straining with every muscle in his upper body, Nick managed to roll on to his side and bring himself to a stop on the ground in the wagon's wake.

The remaining gunmen had scattered a bit when Catherine had fired her shot. Now they were coming back in like a noose closing around Nick's neck. One of them managed to get to his gun and almost drew a bead on his target before Nick pulled the modified Schofield from its holster and took a shot of his own.

The pistol barked once and sent the man reeling back. The pain shooting through Nick's elbow was the only reason his shot hadn't done more than open a nasty flesh wound in his target. Nick compensated for the pain in his arm and adjusted his aim accordingly. When he shifted the pistol toward the next man aiming at him, he squeezed the trigger and put a bullet straight through the gunman's heart.

The other man's arms dropped to his sides and he fell over like a puppet whose strings had been cut.

All of this happened in the space of a few seconds, leaving only a pair of gunmen on their feet and plenty of blood on the ground. Several more shots went off, but none of them found their marks. The men who'd fired them were too busy running in opposite directions and firing wildly over their shoulders.

Nick leveled his gun at the closest one and took aim. He stopped himself before firing, however, since none of his targets were interested in fighting any longer. Even so, Nick didn't holster his pistol until the last of the gunmen had tossed their weapons and found somewhere else to be.

Turning to get a look at where the wagon had gone, Nick jumped a bit when he found it to be no more than ten yards from where he'd last seen it. Catherine had the reins gripped tightly in one hand and the rifle cradled in the other.

"They didn't want to go far without you," she said, nodding toward the horses. "And neither did I."

Nick looked up at Catherine's face and kept his eyes on her for a couple of seconds. The first portion of that time was to make sure she was all right. The second portion was just to enjoy the view. "Is that rifle reloaded?"

She nodded.

"Then cover me while I take a look at something." With that, Nick walked over to the body of the shotgunner stretched out in the dirt.

Some men might have been squeamish about putting their hands on a dead man. Others might have felt peculiar about rummaging through a corpse's pockets. But Nick was neither sort of man. He was one who did both of those things for a living. Of course, it was usually under better circumstances.

Nick pushed the shotgunner over and unceremoniously reached into the man's inner jacket pocket. When he pulled his hand back, he was holding a small piece of paper. He looked it over and then tucked that paper into his own shirt pocket. After that, Nick climbed into the driver's seat and got himself situated. "You all right?" he asked.

Catherine nodded. "What about you?"

Examining his scraped hands and working the kinks from his elbow, Nick replied, "Just a few dents put into my pride, but that's about it."

"Who were those men?"

Nick took another look at the gunmen who were spread out on the ground and shook his head. "I don't have the faintest idea. They look familiar to you?"

"Sorry, but you're the only gunfighter whose face I've committed to memory."

Shifting his eyes over to her, Nick said, "If I didn't know any better, I'd say you were enjoying this."

"It just reminds me of old times, that's all."

"I wouldn't think those times would bring such a smile to your face."

"Then maybe it just feels good to be shooting back for a change."

"Now *that,*" Nick said as he snapped the reins, "I can believe."

Rasa and Kazys rattled their heads a bit and stomped their hooves against the dirt when they felt the leather flick over their backs. After giving Nick a good enough amount of hell, they leaned forward and got the wagon moving in earnest.

# ELEVEN

The town of Jessup slowly faded behind the wagon. Rasa and Kazys fell into a plodding rhythm of digging their hooves into the dirt, leaning forward, and pulling the wagon along the trail. Before too long, the horses were moving well enough that they hardly even needed to be steered.

Nick sat with his back against the seat and his legs propped up against the front of the wagon without giving more than the occasional glance to the trail ahead. At the moment, he was examining the paper he'd found in the shotgunner's pocket. With the sun behind him, he had plenty of light in which to read.

Catherine had moved herself into the back of the wagon, where she sat and sifted through her bags. Although Catherine was a bit lower than him, her back was almost against Nick's as she went through layer upon layer of clothing that had been hastily tossed into the bags. Now that it was folded a little neater, she discovered that she had a good amount of space left to be filled.

"I could have packed more," she said.

"Hmm?"

"I could have packed more," she repeated. Slapping her hands against the top of her folded clothes, she groaned, "I should have packed more. How long are we going to be away?"

"Hmm?"

Frustrated, Catherine twisted around to get a better look over her shoulder. "Are you listening to me?"

"Oh. Yeah. You should have packed more."

Rather than try to carry on the conversation at such a disadvantage, Catherine got to her feet and climbed back into the driver's seat from the back of the wagon. It wasn't the easiest task, but the wagon was open enough for her to move without having to negotiate too many obstacles. The wheels were turning fairly well, but had been moving at the same speed for so long that neither of the passengers even felt the jostling any longer.

Once she was on the seat beside Nick, Catherine took a moment to see if she was noticed. Nick was still studying the paper in his hands carefully. The only time he took his eyes from it was when he felt the quick peck of Catherine's lips against his cheek.

"What was that for?" he asked as he snapped his head around to get a look at her.

Catherine shrugged and smiled. "Mostly to get your attention."

Judging by the look on Nick's face, she'd succeeded.

"What's that?" Catherine asked, nodding toward the paper in Nick's hand.

Twitching back toward the object he was holding, Nick's expression was partly troubled and partly disappointed. "It's a business card," he replied.

"And you found that in the pocket of one of those men?"

Nick nodded.

"Whose card is it?"

"Here," he said. "Take a look for yourself."

With that, Nick handed over the card and shifted his eyes toward the road splayed out in front of him.

The country they were passing through was an expanse of flat fields of tall light brown grass. As they got closer to the Missouri border, those fields would give way to green rolling hills.

" 'RP Collections,' " Catherine said. She turned the card over so she could look at the back and then took a second look at both sides before handing it back to Nick. "It's the same as the one Dan Callum was given. Does it mean anything to you?"

"That was the name of the business Red Parks supposedly ran in Virginia City," Nick said.

"Supposedly?"

"That's right. The titles 'vigilante' or 'leader of a lynch mob' didn't look quite so good in print. I also found one of these cards on the man who was watching me in Wyoming. My guess is that just about every man I've been forced to go up against has been carrying one of those cards."

"You mean every man who tried to stop us from leaving?"

"Them and the others who have been after me."

Catherine settled into the seat and put her feet up onto the edge. The wagon rocked back and forth to the steps of the horses. Rasa and Kazys were moving along at a steady walk, which was just enough to move the passengers as if they were being rocked by a gentle hand. "You know something? Before you came into my life, hearing someone talk about these things would've bothered me."

"And what about now?" Nick asked.

"Now it doesn't bother me so much. Is there anything we can do about it right now?"

"Not really."

"And are you going to tell me where we're headed?"

"Ellis Station, Missouri."

"And you know how to get there?" Catherine asked.

"From what I gather, it's in a spot not too far from where that bridge was blown up a few years ago. Red must be nosing around some more spots he thinks I might show up. Ellis Station sounds close, but it's not quite the place he's after."

"Close to what?"

Nick sighed and looked off to one side. "I grew up in Missouri. My father still lives there, but he's in a town called Saunders Pass. At least, he was the last time I saw him."

"And when was that?"

Still gazing out at the grass which swayed in the breeze, Nick replied, "Over ten years ago."

Nick didn't say much after that and Catherine wasn't about to press him. It had been a long day and their nerves were just beginning to unwind after the fiery way they'd left Jessup. For the moment, it did her some good to sit back, close her eyes, and let the winds shift around her.

There would be plenty of time to talk on their way to Ellis Station.

After a quiet night camping under the stars, Nick had loaded up the wagon while Catherine fixed some breakfast. With their bellies filled and a few hours' sleep under their belts, they found themselves climbing back on to the wagon's seat. Rasa and Kazys weren't happy about it, but the horses got the wagon rolling toward the Missouri border after a few snaps of the reins.

Having grown up in Nebraska, Catherine was accustomed to wide-open spaces. But she hadn't really enjoyed them since she was young enough to take off running in one direction and not stop until her legs got tired. Jessup was a nice enough town, but there was something about not having any walls in sight that made her soul swell up and press against the inside of her body.

Looking over at Nick was enough to make that feeling even better. It was a new day and there was a contented smile on Nick's face that seemed a little out of place simply because he so rarely wore it.

Nick lay back with his feet up and the reins dangling over one leg. The trail was stretched out in front of them and the horses had nowhere else to go but straight ahead. The sun was slowly working its way across the sky, giving the air a warmth that smelled of damp earth and blossoming trees.

"I love it out here," Nick said.

"It is beautiful."

"I've always loved it out in the open like this. Out on the prairie, in the mountains, even in the desert."

"You like to be alone?"

He considered that for a moment before shrugging. "I guess everyone likes that sometimes."

"Is that why you do the job you do?" Catherine asked. "Is that why you're a Mourner?"

"I learned my trade from my father. He dug graves and made coffins. He taught me carpentry and eventually how to chisel rock so we could carve headstones. We learned that one together, actually."

"Were you two always close?"

Nick didn't answer that. At least, he didn't answer in words. The look in his eyes as he stared a hole into the horizon spoke volumes.

"Did your father always live out in the open?" she asked, making a clumsy attempt to steer back toward the subject. "Maybe that's why you like having all that space around you."

Nick let out the breath that he'd been holding and glanced up at the sky. They'd been riding all day and it was starting to grow darker. Stars were just beginning to poke through the veil of sunlight. Lowering his gaze to the earth, Nick held it there and said, "Actually, we did always live in places like this. But that was because of something I said as a kid."

"Really?" she asked, perplexed at the notion of Nick Graves as a child. "What did you say?"

"It was right after we got to this country. We got off the boat, my father and me, and he tried to scrounge up some work. I don't remember too much of it," he lied, "but I do recall it being a rough trip."

"How rough?"

"Let's just say that my father brought me and my mother onto the ship bound for America. Only me and him walked off of it."

Catherine paused for a moment and tried to think of something to say. "I'm sorry to hear that," was the best she could do.

He shook the words off. "When we got off that boat, I said that I hated the sea and never wanted to go near it again. My father loaded me up onto a stagecoach and we headed west. We didn't stop until we reached Missouri. He said it felt close enough to the middle of the country to suit us."

"He sounds like a good man," Catherine said with a smile.

Now Nick had to pause as he chewed on what he'd just said. Judging by the look on his face, he seemed a bit surprised to have heard some of it himself. Before too long, he shrugged and said, "You're right. Still is one, I suppose. He was a good father. I just don't think he knew what to do with me once I didn't need anyone to wipe my nose.

"There just got to be a point, right about the time I stopped growing like a weed, that he sort of reached the end of his rope." Part of that sentence brought a fond smile to Nick's face. He seemed to catch himself in the middle of it and straightened up. "Then again, I guess I was kind of a handful."

Catherine smiled and shook her head. "Something tells me that you were more than a handful."

"I guess you could say that." Nick took hold of the reins and gave them a gentle flick. "You ask him and he'd probably tell you things that would make you wonder why you were foolish enough to listen to a word I said. Coming along with me like this would seem downright crazy."

"So does he still live in Missouri?"

"Probably. After coming to this country, he never had any gumption to travel anywhere else. I got a burr under my saddle and started fixing to leave and he wouldn't have any of it." Nick's eyes took on a faraway quality. "He wanted me to be proper and ply the family trade and I wanted to raise hell and make my mark. Once I broke away that first time, there was no looking back. I may not have been on the straight and narrow, but it sure beat the hell out of digging graves."

Catherine rubbed Nick's back and said, "Things are different now. You're not some wild kid anymore. Maybe your father would like to see how you turned out."

"If I wanted that kind of grief, I'd go straight to Saunders Pass. I think I'd rather see what Red's got going on at Ellis Station and meet up with him there before he gets around to pestering my family."

"Why would meeting your father again be so bad?"

"Let's just say he'd run out of breath ten times over before he got done telling me what a mess I'd made of things. Until recently, we've both been content to tell folks that the other one doesn't exist. I let folks believe my father's dead so they won't go looking for him. He tells folks I'm dead because . . . well . . . to him, I probably am."

"He's your father, Nick," Catherine said while touching his arm. "He still cares about you. I think you need to see him again. He won't be around forever, you know."

"My pa's been digging graves in the same cemetery for so long that he's practically a part of those hills. He's not a threat to anyone, but that won't stop Red from hurting him if he's trying to flush me out. Hopefully, I can get to him before he decides to go into Saunders Pass."

"That's all the more reason to go see your father first. You know, to keep him safe."

Nick shook his head and spoke with steely resolve. "My father wouldn't trust me to protect him. He'd probably just spout off about how I was the cause of all this trouble. Even if he was right, he wouldn't help matters any."

"All right, then," Catherine said with some steel of her own in her voice. "If you won't consider visiting your father, could you at least consider telling me what we're doing out here? I mean, I came along because I trust you, but I deserve to know what's going on."

Nick told her about what had happened, starting all the way back at the table in Petunia's. He told her about meeting up with Shad as well as the man that he'd found in the saloon across the street from Jessup's post office. Catherine listened to the story intently, taking it all in without interrupting him.

When Nick stopped talking, Catherine asked, "And you're certain it's Red Parks who's after you?"

"I was certain the moment I saw for myself that Red wasn't in that coffin."

"Why would he be after you?"

"I'm not sure yet. I would have thought he'd be done with me by now. All I know for certain is that Red sent some gunmen to keep an eye on me and even knew where to send his men once I left Wyoming. If I could, I'd make it so you never got touched by any of this. Right now, I need to keep you safe and make do with the way things are." Nick snapped the reins again and added, "Me and Red have our own business to take care of. It won't be pretty, but it's got to be put to rest."

"I think I recall you mentioning Red," Catherine said after Nick had squirmed enough. "I thought you used to look up to him."

"We didn't exactly start off on the right foot. I was still a kid, and I was riding with some known men. Actually, I was getting to be a known man right around then."

As Nick spoke, he stared at the road ahead without actually seeing it. His eyes drifted from the slow bobbing of the horses' heads to the clouds ambling across the sky. "We were riding through Montana, which was pretty close to lawless back then. It was a great time to be young and full of fire and a great place to ride if you were stirring up trouble.

"We made it all the way to Virginia City before we caught up with anything close to the law. They called themselves the Vigilance Committee, but they weren't much more than a band of killers with masks. Only thing that separated them from us was that they had the support of the folks in town because they ran off young punks like me and my friends."

"You and Skinner?" Catherine asked, thinking back to the mad dog that she'd gotten to know all too well.

"Yeah," Nick replied with no small amount of shame in his voice. "Me and Skinner. Back then, I was learning a hell of a lot from Skinner. Mostly how to shoot and fight and do it all without getting caught. We were pretty lucky that so many of us made it to Virginia City at all. But once we got there, our luck ran out. At least it did for most of us."

"You were caught by the Committee," Catherine guessed.

Nodding, Nick said, "We were set up, actually. I found that out when I got back in touch with another friend of mine who I thought was dead. Barrett Cobb was the smart one among us. He knew Skinner was leading us straight into hell and thought the only way for him to split up with us was to break up the whole gang.

"Barrett scouted out Virginia City, tipped off the Committee, and rode us all in there without a care in the world." As he spoke, Nick could hear the shots that had been fired all those years ago. He could still hear echoes of his own voice screaming with helpless rage.

"We were rounded up," he said in a voice that was getting rougher with each word. "And strung up. I thought I was dead too, but I was knocked out and when I woke up I was looking at Red Parks. He led the Committee. He was standing there right next to Skinner."

Nick's laugh was a short, humorless chopping sound. "He and Skinner pulled me aside so they could talk to me." Shaking his head, Nick glared at the horizon. "Talk to me while the others were off being hung. Red told me that I could do better than what I was doing. Skinner told him that I had talent." That last word came out like a vulgarity.

"Red offered to let my friends go if I joined up with him and I accepted because it seemed like an exciting way to do the right thing. Looking back, I can't figure out which is more absurd: Red's offer or the fact that I took him up on it."

# TWELVE

*Virginia City, Montana*
*1866*

Life in the Vigilance Committee was a good one.

Although nobody in town had elected a single member to the Committee, nobody was about to ask any of them to step down. In fact, the locals seemed to respect the Committee as a whole. They didn't have to see through burlap to know whose faces were under those masks. Everyone who'd lived in Virginia City knew that there was no real law that would protect them. There were no men in badges who were worth a damn to put teeth into the ordinances and decrees that made up a civilized society.

Word had spread over the years that small towns like Virginia City were easy pickings for anyone with a horse and a gun. Roads were unsafe and ravaged by the lawless. Fights broke out, blood was spilled, lives were lost, and nobody had to answer for it.

Nobody, that is, until the Vigilance Committee started hanging the lawless from trees and rafters.

After enough outlaws had been strung up, the killings started to taper off. Roads became safe and the only ones who needed to be afraid in Virginia City were those who had plans on crossing the Committee.

Folks could live their lives again. They could raise their families without cursing the world their kin had been thrown into and they tipped their hats every day to the men who made it all possible. Gratitude was shown in the form of goods and services. But most of all, Committee members were seen as heroes.

Yes, life in the Committee was good. Nick Graves found that out soon after he'd joined their ranks. It didn't take long for folks to notice the new voice in the darkness as the men bearing torches made their rounds. There was a fresh set of eyes staring out through holes in a newly slashed burlap mask.

Weeks passed into months and months into years. All this time, the locals grew accustomed to their new protector and tipped their hats to young Nick Graves, who'd moved in to sink some roots in Big Sky

Country. They hadn't warmed up to him at first. After all, Nick's roughness was worn proudly in everything from the strut in his step to the fire in his eyes.

Talk had circulated throughout town about Nick Graves, but nobody dared to say a word in front of Red Parks. When Red was around, they gave him a few kind words, a friendly wave, and then moved along.

But as time passed, Nick was accepted among the Committee as well as the rest of Virginia City. In fact, both groups were real glad to have him on their side. Especially on days like this one.

Four days ago, two cowboys had drifted into town looking to get drunk and paw the first working girl they could find. The cowboys had been rowdy, but no more so than any other young man who'd been on the trail for a bit too long. They'd made some noise and hadn't started more trouble than the saloon owner could handle.

That changed, however, once the rest of the cowboys showed up.

Two more of them rode into town late on the fifth day. The sun was just setting and the sky had turned the color of freshly spilled blood. After the sun had set and the music had started pouring from the piano inside the town's biggest saloon, another three cowboys joined the rest.

Once the liquor flowed into all seven of them, the shots had started to go off and bodies started to fall. The first one to hit the floor was a kid who'd made the mistake of calling one of the cowboys the cheater that he was. That kid now lay on the floor with a gaping bloody hole where his right eye had formerly been.

"What the hell is going on over there?" the barkeep shouted. "I told you boys there's to be no shooting in here!"

One of the cowboys got up from where he'd been sitting, still holding the smoking revolver in his fist. "He was cheating."

The barkeep stepped from behind the bar. When he was clear of the large wooden structure, the shotgun in his hands was plain enough to see. "Put that gun down," he said in a steady voice. "Right now."

Every voice fell silent.

The music stopped.

Even the clock on the wall over the door seemed reluctant to tick.

"Sure," the cowboy said. "I wasn't the only one at this table to see this prick was cheatin'. I was just the first to do anything about it."

"We'll decide that later. For now, just put

the gun down."

The cowboy was of medium height. He had a dark complexion, which had gotten that way after spending years under an unforgiving sun. An unruly mustache covered his upper lip in a mass of thick dark curls. As he lowered his gun to the table in front of him, he smiled accommodatingly.

Nodding, the barkeep said, "All right, then. You need to come along with me and we can get this straightened out. Anyone else who saw what happened will need to come along as well, so —"

"Hold up now," the cowboy interrupted. "I'm not going nowhere."

The nervous pain in the barkeep's chest came back with a vengeance. He gripped his shotgun and struggled to keep his fear from showing on his face.

"I'm not through with my game," the cowboy said. "And my friends aren't through with their drinks."

"I . . . I'll have to ask you to leave," the barkeep stammered. "You and your friends."

"You want them to leave? Then you can say it to their faces."

Taking that as a signal, the other cowboys stood up so quickly that their chairs were knocked over behind them. Three of the remaining six slapped their hands against the guns at their hips. The other three had cleared leather before their legs had brought them up to their full height.

Where there had so recently been silence, there was now chaos. Gunshots filled the air for no more than a few seconds as hot lead pierced the veil of cigar smoke that hung in the saloon. Wood was splintered, women screamed, and men dove for cover. Glass shattered and flesh was ripped open as two of those cowboys' shots found their mark on the barkeep's body.

As he went down to one knee, the barkeep tightened his finger around the trigger of his shotgun. Fire and smoke roared from the twin barrels, filling the room with so much noise that it seemed the mouth of hell itself had opened up and yawned. Although the buckshot mostly dug into the floor and some furniture, the shotgun definitely had an effect upon the cowboys.

The cowboys who'd stood up now dropped straight down again. A few of them crouched behind whatever cover they could find while the card player of the bunch took hold of his table and flipped it on to its side. The body of the kid accused of cheating flopped onto the floor like a discarded rag doll.

"Jesus Christ," the barkeep muttered as

the pain from his fresh wound began to assert itself. Reaching down with one hand, he felt along the spot on his side where heat and cold were mingling beneath his flesh. His hand felt something wet. When he pulled it up to take a look, he saw dark crimson smeared over his fingers. "Aw Jesus."

"I'm going for help!" shouted a bespectacled man who practically lived at the table closest to the front door.

Before anyone could say a word or try to stop him, the bespectacled man was gone. The door leading out to the street rattled against its frame in his wake.

"Goddammit, stop him!" the lead cowboy screamed.

One of the cowboys was a squat blond kid in his late twenties. His face was covered with stubble and his hair hung down low enough to cover his ears and forehead. "Too late, Jace. He's already took off across the street."

Picking up the closest one of his partners that he could reach, Jace hauled a cowboy with greasy black hair onto his feet and shoved him toward the narrow window at the front of the saloon. "Take a look for yourself, for Christ's sake! He's probably out there just screaming for the law."

"Ain't no law here," the cowboy grunted as he was shoved toward the window. The last of those words fogged up the window as they came out of his mouth. That same piece of fogged glass suddenly exploded inward as a pistol barked from the street outside.

The bullet shattered the glass along with the cowboy's greasy skull, snapping his head to one side as if he'd been knocked with an unseen punch. His mouth opened, but nothing came out. The expression on his face was so surprised that it might have been funny if it wasn't painted on to a dead man.

Jace ran to the window so quickly that he could have caught his partner as his body keeled over. Instead, he let the corpse drop so he could focus on what was outside. "Hey, Travis," he called over his shoulder. "Come here and take a look at this."

Everyone else in the saloon was finding the courage to poke their heads up, now that the number of cowboys had been whittled down by one. One of the men at the bar found a bit too much courage and made a reach for his gun. The blond cowboy shifted his aim toward the overanxious drunk and put him down like a rabid dog.

The other remaining cowboys jumped at

the sound of the shots, but calmed when they saw it was one of their own doing the shooting.

"Jesus, Thirsty, what was that for?" asked one of the younger cowboys. His face and body were so narrow that his clothes seemed to be hanging on a dressmaker's dummy rather than a person. His dark hair was shot through with light streaks, making him appear even more boyish in contrast to the others.

Thirsty's teeth were gritted until the skin around his jaw was whiter than the sun-bleached tips of his hair. "He was going for his gun."

"That was a mistake, asshole."

Everyone in the saloon turned to look at who'd spoken those words. The man they spotted was stepping through the front door, flanked by three others. It was difficult to pin down which of them had actually spoken, since none of them had a mouth or even a face that could be seen through the rough burlap sacks covering their heads.

All four men wore long coats over simple brown trousers and shirts. They carried guns in hands wrapped in work gloves. They varied in height and weight, but it was impossible to say by how much. The way they were dressed, there could have been anything under those coats. The burlap sacks covering their heads and tied at the neck could have concealed any sort of demon.

But it was the eyes staring out from behind the burlap that rattled the six remaining cowboys. Those eyes were the only pieces of humanity that could be seen on any of the four men. It was like seeing breath come from the jagged mouth of a scarecrow.

"What's going on here?" the masked man in front of the others asked.

The youngest cowboy practically tripped over himself to put a few more steps between himself and the masked men. "That's them, Jace. That's the ones I warned you about."

Now that more of his buddies were making their presence known throughout the saloon, Jace smirked confidently. Here and there, other cowboys were standing up or shifting to get their hands closer to their weapons. "So this is the big, bad Vigilance Committee?" He took a step closer and met the leader's gaze. "They ain't but a bunch of cowards who hide their faces."

"Maybe they're just ugly," said one of the other cowboys who'd just now gotten up the courage to step forward. "Maybe they's afraid to scare the ladies."

For a moment, it seemed as though none of the eyes staring out through those holes were capable of blinking.

The leader's glare shifted from the cowboys to the dead body in front of the overturned card table. "Did you kill this boy?"

Having found a bit more courage, the cowboy from the back of the room took another step forward. "So what if we did? The little bastard had it —"

"He shot Milt too!" came a voice from the crowd.

The leader of the Committee shifted his gaze once more. "That true, Milt?" When he saw the barkeep nod and hold up his blood-covered hand, the eyes beneath the mask shifted to the Committee member on his right.

Seeing that, the Committee member next to the leader snapped his arm down to his side and drew a pistol amid the flutter of his open coat. The sound of iron brushing against leather was still floating through the air as the gunshot blasted straight down the middle of the saloon. Smoke and fire blossomed in front of the second Committee member, briefly illuminating the curve of nose and chin beneath the rough mask. His eyes blinked once as the gun went off. Other than that, he might as well have been a machine.

The cowboy at the back of the room dropped as if he'd been kicked by a mule. His back hit the floor with a definitive *thump,* driving the last bit of air from his lungs. It was plain to see by the unnatural tilt of his head and the position of his body that those lungs would never fill again.

"Anyone else got something to say?" the Committee's leader asked.

There were a few excited murmurs throughout the saloon, but those came from the locals.

The eyes behind the Committee leader's mask shifted from one cowboy to another. "No? Well, then, I guess I'll take you boys into custody."

"The hell you will," Jace snarled in a voice that seemed to have clawed its way out from the back of his throat.

When they saw Jace lift his gun while wearing that crazy look on his face, the other cowboys followed suit. It was hard to tell if they were backing his play or if they simply knew they'd run out of options. Whichever it was, they raised their guns and started pulling their triggers while following

Jace toward the saloon's front window. As the fire exploded from the barrels of their guns, everything else inside the saloon seemed to explode as well.

Two of the Committee members stepped to one side and ducked behind the closest table. Along the way, they took quick aim and pulled their triggers. The leader and the man to his right held their ground, but only to put themselves in slightly better position to fire upon their targets.

With every shot that was fired, the smoke inside the saloon grew thicker and thicker. Finally, it formed a swirling black mass that writhed in the air like a living thing as lead hissed back and forth through it. The stench of burnt powder caught in the back of everyone's throat, turning panicked screams into hoarse hacking coughs.

By the time the front window shattered completely, the rush of fresh air was like a gift from the outside. Glass shards spattered onto the dirt, soon to be followed by the heavy impact of Jace's body flying from the saloon.

Once outside, Jace looked up and did his best to suck in a breath to replace the wind he'd lost in his fall. Shots were still blazing inside the saloon, but it was too late to worry about that now. He was more concerned with taking his next breath.

Just then, another one of the cowboys dropped to the ground outside the window. Jace twisted around to get a look as he struggled to get back onto his feet. He caught a glimpse of a familiar face, but the eyes were already glazed over and blood caked a gaping wound in his head. The last few moments of fear and panic were still plain to see in the cowboy's face, but the last flicker of life was already gone from it.

Jace struggled to keep from shaking while he got to his feet. More of his partners were exiting through the window. Though they were bloodied and swearing up a storm, at least they were alive.

Thirsty grunted as he dropped onto the ground outside the window and fired another shot into the saloon. "Travis is right behind me."

As if on cue, Travis leapt through the broken window. The moment he turned toward the street, he froze and lifted his gun. Spread out in front of him were the remaining Committee members, walking straight toward the saloon with their guns held in steady hands.

Jace and Thirsty's eyes were red and watering from all the smoke inside the saloon. Because of that, they hadn't seen the masked men until it was almost too late. The Committee members closed in on them like devils coming in to take a fresh soul to hell. Their guns went off at almost the same time, spitting smoke and lead in their direction.

The cowboys' screams were washed away by the roar of the gunfire, but their bodies kept moving. Blood sprayed into the air, but that didn't stop them from running flat-out to the horses waiting for them nearby. Although the animals were rearing and kicking due to all the noise, they responded to their riders' touch and allowed the cowboys to climb into the saddle.

By this time, the Committee members who had been inside the saloon were stepping out through the window and front door. Cowboys were scattering in every direction, running into the street like headless chickens.

Once all the cowboys had made it to their horses, they got moving like they'd been shot from a cannon. The Committee was close behind them, mounting horses that were every bit as immune to the gunfire as the men who sat in their saddles.

"Let's show these boys the error of their ways," shouted the leader of the masked men.

# Thirteen

The Committee rode back in high spirits. After tugging the ropes from around their necks, they pulled off their masks and draped them over their knees. Riding toward the stable, they swapped stories and even jokes about the men they'd successfully run out of town.

"Did you see the look on that skinny one's face?" Pete Masters asked. "I swear he was about to shit himself."

Pete was a good-natured sort who always wore a smile on his round face. A brushy mustache covered his lip like a row of black weeds sprouting from his nose. Thick callused hands grasped the reins. He sat with a slouching, easygoing posture in his saddle.

Will Culligan was another of the Committee members who rode at the end of the row. "I think he did shit himself after ol' Nicky there dropped his friend. Brad'll laugh his ass off when he hears about that."

Riding next to Will, an older man by the name of Bob Ralston started laughing in a series of scratchy snorts erupting from the back of his throat. Bob was in his early fifties and had the gray streaks in his otherwise dark hair and beard to show for it. He also had the scars on his face and arms that came from a life spent in wars of one kind or another. Whether he was battling Indians, Rebs, or outlaws, he always had a gun strapped around his waist.

Although the men rode on in more or less of a straight row, the ranks were shown in the subtle way that the middle of that row was allowed to ride one or two steps ahead of the rest. At the top of the pecking order was Red Parks, a skinny man with a steely edge to him that was shown in the angle of his chin to the spark in his eye. Red never allowed himself to relax too much, but he did smile and nod to the jokes that were being tossed about.

Pete Masters rode at Red's left and a little behind. The man keeping pace with Red was named Owen. He had sandy blond hair and a crooked smile etched on to his face. Owen only rode with the Committee every now and then, but since he was Red's brother, nobody put up much of a fuss. Riding on the other side of the Committee's leader was its newest member: a kid by the name of Nick Graves.

Nick looked an awful lot like most of the trash that the Committee either strung up or kicked out of town. He was wide at the shoulders and broad through the chest, sporting the muscle of a young man who was plenty used to fighting for what he wanted. His posture was straight as an arrow and the upward lift of his chin reflected a cockiness that meant he didn't mind looking down his nose at the rest of the world. But his eyes were the feature that gave him the look of a dangerous man. They were predator's eyes that saw everything, figured all the angles, and did so without a trace of feeling.

After all Nick had been through, he figured he'd done pretty well for himself. Barrett and the rest of the gang were long gone. Skinner had moved back to his old ways, but at least he was raising hell somewhere else. That one was like an arrow broken off inside a wound. He couldn't be removed without making a mess, but things sure felt better once he was gone.

After proving himself time and again in the eyes of the Committee, Nick felt like he was truly one of them. He laughed and joked right along with the others. He missed his gang, but at least the Committee gave him something to do that was worth doing.

"I barely meant to kill that cowboy," Nick said. "I thought he'd duck or something when I made my move."

"No need to apologize," Red said. "That's just one less noose to fill if them boys ever decide to show their faces around here again."

"If we need to find them," Owen said, "we can just follow the trail of piss they left behind."

Everyone got a laugh out of that. Owen was always good for a few laughs when he came along for a ride, which was another reason the Committee didn't mind him tagging along.

"You mean we're not going after them?" another Committee member asked from farther down the line.

"We dropped three of them by my count. That makes up for the boy they killed today." After a few quiet seconds had gone by, Red shifted in his saddle so he could look at each member of the Committee in turn. "Don't worry about nothing. We'll cross paths with those cowboys before too long. We only let them think they shook us in them hills so we could be home in time for supper. They might want to live like animals, but that don't mean we have to."

The rest of the Committee nodded and relaxed a bit, but still seemed a little on edge. Even Owen wasn't smiling as much as usual. Ever since they'd chased the remaining cowboys into the open range outside of town, they'd been set for a hanging. Since plenty more had swung for doing less, letting those cowboys go just didn't sit right among the vigilantes.

"Hey, Bob," Red called over his shoulder. "You recognize that young fella that nearly messed his trousers?"

Bob squinted and then nodded. "I think I seen him in town before. Could'a been around Missy Weyland's place."

"That's exactly right. And that's exactly where we'll meet up with them cowboys again. At least, that's where we'll meet up with that young one. When we do, he'll lead us back to them others."

Nick shook his head. "After they cool their heels, they might just work up the courage to come gunning for us. If we head back out right now, we might be able to catch them when they're still rattled."

"Rattled ain't necessarily good, Nick. They're twitchy right now and that means they'll start shooting at us the moment we're in sight. Once they calm down a bit, they'll get sloppy and we can get in close to finish the job we started."

"I'll want to be along for that," Owen said. "I think one of their shots ripped my favorite jacket."

There was a little more laughter, but it was forced at best.

Nick, on the other hand, didn't even try to slap a smile onto his face. He didn't much like the idea of letting those cowboys go, even if it was only for a little while. Despite his misgivings, Nick agreed to it all the same. After all, there wasn't much else he or anyone else could do to change Red's mind once it was set.

Once the Committee put their horses up for the night, they went their separate ways. Each of the men had a home and family to tend to. Each of them except for Nick, that is. Nick had a home, but he saw it mostly as a house on loan for the time being. It was filled with the necessities of life, but not much else. Most of the time, it wasn't even occupied.

Nick spent most of his time outside. He sat on the ground with his back against his house and his legs stretched out on the ground. One hand was usually draped over his stomach while the other kept itself busy plucking grass from the dirt. This night wasn't any different and Nick was outside under the stars when he heard someone approaching. Nick's hand went reflexively to the grip of his gun as he turned to see who was paying him a visit.

"Evening, Red," Nick said as his hand left his gun and went back to pulling weeds.

"Howdy, Nick."

"I thought you'd be paying a visit to Missy Weyland."

Red stood next Nick and leaned against the house. Staring out at the horizon, he said, "Actually, that's what I came by here for. I want you to go over and pay a call to Missy. Owen's wife is cooking up some mess or another tonight and wants me to give it a try."

"Is he still with that Chinese woman?"

"Mei Li," Red said as if the words themselves were sour. "I tried to talk him into shipping her off to California, but he seems to like whatever them celestials have between their legs. If she didn't keep my brother so happy, I would've shipped her off myself. It ain't like he couldn't get another one if he wanted. Anyway, I ducked out of the last few dinners she slapped together, so I'd best go to this one, just to keep her from squawking."

Even though Nick wasn't exactly the sensitive sort, he didn't see the sense in the way Red and Owen treated Mei Li. As far as he could tell, that Chinese woman did her best to keep Owen happy when the blond prick barely deserved half as much. Since arguing about it was less than useless, Nick had learned to keep his mouth shut on the matter or change the subject completely.

After a few seconds, Nick looked up at Red and asked, "So it's just me who'll be going over to the Weyland place?"

"Just you."

"You think that cowboy brother of hers will be there?"

"Not yet, but he will be. He knows he'll get killed if he shows his face anywhere else. Them boys are desperate and wounded. They'll come sneaking back because they got nowhere else to go and the best way in will be through Missy Weyland. When he shows his face at her house, I want him to have a little surprise waiting for him. That'd be you. Once he sees you there with his sister, he'll come around."

"And Missy will agree to this?"

"It doesn't matter what she agrees to."

Nick pulled another clump from the ground and tossed it. "She might not see it that way. She might just run off and disappear with the rest of them cowboys."

"She won't go anywhere," Red replied simply. "Like I said, that's where you come in, Nicky." Easing himself down to sit beside Nick, Red took a cigarette from his shirt pocket and put it between his lips. He struck a match against the wall behind him and touched the flame to the cigarette. After inhaling and exhaling a stream of bitter smoke, he asked, "Do you trust me?"

"Yeah. I do."

"Truly?"

Nick had to think about that for a moment. Images went through his mind of when he and Red had first met. There were images of his own gang of outlaws, boys who had been like brothers to him. Nick had been knocked out right before most of those brothers were strung up by the Vigilance Committee.

But Nick had come to an uneasy peace with the sacrifice he'd made. He'd signed on with Red to start a new life with the Vigilance Committee.

"I guess we didn't get started on the right foot," Red said, recognizing the haunted look in Nick's eyes. "But I knew you didn't belong with them outlaws. You sure as hell didn't belong with the likes of Skinner. That one would turn a saint into a mad dog killer if they spent too much time in the same room. I saw something in your eyes that told me you were better than them others."

"You mean when you had me and the rest of my gang at gunpoint in that same saloon?"

Red smirked and nodded. "That's right. I've seen plenty of killers and thieves. They're animals. Skinner's an animal. You're no animal. You kept your wits about you, even when faced with all them guns. Now that you've been on the Vigilance Committee for a stretch, you know how rare it is for someone to look into our eyes without flinching. That takes real sand, Nick. It takes character."

Pushing his fist into the dirt, Nick thought about some of the men he'd faced down now that he was the one looking out from behind that mask. Some of them cried when the noose tightened around their necks and others spit right back into their executioners' faces. They all talked tough, but those were all just hollow words.

Nick had been afraid when cornered by the Committee that first time. But more than that, Nick had been angry as hell. He could still feel the fire in his belly, just thinking about it. That fire was hot enough to burn away everything else, fear included. The promises back then were anything but hollow.

"I guess that is kind of rare," he admitted.

Red nodded. "You're damn right it is. I may have been with some of these other boys for a while, but that don't mean I want to turn over the Committee to just any of them. You got the potential to be with this Committee long after I go."

"You don't really think the Committee will be around forever, do you? I mean, the law's got to come to Montana sooner or later."

"The law's got its place, but there will always be a need for this Committee. There will always be a spot for men who step up and do what's needed, even though it might not sit right with the law. That's why I didn't mind recruiting you from that gang you were riding with. In fact, I was looking for someone with your perspective."

"You mean an outlaw's perspective," Nick corrected.

Red didn't reply to that with words. Instead, he leaned back and took a long pull from his cigarette. The smoke curled out of his nostrils before being expelled like a burst of steam. "That brings me back to Missy Weyland," he said without touching back on what Nick had brought up.

"You think Missy will help in turning over her brother to us? I still don't know about that, Red. Folks around here may respect us, but —"

"Folks around here need to pay for the services we provide. They get to breathe easy and sleep like babies at night because we're out there doing what we do," Red interrupted. "Missy had damn well better help us. Otherwise she's no better than her asshole brother." Softening his tone, Red added, "Don't hurt her, but don't let her leave that house. You sit with her and keep her company until her brother shows up."

"What happens if she tries to get away?" Nick asked.

"I know you can keep a little thing like her from getting the drop on you. Tie her to her bed when she sleeps. Tie her to a chair during the day. Keep a gag on her mouth to keep her quiet. Do whatever it takes to keep her in that house until her brother comes calling. When he gets there, signal to the rest of us and we'll come. You know those cowboys will be watching for the Committee to be doing its business."

Nick nodded.

"So that's what we'll do," Red said. "We'll be out riding like we're looking for them and make sure they get a nice, wide open-ing to slip back into town. Just when they think they got the drop on us, we'll sur-round them, round every last one of them up, and then do what we do."

"By that, you mean hang them," Nick stated.

Red looked down at Nick. With the smoke seeping from his nose and mouth, he looked like a monster from a kid's story who was just about to breathe fire onto a helpless vil-lage. "I mean we make an example out of them, just like we do to all them others that ride through here like they own this country. We show them why they should ride some-where else and leave the good people of Virginia City in peace."

Nick let out a short laugh. "You mean avoid this town like the plague."

"Same difference."

# Fourteen

Nick rode a quarter-mile out of town to a square house with one window illuminated by a flickering candle and a bit of smoke curling up from the chimney. After tying his horse to a post, he walked up to the front door. He could smell bread baking and could hear a woman singing to herself inside the place. When he knocked, the singing came to an abrupt halt.

The door swung open just enough for a pretty blonde to take a peek outside. Even though he couldn't see more than an inch of her, Nick could tell that Missy Weyland was every bit as pretty as the last time he'd seen her. Blonde hair covered her forehead in thick curls. The skin of her cheek was smooth and pale, making the blue of her eyes stand out even more. Her lips were plump and ripe with youth, trembling just a little bit when she got a look at who was standing on her front porch.

"Oh, it's you," she said, doing a bad job of hiding the nervousness in her voice. "You're Nick Graves, right?"

"I am."

"Oh. All right, then, Nick," Missy said. "What can I do for you?"

"I was wondering if I could come in for a moment."

She paused and glanced behind her. "I . . . don't know if that's a good idea."

"It's about Travis."

Nick wasn't going to mention her brother until he was inside. When he let the subject slip, he knew right away that it was a mistake.

"I don't know what you're talking about," she quickly said while starting to shut the door. "Now if you'll excuse me, I need to get back to fixing supper."

Nick's arm extended straight out, grabbing hold of the door a split second before it closed. There was barely enough space for his fingers to slip inside and curl around its edge. "I need to have a word with you," he said. "It's important."

It seemed that Red had been right about Nick and his outlaw's instincts. At that moment, every bone in Nick's body told him that Missy was going to run. It was an instinct that came after years of being a predator and becoming very good at reading his prey.

Missy pushed against the door a little harder and Nick responded in kind. With just a bit more effort, he was able to force the door open while knocking Missy back a few steps in the process. Before completing his first step into the house, Nick had gotten a good enough look around to know where she would head.

There was very little furnishing in there, apart from the kitchen and stove on the left. If she meant to put up a fight, she would head in that direction to get her hands on anything from a skillet to a knife. On the right, there was one door leading into a bedroom. If she meant to hide, that was where she would go.

Tears sprang into Missy's eyes and her breath started coming in short, frightened bursts. Her feet skidded against the floor, threatening to come out from under her, even though she knew every splinter and loose board like the back of her hand.

As the tears streamed down her cheeks and her breaths turned into sobs, she dashed to the right, where the salvation of her bedroom beckoned to her. Before she could get within arm's reach of that door, she felt an arm wrap around her midsection and pull her back.

Nick had somehow managed to act before she did and circled around so he could catch hold of her when she finally did decide to bolt toward the nearby room. His arm wrapped around her waist and he easily pulled her in. When she bumped against him, Missy's eyes were filled with surprise at first, which soon turned into dread.

"Wh . . . what are you going to d . . . do to me?" she stammered.

Although she was asking a question, it was plain to see that she'd already arrived at some conclusions on her own. Nick could feel her body trembling. Although she struggled to get free of him, her efforts were halfhearted at best. It seemed she was already convinced that there was no escaping the Committee.

"I'm not going to hurt you," Nick said as he pushed forward into the house so he could close the front door. "I just want you to take a seat and be quiet."

Even though he spoke those words as soothingly as possible, Nick recalled saying those same things to other hostages over the years. He'd never been partial to taking women as prisoners, but plenty of those in his old gang weren't so high-minded.

When Missy dropped down into the closest chair, Nick removed the rope that had been coiled around his left shoulder. He wrapped her up nice and tight, bringing the rope together at a point that she couldn't reach even if she could move her hands.

Missy was no longer sobbing. The tears were leaking from her eyes and her lips were drawn shut so tightly that they'd lost their dark pink hue. The blue in her eyes was overpowered by the jagged red lines surrounding it. Soon sweat had broken through the pores of her skin to make her entire face a slick, glistening mess.

"Travis only came into town to see me," she whispered.

"But he and his friends sure didn't mind staying for a while, did they?"

Wincing as if she expected to be backhanded at any moment, Missy averted her eyes from him. "No . . ."

Nick could feel the blood pumping through his veins. He'd never forced himself on any woman, but at that moment, after dominating Missy so completely and seeing her cower before him like a whipped dog, he could understand how a mind sicker than his might get a thrill from going that extra step.

Letting out his breath, Nick walked around the table and pulled out another of the chairs similar to the one in which Missy was now tied. He sat down, placed his hands where she could see them, and looked directly into her eyes. "I'm not going to hurt you, Missy. I'm not here for that or anything else. You've got to believe me."

"Why should I believe you?"

The aggression in Missy's voice was so sudden and so out of her character that it shocked Nick.

Her face was still a mess, but under all the tears and sweat there was something more primal. It was the face of someone who had nothing left to lose.

"Answer that," she demanded. "Why should I trust you when you're the one who kicked in my door, took me prisoner, and tied me up to my own chair! Why should I believe a damn word you say?"

"Your brother started this. He was the one who brought those assholes into town so they could stir up shit and start shooting. You know that they killed a man over losing at cards? He wasn't cheating. He just won too many hands."

"Riding into town and shooting?" she repeated with disgust in her voice. "That sounds real familiar."

Nick's eyes narrowed and he leaned forward. "You talking about me?"

"Yes, I'm talking about you. The Committee should've strung you up with the rest of those bastards you called your friends and been done with it. But Red had to keep you around like some sort of trophy. You're just a dog on his leash. You know that, right? Everyone else knows it."

"Shut up."

"What's the matter? Big, bad gunfighter doesn't like it when he hears something he don't like?"

"Shut up."

Now Missy was leaning forward as much as her bonds would allow. The effort of raising her voice and straining against the ropes had given a scarlet hue to her face. "Red got himself a new little doggie and he takes him out for a walk every day so the whole town can see how he and his Committee can tame them animals they don't kill. And he can show the rest of the world how a gunman like you can either die or work for him while the rest of Virginia City smiles and pats his doggie on the head to make sure he feels nice and comf—"

Nick stood up and drew his gun in the blink of an eye.

Missy's voice caught in her throat, preventing her from taking a breath just as surely as if she'd swallowed a cork. Her muscles froze inside of her and her blue bloodshot eyes focused on the pistol that had materialized in Nick's hand after a quick flutter of motion.

"I said be quiet," Nick whispered.

The gun in his hand didn't move. It remained pointed at a spot between Missy's eyes.

Keeping his voice soft and measured, he asked, "Now are you going to keep quiet or do I need to quiet you myself?"

Her lips trembled a bit as fear once again cinched its grip around her. "I'll be quiet," she replied in a little girl's whisper.

Suddenly Nick glanced down at the gun in his hand. As surprised as Missy had been by the speed of his draw, he was just as surprised to have drawn at all. The weapon was so natural in his hand that he barely felt it when it was there.

Nick lowered the pistol and eased it back into its holster. From there, he lowered himself back into his seat and let out the breath he'd been holding. "That's not true what you said," he announced.

"I'm not lying."

"Maybe not. But maybe you just don't know the truth either."

Slowly, she shook her head. "Everyone knows about Red and his Committee. Most

205

folks even welcomed them here at first. They do some good now, but we're all paying for it. You men take so much from us that we barely make any profit anymore."

"Who are you talking about?"

"You name it. Stores, ranches, even the saloons need to pay tribute."

"You'd pay taxes to a sheriff if you had one," Nick said calmly. "The town would pay his salary. It's the same thing."

"Sure it is. But a sheriff don't kill folks for opening their mouths against them or refusing to pay because they need to feed their families." When she saw Nick shaking his head, Missy added, "You try asking Red about the money he takes. Then ask him about what happens to them who can't pay. Do you really think all the folks you hang and run out of town are guilty? Or do you even care what they did to be strung up?"

"People call us heroes," Nick said. "They know we protect them."

"They're scared. Living here is like living in a wolf's den. Anyone can get eaten at any time, but it beats being out there on your own, where any number of beasts can tear you apart. At least here we know where the wolves are. When we see you coming, all we need to do is wave and pat you on the back to keep you happy."

As much as Nick wanted to argue with her, she was too frightened to pull together such a convincing lie. Besides, too much of what she said made sense. Although part of Nick's duties was to collect "donations" from various shops around town, he never pressed anyone on where all that money went. Judging by the looks on some faces, other Committee members weren't as forgiving when it came to late payments that Red had described as simple taxes.

There were plenty of other instances as well that had festered in the back of Nick's mind since he'd shoved them back there and did his best to ignore them. For every instance where the Committee made a trespass, they also did some good. For every lynching that happened at a dark tree or in a lonely shack, there was a hanging that would have been carried out by any lawman in any other town. Nick didn't acquaint himself with every man buried by the Committee. But for every one of them who proclaimed his innocence as the noose tightened around his neck, there was another that any blind man could tell was guilty.

One man's taxes was another man's extortion.

Wasn't that the way it seemed everywhere

else in the world?

Didn't every man say he was innocent when being called out for his crimes? When Red had pointed out that very thing, Nick was inclined to agree with him. Now, as he looked into Missy's haggard face and saw the defeated way she turned her eyes from him, Nick wondered why he'd joined up in the first place.

At the time, the Committee had been the best shot of respectability a man like him could afford. Now, when he took a hard look at the Committee through someone else's eyes, even for a few minutes, Nick didn't like what he saw.

He closed his eyes tightly enough to set off a blurry fireworks display behind his eyelids and shook his head to clear it away. "Red wants to keep this place safe. He kept me alive and stayed true to his word. I know you're scared right now, but you got to believe that you won't be hurt. Your brother stepped out of line and needs to pay for what he's done. If you talk to Red, I'm sure we can come to an arrangement. Maybe we can spare them cowboys who were just caught up in what them other ones started."

"Spare them?" Missy asked with a dumbfounded look on her face. "You think Red's capable of something like that? You really believe that, even after all you saw for your-self?"

"It's because of what happened to me that I know there could be a chance."

"You mean that gang you rode in here with that first time?"

"Yes."

Missy stared at him for a few long moments. She even glanced to either side, as if she expected to find someone else in the room listening to their conversation and snickering at what they heard. But it was only her and Nick in there. The fragrant scents of cooking had turned into the stench of burnt bread. Pots rattled on the stovetop and spat steam out from beneath their lids.

"Red killed them others you rode with," Missy spat out.

"That's not true. He let them go. He told me he would if I stayed. That was the deal."

"There were a few that got away, but not the others." She looked at him now in disbelief. "How could you not know that? Red doesn't let anyone go. Not your friends, not you, not anyone."

Although he could still hear Missy's voice, Nick wasn't listening to what she said. The rush in his head was like whitewater over jagged rocks. The noise filled him up and shook his mind like an impatient father trying to knock some sense into a screaming child. Nick started to feel dizzy. Then something else took root inside of him.

Rage.

It started as frustration, grew into aggravation, and blossomed into the fire that now torched his innards.

Nick hardly even noticed the little blonde tied to the chair in front of him. Instead, he gritted his teeth and thought back to all the things he'd ignored in the last few years. So many things he'd missed completely at the time now became clear to him in a rush.

Seeing the rage inside of him, Missy started to cry. Her shoulders and chest heaved beneath the ropes binding her as her head drooped straight down. There was no way for her to see what Nick was thinking. All she saw were his cold eyes shifting to the color of gunmetal. The muscles in his jaw clenched and one corner of his mouth had started to twitch.

As far as she could tell, he was one breath away from sending a bullet through her skull.

"Does everyone really know this?" Nick asked in a voice that was like an icy current running beneath a frozen lake.

"I . . . I don't —"

Nick's hand slammed against the table so

hard that it made everything on top of it jump. Even Missy almost cleared the floor.

"No!" Nick snarled as his hand came down on the tabletop. "Don't try to put your words together. Just answer me!"

"Everyone knows all about the Committee. Everyone knows Red doesn't tolerate anyone breaking the rules here in town and everyone knows that you either do what Red tells you or you get hurt. That's how it's been ever since the Committee was formed."

"What about the rest of it? What about my friends?"

Her head came up for a second so she could get a look at his face. There wasn't so much as a hint of emotion there anymore. All that was left was a stony visage with less expression than a burlap mask.

Letting out her breath, Missy looked around at her house as if for the last time. The tears were coming again, but she no longer had the strength to put anything else behind them. "Ask Pete," she sighed.

"Pete Masters?"

Missy nodded. "He'll tell you. He'll even show you."

"Show me?"

She nodded.

"Show me what?"

"The pictures for the newspaper," Missy said in a rush. "The ones the Committee take of the men they killed. The ones that get printed in the newspaper."

"How do you know about this?" When Nick saw that his answer wasn't forthcoming, he slammed his hand down upon the table one more time. "Tell me!"

"Pete used to brag about printing up a special edition, just to put you in your place if you got full of yourself, but Red wouldn't hear of it. They used to fight about it when you were away. It wasn't no secret. Everyone in town's seen those pictures in the paper. The Committee wants them printed as an example to keep folks in line."

It wasn't a secret. Nick had seen plenty of pictures like those splashed across the front pages of newspapers in plenty of towns. He'd even seen family men having pictures taken of themselves at hangings, as if it was some sort of goddamn picnic.

"Why didn't anyone tell me?" Nick asked.

"Because Red wouldn't like it. Besides, we all know about you. We heard of the things you've done. The people you killed."

Nick could hear the fear in her voice, just as he could hear it in the voices of everyone else who ever spoke to him in that town.

Missy turned her head to look away from

him until her neck hurt. Although she couldn't sob, she let out a high-pitched moan dredged up from the bottom of her soul, which sounded as though it was tearing apart the back of her throat on its way out of her mouth.

Before much longer, she didn't even sound human.

Listening to her moan like that, Nick felt his blood start to boil. He found himself rising from his chair and moving toward her with his fingers getting ready to clamp on to her and squeeze for all he was worth. The anger at what she'd said was only matched by the anger of knowing she was right. And when she could no longer bring herself to answer a simple question, he started to wonder what the hell good she was to anyone else for any other purpose.

He hadn't harmed a hair on her head and the stupid bitch was blubbering like she'd been gutted. The overwhelming display of weakness was like dangling raw meat in front of the hungry predator inside Nick's soul.

Choking the life out of her wouldn't only be easy, it would make him feel so much better just to know that he wouldn't have to hear that pathetic fucking whining.

Nick stopped.

He hadn't been reaching out to grab hold of Missy's neck.

He hadn't been leaning in to grab her or touch her in any way.

He hadn't moved much at all, but the intentions had been right at the surface of his mind, which was close enough to make him realize they were truly there.

And that, he decided, was enough.

# FIFTEEN

Pete Masters lived in a modest home with only a few niceties. Like most of the rest of the Committee, he lived within his supposed means as a way of maintaining the charade that he was an upstanding member of the community. He sat on his porch with his feet propped up on a rail, savoring a cigar the way any man might do after a hard day's work.

When he saw another figure walking toward his front step, he didn't think much of it. "Nick? Is that you?" Pete asked.

Nick didn't answer. His face was calm and expressionless. As he walked up the two steps leading on to the porch itself, he didn't say a word.

Pete swung his feet down and his hand drifted toward the gun at his hip. He paused there for a moment, wondering why he'd made that particular move. "Shouldn't you be over at the Weyland place?"

"Tell me about my gang, Pete." Nick's voice was steady and calm, just like the rest of him.

Nick's calmness started to gnaw at Pete's gut. Without making any sudden moves, he got to his feet and stepped back. "*Your* gang? What are you talking about?"

Nick pulled in a breath. When he let it out, he flashed a quick smile. "You recall my old gang. I let you run them out of town. You and the rest of the Committee chased them out instead of hanging them because I agreed to stay."

"That's right. And that's just what we did."

Nick's eyes burned a hole through Pete's face with an intensity that rooted the other man to the spot. "Did you?"

Although Pete did his level best to keep from squirming, he could feel his hand itching to wrap around the gun holstered at his side. If it was any other man but Nick standing in front of him, that gun would have already cleared leather. But it was Nick standing in front of him and Pete knew damn well that he might have trouble outdrawing him.

"We told you what happ—"

Pete was cut short as Nick's hands snapped up and slammed hard against his

216

chest. The powerful shove knocked Pete's back against the door leading into the house. One more shove knocked the wind from Pete's lungs and a third opened the door and knocked him straight through it.

"I know what you told me, Pete," Nick snarled. "Trouble is, I'm not so sure I believe you anymore."

They were both inside Pete's house by now. Pete had stopped himself from stumbling any farther back, but he was still a bit wobbly in his stance. Nick had taken a few more steps inside before stopping. Without taking his eyes off of Pete, Nick reached behind him with his left hand and pushed the door shut.

The *thud* of that door closing sent a chill down Pete's back. "Red took you in like you was his own," Pete said. "Them asshole friends of yours were small fish and he tossed them back because he needed a man who was quick with a gun."

"That was the deal, sure enough. Now tell me what really happened."

Reacting to the cold fear he felt working its way down his body, Pete straightened up and leered at Nick. "What the hell is this about? Red told you to stay and watch over that Weyland bitch."

Before he even knew what he was doing,

Nick reached out and smacked Pete across the face. Although he kept his hand open, he put enough muscle behind it to knock Pete back again.

"I know what Red told me. You should be more worried about what I'm telling you." Nick paused and eased himself back. "You want to go for that gun?" he asked as a cruel smile slid on to his face. "Go on," Nick taunted. "Lay one finger on that gun and see what happens."

Pete thought about it.

He thought about it for a few seconds that dragged by like hours.

His hand inched toward his holster and his eyes took in the sight of Nick standing like a statue in front of him.

Nick's eyes glinted with expectation. The corner of his smile twitched as a quick chuckle rumbled in his chest.

"You're nothing but talk, are ya, Pete?" Nick waited for a few more seconds to see if that would be enough to push Pete into a mistake.

It wasn't.

"All right, then," Nick said with a disappointed sigh. "Since you like talking so much, how about you tell me what happened after I was knocked out? And don't try to tell me it was nothing because we're way past all that now."

For a moment, Pete looked as if he was going to shake his head and shrug his shoulders. The confused expression was like the rouge applied on to the cheeks of an inexperienced whore.

Finally, Pete shook his head. Although he didn't say anything, his eyes flicked over toward a locked chest against the wall next to his bed.

When Nick followed his glance, he found himself taking in details of the room itself for the first time. The house was a single space divided up by clusters of furnishings. The kitchen and dining area was marked by a small table and pot-bellied stove. The sitting area was marked by a chair facing the fireplace and the bedroom was just a collection of a bed, a wardrobe, and chest.

"Go over there and open that chest," Nick ordered.

Pete was already starting to shake his head. "There's nothing in there. It's just pictures." As Nick moved closer to him, Pete found his voice rising in pitch and his words spilling out of him faster and faster. "You know, for the newspapers, just like Red wanted. Hell, you were there when most of them were taken. Jesus Christ, Nick!"

Red did enjoy seeing pictures of the Committee's exploits in the local newspaper. A few of the more grisly photographs even made it into the papers of neighboring towns. Red declared it was to "spread the word of the Vigilance Committee's intentions." Nick had come to realize that most folks were just morbid and curious enough to enjoy seeing dead men while they sipped their coffee. That is, the pictures served well enough if those same folks couldn't make it to the hangings in person.

While Nick thought about that, Pete threaded the fingers of both hands together and lashed out with them as though he was swinging an axe. Nick sidestepped the desperate swing, but still caught a few of Pete's knuckles against his ribs. Although the jolt of pain stabbed through Nick's gut, Pete was too committed to his swing to follow up on it. By the time his arms had reached the end of their arc and he was pulling them back again, Pete felt a solid impact below his belt.

Pete doubled over with his hands still clenched together, wheezing as Nick's knee slammed one more time into his groin.

Taking hold of Pete by the shoulder, Nick straightened him out and said, "That was just sad. Is that all you could muster? Did you forget about that gun you're wearing or are you too chickenshit to draw it?"

As Pete started to form an answer, his lips flapped together uselessly. The sight of that was too much for Nick to stomach, so he smashed his fist into Pete's face as if he meant to knock it clean off his head. Pete reeled back and dropped onto the floor. Once there, he curled up and pressed his hands flat against his aching crotch.

Calmly, Nick walked over to the chest next to Pete's bed. It was locked, so he drew his gun and blasted it open with one shot. After that, Nick dropped the gun back into its holster and knelt down to reach into the chest.

"Bob Ralston's not far from here," Pete groaned while trying to push through the pain that still filled his lower body. "He's probably already been to the Weyland place and seen that you're not there."

Nick paid no attention to the man shouting from the floor behind him. He was too busy rooting through the clothes, personal items, and trinkets inside the chest to concern himself with Pete's nonsense.

And then he found it.

The moment his hands brushed against the bundle wrapped up in a used pillowcase, Nick knew that he'd found what he was after. Knowing that his time was drawing short, he unwrapped the bundle and found the pictures that Pete had talked about.

Nick recognized them right away. They were photographs of the Committee's handiwork and, sure enough, Nick had been present when most of them were taken. They were part of Red's effort to let folks outside of Virginia City see what happens to the lawbreakers who are stupid enough to come there. Truth be told, most newspapers printed similar pictures just to boost their sales.

The pictures were eerie in the way they seemed both staged and real at the same time. Bodies hung from trees with their necks bent at unnatural angles. Nooses dangled from flowering branches. Men with holes in their heads lay propped up against familiar buildings.

Horses grazed in fields where groups of corpses were piled up like firewood. Hands were tied behind backs and feet dangled inches over the ground while gaping, waxy faces stared up at the rope that delivered them into the next world.

Nick had been present for a good number of those executions. The men in most of those pictures deserved to be dead. The men in one of those pictures, however, were men that Nick had grown up with.

It was at the bottom of the pile, stuck away as if that would be enough to hide it. When Nick got a look at the picture, he felt as if he was tossed back in time to when he'd been in the very space that it had been taken.

The photograph was faded at the corners and depicted the inside of a barn. A white horse was eating some hay on the right side and crates were tossed about on the floor along with a few discarded wheelbarrows. Nick had been there, but before the picture had been taken. When he'd been in that barn, his friends had been fitted for nooses and were still standing on crates. They were the same crates in the picture that were on their sides and well away from the bottom of the feet that hung over the floor.

Under each of the bodies strung up from the rafters of that barn, there was a name written in Pete's childlike scrawl. Cooley, Fargo, all were names of men Nick had ridden with into Virginia City that first time those years ago. The names were written on the picture beneath the bodies that hung from the Committee's nooses with their hands tied behind their backs and their faces lolling to one side.

As Nick took in the sight of those dead faces, he recalled each of them in life. Each of those boys had trusted Nick as their leader. They'd trusted Barrett as the planner and Skinner as their wildest gun. That trust was still written across their pale, waxy faces, as if they went to their deaths believing that one of their buddies would show up at any moment to cut them down from those rafters.

"It was Red's idea to keep it," Pete said in a whiny voice.

"He's not that stupid," was Nick's reply.

Nick didn't know how long he stood there looking at that picture. He barely even realized he was turning back around and heading for the door until Pete Masters ran up and tried to stop him.

Maybe Pete had gotten enough time to dredge up some courage. Maybe he spotted the dazed look in Nick's eyes or the way he clutched the picture of his dead friends in his gun hand. Either way, Pete picked that moment to take his stand.

Nick reacted with startling quickness. He grabbed Pete by the collar and hefted him up until Pete's face started to loll like the men in the picture he was holding. Pete had drawn his pistol, but was too shaken to use it.

"You had to have known about this," Pete said. "You had to know it after never hearing from them in all this time. You had to know it after seeing how this Committee works."

Nick didn't say a word. Those same things that Pete had said were already swimming through his brain. Hearing them come from Pete's mouth was more than Nick could bear.

He let Pete go with a shove toward the front door. After tucking the picture into his pocket, Nick took a step back from Pete and squared his shoulders. The stance he took was easy enough to recognize and it caused Pete to raise the gun he'd almost forgotten was in his hand.

Nick's hand flashed to the holster at his side and wrapped around the grip of his pistol. After clearing leather in less time than it took to blink, he bent his elbow and aimed at the hip before pulling the trigger. His round punched a hole through Pete's chest and burrowed straight through his lung before lodging into bone.

Pete reeled from the impact and pulled his trigger reflexively, sending a bullet into the frame of his bed. With the dazed look still on his face, Nick took hold of Pete's shoulder with his left hand and pulled him close. He wedged the barrel of his gun up into Pete's stomach just below his rib cage and pulled his trigger.

The gun's muffled roar sounded again and again as he sent blast after blast into Pete's body. With each *thump* that sounded, Nick heard another lie that he never should have been stupid enough to believe in the first place.

"They got their scare and left town," Skinner had vowed on that day when Nick had asked him what the Committee had done to the rest of the gang. "Barrett was the first to go. He told me to tell you he'd head up into Leadville and would wait for you there as long as he could. I already met up with the rest and told them to go their separate ways."

*Thump*

"If this gang sticks together, we'll be rich," Barrett Cobb had promised him when they were boys aching to get away from their homes and raise hell out in the world. "We can do what we please and be known men. It's the best kind of life there is!"

*Thump*

"Let your friends go," Red had urged in a quiet moment just before Nick had signed on with the Vigilance Committee. "They have their lives and you have yours. There's no reason you can't all live well."

*Thump*

Nick took a step back and looked at what he'd done. The shots he'd fired had hollowed out Pete's chest almost to the point that a man could reach straight through his torso. After letting Pete go, Nick sent one more shot through Pete's face as he was falling backward.

Now that Pete was out of the way, Nick could see Bob Ralston standing at the doorway wearing a shocked expression on his face.

"What the hell did you do?" Bob asked as he stuck his head inside.

Nick walked toward the door. When he got close enough, he swung his gun up and out until it connected with the bridge of Bob's nose. He kept right on walking and left Bob to fall back onto the porch in a bloody, unconscious heap.

*Thump*

"You've got to get out of here," Nick said as he busted into Missy's house and grabbed the first knife he could find.

Missy was staring at him in stark terror, her eyes bulging out over the gag that covered the bottom portion of her face. When she saw Nick grab the knife from her kitchen and walk toward her, she started wriggling and struggling against her ropes.

"You were right," Nick said. Reaching out with the knife, he slashed it through the ropes wrapped behind the back of Missy's chair. "They're dead. Jesus Christ, how could I not know they were dead?"

As if sensing that Nick was barely aware she was there, Missy stopped her struggling and let Nick cut her ropes. She could hardly even believe it when she felt the ropes loosen and give way after she leaned forward. Missy then reached up to pull the gag away from her mouth. To her surprise, she found a new man looking back at her.

Nick's eyes were no longer those of a barely domesticated predator. The fierce coldness was still there, but it didn't stem from the same spot as before. She couldn't quite put her finger on the specifics, but Nick Graves seemed more . . . human.

"I'm sorry," he said. "I'm so sorry for doing this to you."

Staring at him, Missy felt as though she'd witnessed a miracle. She no longer feared Nick. It was as though, somehow, the meanness and hostility that had been such a vital part of the man had been wiped away. She found herself reaching out to touch his cheek, just to see if he would snap at her.

Instead, Nick let out the breath he'd been holding and placed his hand over hers. The moment lasted for half a second, but would mark the most vital change in Nick's life. It was a moment devoid of all lies — too pure to be marred by words.

Suddenly Nick's eyes snapped open and he pulled away from her. Everything that had happened came back to him in a rush. The foolishness of his youth had hurt him bad enough. To keep being foolish once his eyes had been opened would be a sin against the brains God had given him.

Pete Masters was dead. Hell, he'd almost been blasted in half.

Bob Ralston had seen it happen and was still alive.

The rest of the Vigilance Committee was nearby and surely out to find him by now.

Missy looked at him, confused and terrified.

As much as Nick wanted to comfort that poor, fragile little blonde, there simply was no longer any time. "Run," he told her.

She did.

He could hear her screaming less than a second later.

# Sixteen

Nick bolted outside and found the remaining members of the Vigilance Committee circling Missy Weyland like a pack of hungry dogs. Their faces were covered in the familiar burlap masks, but Nick knew the men well enough to pick out who was who by their build or the glint of their eyes from behind the roughly cut holes in their hoods.

Shad had his arms wrapped under Missy's arms and was lifting her off her feet. Owen took hold of her by the ankles while wearing a grin that was more enthusiastic than ever. The other members of the Committee closed in, but quickly parted to make way for one man to pass.

That man was Red Parks. His cruel eyes were distinctive enough to blaze themselves into Nick's memories and nightmares alike. There wasn't a mask in existence that could hide their cruelty.

"I thought it couldn't be true," Red said.

"I heard there were shots and that Pete was dead, but I thought it had to be some kind of mistake. Then I heard that you'd turned on us and I thought for certain someone had gotten their signals mixed."

Nick planted his feet and lowered his hand toward his gun. That single movement set a whole other chain of events into motion.

Shad and Owen dropped Missy and held her down while drawing their pistols using their free hands. Everyone else had their guns out as well and the snapping of hammers being thumbed back rattled through the air. Only Red remained still.

Red appeared to be taller than the rest, even though he was only of average height. He never backed down from anyone or anything. The close-set eyes peering out from his mask narrowed a bit to betray the smile that grew on his face. "You see, things like that tend to give people a bad impression."

Nick's gun had cleared leather, but he stopped before bringing it up any farther. In the years to come, Nick would curse himself for not pulling his trigger at that moment. He would curse himself, even though he knew to do so would have caused his own death a moment later.

"Take his gun from him, Will," Red ordered.

Will Culligan stepped forward, keeping his pistol aimed at Nick's chest. He reached out with his free hand to rip the gun from Nick's grasp.

Red nodded and turned his back to Nick. "Come on. Let's all have a little chat."

With one wave of his hand, Red sent another Committee member into motion. The burly man grabbed hold of Nick by the back of his neck while Will jammed his gun into Nick's ribs. Together, the two men herded Nick along behind the others.

The entire time, Nick's mind was filled with ways to break free of his captors and get his hands on a gun. He knew he would probably take some lead, but he figured he could get out alive. Whether that was youthful bravado or self-confidence, he couldn't say. The only thing that kept him in line, however, was the fact that he couldn't think of a single way to get to Missy through both Shad and Owen.

Red took them to a small barn on the edge of town. The building had been there since Virginia City was founded and leaned slightly to one side. It was meant to be used for storage and to keep a few horses out of the elements, but the Vigilance Committee had put the place to a darker purpose.

When he looked up at the rafters crossing over his head, Nick saw ghostly images of his friends hanging there with their hands tied behind their backs and their heads lolling at an unnatural angle. The moment Missy saw where she was, she broke into a hysterical fit of crying.

"Shut that bitch up," Red barked once he and his men were inside the barn. "And keep her busy so me and Nicky here can talk."

With that, Shad kicked her on to some straw and dropped down on top of her. One of his hands pressed against her mouth while the other got busy unbuckling his pants. Owen positioned himself so he could stretch both of her arms over her head and then pin them down.

"She's not a part of this, Red," Nick snarled. "She didn't do anything."

Red's eyes looked on in an amused kind of way, almost as if they were watching two children roughhousing. "It's not about anything she did. It's what she might do. You see, I can't have anyone spreading bad words about my Committee."

As he spoke, Red paced the barn with his arms clasped behind his back. On one side of him, Bob Ralston was slamming his fists into Nick's stomach and face while someone else held Nick by the arms. On his other side, Shad and Owen were pulling Missy's skirts up around her waist and forcing apart her legs.

"It just wouldn't be right for our good name to be smudged like that."

One after another, the fists landed on Nick's face and torso.

The filthy, probing fingers scratched their way up along Missy's thigh until they found what they were after.

"I can't allow something like that to happen," Red continued.

Nick forced open his eyes and blinked away as much blood as he could. "Why are you doing this?"

"You killed Pete," Red answered without an ounce of emotion. "For that, you've got to pay the price."

Another fist smashed into Nick's side, driving all the wind from his lungs. When he took his next breath, it felt like a fire had been set inside of him and it was being stoked by hunting knives.

"Not me," Nick wheezed. "Why . . . are you doing this to her?"

Red glanced over to where Missy was laying. She was beyond screaming now and had her head turned to one side so she at least didn't have to look at the man violating her. Shad rode her roughly, grabbing her anywhere he could reach while his hips pumped viciously back and forth.

"My men aren't doing a thing to her," Red stated. "That's all your doing."

"Wh . . . what?"

With a snap of Red's fingers, all the Committee members stopped what they were doing. Once they saw Red coming toward them, Bob Ralston took hold of Nick and hoisted him up.

Red leaned in close until Nick could make out every last stitch in his burlap hood. When he spoke, Red's breath steamed out from behind the rough weave. "You could have had a good life here, but instead you chose to root around and find dirt on the ones who you've been riding with for over a year. Ever hear of looking a gift horse in the mouth? That's never a good idea."

Blood trickled from Nick's split-open lip. His eyes were swelling and it hurt just to keep his head up. But after the damage he'd already taken, the pain was starting to wash away into a throbbing numbness. He did, however, feel the touch of iron against his shoulder.

"You found them pictures, didn't you?" Red asked. "Brad always said we should have gotten rid of those. Or we should have gotten rid of that one, anyway. Of course, your friends did look real good swinging from these rafters. But I wanted you to find that photograph. I guess it was a good test to see where your loyalties truly lay."

Nick felt a jab in his shoulder and then a muffled explosion filled his ears as Red pulled his trigger.

At first, Nick felt nothing. The shock hit him like a club and lasted for a full second. Then the smell of gunpowder hit his nostrils, followed by the stench of his own burnt flesh. After that, the pain hit and he felt the part of his shoulder that had been scooped out of him by hot lead.

Nick's teeth clenched together and his entire body convulsed. His eyes fixed upon Red and his ears were suddenly filled with the laughter of the Committee members.

Red hadn't looked away either. His eyes were cold and emotionless as he observed Nick buck and twitch against the grip of his captors.

"That had to hurt," Red stated. Looking over to Missy, he added, "But it serves you right for raping that poor, sweet girl. At least, that's what we'll tell folks around here when they ask why we had to punish one of our own. We'll just have to tell them that you turned back to your savage roots and outlaw ways. Pity, seeing as how far we all thought you'd come."

Shad laughed and got up so the next man could have his turn. Will Culligan had stepped up to her, but it was Owen who now dropped down and started moving between Missy's legs. Even as Owen started squirming and moaning on top of her, Missy kept her bloodshot eyes aimed at Red.

"I'll tell them the truth," she said in a soft yet determined voice. "I'll tell them everything that happened and everything your damn Commit—"

She was cut off by the sound of another gunshot.

In a heartbeat, Red had snapped his pistol toward her and pulled the trigger. The bullet caught her in the neck and opened her up to spill a gout of blood onto the floor.

"Jesus Christ," Owen said as he jumped up off of her. "You should'a warned me you was about to do that!"

Red walked over to Missy, squatted down, and cocked his head so he could look her in the eyes. "You shouldn't have said that," he told her.

Struggling to pull another breath through her mutilated throat, Missy looked at Nick as if to apologize. Then she took one more look at the murderous scarecrow pointing his gun at her.

Red's next shot caught Missy right between the eyes.

Standing up, Red looked over to Nick. Before he could say anything, he snapped his head around to take a look at the front of the barn.

Nick looked that way as well and found a group of men standing at the door. They were locals who Nick recognized as owners of the corral not too far from the barn itself. One of the three locals held a shotgun. The other two were brandishing what appeared to be axe handles.

"What's going on in here?" asked the man with the shotgun. As he spoke, he looked around at the masked Committee members. "We heard shots. Is that Nick Graves you got there?"

One of the other men stepped forward, gripping his axe handle like a club. "Holy shit, that's Missy Weyland! She's dead."

"Grab them," Red ordered.

With that, the two men who'd been with Missy sprang forward. They were joined by the rest of the Committee members, including the ones who'd been holding Nick upright.

Nick dropped to the floor. The impact was

enough of a jolt to his system that he couldn't so much as move after he hit. His lungs burned with the effort of breathing and his torso was on fire with the wounds he'd already taken. Adding to that was the horror of what he saw through his tired, aching eyes.

The members of the Vigilance Committee overtook the unlucky locals with ease. Red stood by and watched as his men rushed forward to carry out the orders they'd been given.

Already nervous from the gunshots they'd heard, the local men barely knew what to do when they saw their supposed protectors come at them like a pack of wild animals. The man with the shotgun quickly took aim, but couldn't pull his trigger before the barrel had been knocked aside by one of the Committee.

Before either of the other two local men knew what to do, the axe handles they'd been wielding were ripped from their hands and savagely turned against them. Now that Missy wasn't able to amuse them any longer, Owen and Shad used the crude wooden clubs on the three local men. Will landed a few boots and fists of his own for good measure.

While his brain screamed at him to get up

and do something, Nick's body was unable to comply. Instinctively, his hand went for the holster at his hip.

"Looking for this?" Red asked. He held out the gun that belonged at Nick's side. It was the same gun that Nick had thought to use to make a name for himself when he'd been a stupid kid with a taste for blood.

Once Red was certain that Nick had gotten a good look at the gun he was holding, he turned it toward the scuffle going on nearby. He waited until one of the local men hit the floor in a bloody heap before taking aim.

"Stop it!" Nick shouted. "For the love of God, don't do this!"

"Too late now," was Red's reply. "The Vigilance Committee needs full cooperation from the folks around here. We can't abide with anyone who'd threaten that, just like we can't abide killers like you in our town."

"You're the killers!"

"And so are you. The difference is that we act as the law around here. We don't get to wear badges and we don't have a bunch of judges and courts to back us up. Therefore, we need to back ourselves up and that takes methods that most normal folks can't stomach.

"The folks around here don't much care

about our methods, so long as they only hurt the bad man. It's that reputation that we got to preserve and if someone comes along who can tarnish that reputation, we need to put them in their place in a big way so this Committee can live on.

"We can't abide with a mistake like you," Red explained in a tone that was the same he might use if explaining arithmetic to a slow child. "We also can't abide nosy neighbors getting into our business and seeing too much of what we do."

Nick could feel the rage blazing inside of him. Every command he gave to his body, however, was met with a new rush of pain through every one of his nerves.

"When this town sees what you did to these good people," Red continued, "they might just elect me mayor. You see the beauty in that?"

The rage inside Nick was winning out. It had grown powerful enough to get him climbing to his feet. His hands pushed himself up while scraping against the floor and tightening around fistfuls of straw.

Red took notice of that, stepped forward, and cracked the butt of Nick's gun against its owner's temple. Nick dropped down so his chest and chin knocked against the floor at the same time.

"Shad," Red barked. "Get the rope we stashed and tie him to the floor. Will, set up some boxes."

"What about these three?" asked Owen as he nodded toward the unfortunate locals.

Making certain he was speaking directly to Nick, Red gave his command. "Shoot them and then string them up. We need to make sure it looks like a job our boy Nicky here could do on his own."

The shot cracked through the barn amid a chorus of laughter and one youthful scream.

# SEVENTEEN

The Committee had gathered into a cluster in the middle of the barn with their backs turned to the rest of the civilized world. Although the weathered planks and rotting beams that made up the structure weren't enough to hold back the hot summer breeze, it was a formidable prison to the one kid trapped in the middle of that group.

"You better kill me, Red," Nick grunted as he squirmed on the straw-covered floor. "I swear I'll come back for you! I swear it!"

The Committee had toyed with him for what felt like hours. The door to the barn was shut tight to prevent another group of curious onlookers to come wandering by. One of Red's men was posted outside to let folks know that they were handling important business in there.

Forming a crooked circle around Nick, the Committee members had become creatures harvested from a nightmare. Tattered

243

jackets and torn shirts covered sweaty, muscled backs. Cruel eyes peered anxiously through holes cut into the burlap masks that covered their faces. Sweat pooled into dark stains just above the ropes that tied those masks shut around their necks. They shuffled on feet wrapped in weathered boots, clutching weapons with gloved hands.

Nick had been shot so many times that he barely even felt it any longer. The wounds all looked worse than they were, since the Committee had merely been chipping away at him with their bullets without hitting anything too vital. The pain was so overwhelming that it had come full circle to become just a hot cramp under his flesh.

Not one of the men seemed to notice the heat in the air. The sun had long since gone, but its touch could still be felt in the wind that blew as if from a furnace. The excessive heat combined with the normal contents of the barn to create a stink that coated the back of every man's throat.

"I know, Nicky," Owen said. "You're a real bad man and we should all be real scared."

That set a ripple of laughter through the masked men, but had the opposite effect on the kid in the middle of their circle.

Sometime during the last few moments, Nick had wound up tied by a rope that had one end wrapped around his waist and the other knotted to a steel ring bolted to the floor. The rope had been used to hang more men over the years than Nick could ever imagine. The ring had been put there by the Committee for moments exactly like this one.

"There was no need for you to kill them, Red!" Nick said, trying desperately to keep himself from sounding as desperate as he felt. "I would've stuck by you."

The only masked man to do any speaking looked down at the kid while still holding a smoking pistol in his hand. Hearing his name had struck a chord in him, which made him reach up and pull the mask from over his head. Although the burlap sack came free, the rope still remained around his neck. Red's face was scarred as well, but in a way that made Nick look clean by comparison. Cold, calculating eyes sat over a narrow nose. Under that, a thin line of a mouth curled into a humorless smile. "You did stick by me, Nicky. Right up until now, that is. Here I thought you were better than those wild dogs you used to ride with, but it turns out you're just a shit-eating cur who can't be trusted by nobody."

Although the other men in the circle were plenty anxious to follow Red's lead, they didn't go so far as to take off their own masks. Most of them were bigger than Red and all of them were better armed, but they still kept their distance.

Nick looked from one masked face to another, recognizing each as though he could stare right through the dusty burlap shells wrapped around their heads. The pain from the wound in his arm had already been wiped away by the rush of blood through his veins. All he could feel was the warmth of his blood soaking into his shirt.

"I know what you did to my friends," Nick said. "You men will pay for what you done. Every last one of you will pay!"

Shaking his head, Red looked down at Nick with a hint of pity in his eyes. "We're the law around here, Nick. We're the only thing that keeps these parts from being taken over by scum like those punks you used to ride with."

"They were my friends."

"That's not what you said when you joined up with me," Red pointed out as he hunkered down to put himself closer to Nick's level. "That's not what you said when you threw in with us and strung up the pieces of shit that would murder our neighbors and rape our sisters."

"You aren't any better than the men you

killed," Nick said in a low, steady voice.

"You mean the men *we* killed," Red corrected. "You, me, and all of us here."

Nick's breaths were like assaults on his lungs. Pulling them in was a hardship and letting them go was an unfortunate necessity. "Yeah," he finally said. "All of us."

Nodding victoriously, Red squatted a little more with his elbows perched on the ends of his knees. "I took you in when I should have killed you. I tried to show you the right path when you were just another piece of shit that I shouldn't have taken off my list to hang. You're just a piece of trash, kid. Even your friends knew that."

Hearing those words lit a fire inside Nick's chest that exploded in the blink of an eye. His legs sprung forward, along with both arms. His eyes saw nothing but Red's smiling face as memories of his former companions filled his mind.

Red didn't so much as twitch when he saw Nick lunge for him. Instead, he started to chuckle as Nick shot forward and immediately found the end of the rope that kept him in his place.

The breath that he'd managed to suck in through his flaring nostrils was immediately knocked out of him as the rope around his waist dug in like a kick to the gut. That rope was tied to a steel ring set into the floor, yanking Nick right back down onto the dirty planks. He landed with a solid *thump,* but that didn't stop him from scrambling up again and trying to get his hands on Red Parks.

The more he tried, the more Nick failed. And every time he was snapped back by the length of rope tied around his waist, the more the masked men around him doubled over with laughter. Finally, even Red gave in to the festive atmosphere in the barn.

"Goddamn, you are one amusing son of a bitch," Red said. "It almost makes me want to keep you here for whenever things get too dull."

Nick was well past caring about all the guns pointed at him. Rather than try to keep them from going off, he pretended he wasn't staring down a dozen barrels and focused on getting himself free of that rope. "You're a dead man, Red. All of you are dead."

"That's the spirit! I'll wager you picked that up from riding with Skinner." Turning to the man to his right, Red asked, "Hey, Shad, wasn't it Skinner who told us that Nick and all them others would be coming through here?"

"I think so, Red," came the muffled reply.

Cocking his head, Red made a show of rubbing his chin and pondering the question. He then snapped his fingers and said, "Wait a second! Skinner was the one who brought you to me to keep us from stringing his sorry ass up along with all the others. But he wasn't the one who told us you'd be coming. That would have been your friend Barrett."

The blood was still seeping from Nick's wound. The warmth of it was like a hot brand searing into his flesh. His fingers worked desperately at the knot he'd found in the rope.

"Barrett Cobb was his name," Red explained as if he was lecturing a child. "And he wasn't just your friend. He was your *best* friend. Might as well have been your brother. Isn't that right, Nicky?"

Nick gritted his teeth, which made the muscles in his jaw stand out on his face. His hands were wrapped around the rope, but all the energy had drained from his body. His legs curled up beneath the rest of him before becoming still. After that, he slumped over and remained on the floor, crumpled and bleeding upon his knees.

When he spoke, Nick's voice came out of him without more than a trickle of breath behind it. "If you're gonna kill me . . ." he sighed.

Red's eyes widened and he leaned in closer so he could catch the last whimper to come from the kid's mouth.

"If you're gonna kill me," Nick repeated, "then you should have done it when you had the chance."

As he said that, Nick snapped both hands out from where they'd been resting. One hand had been covering the other, so nobody else could see that Nick had finally managed to slip his fingers through the middle of the knot keeping him tied to the floor. With that single tug, he jerked the knot loose and instantly felt the rope give way around him.

Where before he'd been kneeling like a martyr waiting for the final blow, Nick now sprung up, using both legs that had been coiled underneath him, just waiting for a chance. He launched himself up from the floor, feeling strong enough to burst through any amount of ropes intended to hold him back. Before both legs were straightened, he'd balled his fists and aimed them at Red's jaw.

Although Red was quick enough to turn away from Nick's right hand, there was no way for him to dodge Nick's left. Knuckles pounded against the base of Red's skull, causing his legs to wobble and the rest of him to lurch to one side.

Everyone else in the barn exploded into action as hands tightened around guns and fingers clenched around triggers. All the while, the eyes framed by tattered burlap were gazing at Nick as if they'd caught a glimpse of the devil himself.

With Red stumbling from the punch he'd taken, Nick took hold of the man by the shoulder and spun him around to face the others in masks. Shots were fired and chunks were blasted out of the floor and walls, but none of the rounds drew any blood. The masked men had fallen into a panic and their target had nothing to lose.

That was never a healthy combination for the ones who'd lost their heads.

The only thing on Nick's mind was staying alive for one more second so he could do something more than bleed on the floor. His instincts screamed at him with a primal howl inside his head, drowning out the gunfire like the meaningless ruckus it was. Those instincts told Nick to get himself a gun and the closest gun he could see was Red's.

Nick's free hand moved in a quick, snapping blur to reach down and pluck the gun from Red's hand. All it took was a twist of his wrist and the pistol came free to settle comfortably in Nick's grasp. His finger slipped around the trigger and he took quick aim at the first Committee member he could see. Owen stared back at him with wide, frightened eyes. Before he could pull the trigger, Nick felt a blinding pain explode in his stomach.

Snarling like an animal, Red had jabbed his elbow into Nick's midsection and then dug it in a little deeper. He pulled his arm forward and drove it back again, sending his elbow into the same tender spot. This time he felt Nick stumble back. The grip around Red's shoulder let up just enough for him to slip free of it. While he wheeled around to get some space, Red shouted, "Somebody kill this bastard!"

The few shots that had been fired until now had been more of a twitching response than anything else. Now the masked men had gotten a chance to back away and see what was going on. They also had a clear shot at the raging youth in the middle of it all.

A few smiles formed behind those burlap masks, along with a few bad-intentioned scowls. But the masked men didn't draw their guns until Nick managed to pull in a breath, pick his first target, and send him straight to hell.

The gun in Nick's hand jumped as a plume of smoke billowed from the barrel. Sparks danced in the air as one of the men to Red's left doubled over and toppled to the floor. It wasn't Owen, but he was the closest to where Nick was standing and had been wielding a shotgun. Those two factors were the only things that put him ahead of Red in Nick's list of targets.

Seeing that first one drop was like a breath of clean air in Nick's lungs. It cleared out the cobwebs that had been forming in his head and gave him a faint glimmer of hope that he might make it out of that barn alive.

Boots scraped against the floor just behind Nick as three more men fanned out to a better position. Once they were able to fire without putting their own men at risk, they tightened their fingers around their triggers and got to work. Pistols and even a hunting rifle lent their voices to the mix as the inside of the barn filled with enough thunder to shake the rafters.

But the kid wasn't about to sit still and accept the lead that was being thrown in his direction. Nick had already dropped backward and thrown his legs up toward his head. The roll wasn't exactly graceful, but it was enough to get him to a better position behind a few bales of hay.

From there, Nick got himself situated so he could crouch behind the bales as bullets started chewing into them. When he took a glance around his cover, he saw that only a few of the masked men were foolish enough to remain where Nick had left them. Shad was one of them and had picked up the dead man's shotgun. He held it in one hand while gripping his pistol in the other.

"I see you, you son of a bitch," Shad growled. He let out another string of obscenities that was swallowed up by the combined roar of the shotgun and pistol.

The shotgun's blast sent straw flying in every direction and was enough to knock the bale back a few inches. None of the buckshot made it all the way through, however, despite the impressive show of force.

Before Nick could enjoy his good fortune, he felt something nip at his thigh. When he looked down, he saw a smaller batch of straw fluttering in front of a bloody crease in his leg. Although the shotgun hadn't gotten through the bale, the pistol's round had cut through it nicely.

Nick let out a howl that was loud enough to be heard over the ringing in his ears. He barely knew he was making the noise, which sounded more like the howl of a wounded animal.

"Not so tough now, are you, kid?" Shad taunted. "Time to join yer friends that we strung up in this here barn. You'll make a nice little addition to our picture collection."

The shotgunner's steps thumped against the floor. Nick could feel every one of them as they grew closer to where he was hiding. Although the pained groan was still leaking from his mouth, the rest of Nick's body was pressed flat against the floor. When he felt the other man walk up to stand in front of the hay bale, Nick stuffed the barrel of Red's gun into the blackened hole that had just been shot through the straw. The hole wasn't big enough to see through, but it granted him just a bit more accuracy when he pulled his trigger.

The gunshot was a muffled *thump* as the pistol bucked against Nick's palm. The air above him filled with the fury of the shotgun's second barrel, but the smoke and lead were all aimed well over Nick's head.

Shad's eyes were wide as saucers and his mouth was gaping wide enough for his chin to push against the bottom of his burlap mask. His jaw moved up and down and his mask alternated between pulling tight against his mouth and ballooning outward as he sucked air into his lungs. Even after all of that, he simply couldn't get himself to make a sound. Nick's shot had drilled a hole through one of Shad's kneecaps and the pain was so intense that it kept him from doing much of anything but feel it.

When Nick rolled out from behind the hay bale, he found Shad standing over him, still gaping up at the wall. The shotgun fell from Shad's hand and he dropped over like a tree that had lost a fight with an axe. He found his voice well enough when his shattered knee hit the ground and all of his weight pressed down on top of it.

Nick couldn't have asked for a better way to come out of cover than with Shad crying out like a beaten little girl. Putting Shad behind him, Nick took aim at the other men in the barn and pulled his trigger again and again while running for the door. Although Nick could tell a few of his shots had found their mark, he didn't stand still long enough to get an accurate count.

There were so many other shots being fired around him that Nick's senses were already immune to the hiss of lead through the air and the stench of burnt gunpowder. All Nick allowed himself to think about was getting closer to that door. A few shots burned a little too close for comfort, so Nick dove for the closest spot that could shield him from the incoming lead. Once he got there, he took a moment to catch his breath.

"Hot damn, Nick!" Red shouted from somewhere inside the barn. "I sure am gonna miss you when you're gone."

"That might be a while yet," Nick shouted back as he flipped open the pistol to get a look inside the cylinder. He was all out of fresh rounds. Part of him had already known that much. Years of living by the gun had taught him to count the rounds he'd fired out of instinct. Just when he was about to lose the flicker of hope he'd developed, Nick patted his waist.

While the holster strapped there might have been empty, there were still fresh rounds laced into the gun belt. Nick took one of the rounds from the leather loop and compared it to the gun he was holding. He looked up to the barn's dusty roof and gave silent thanks. After that, he dumped the spent shells from the pistol and quickly replaced them with ones from his belt.

The footsteps hadn't stopped. They were still scraping around in the barn as the masked men carefully closed in around their target. Unfortunately, there were so many of them that it was hard for Nick to pick out the location of any one in particular, since all the noises blended together within the airy space.

"Come on, Nick," came Red's voice from a spot closer than when he'd last spoken. "You didn't always want to go against us. I know that for certain. You agreed with what we were doing."

"The Committee ain't nothing but a bunch of killers!" Nick shouted.

"Maybe, but we kill the ones that need killing. That was never a secret."

"You're not the law," Nick replied in a voice loud enough to mask the sound of him snapping the cylinder shut and cocking back the pistol's hammer. "My friends were one thing, but you went too far and the wrong folks started getting hurt. I could have just left, but you had to push it."

"You're the one that pushed it, boy," Red said in a tone that was smooth enough to slip through the cracks in every wall like a narrow snake. "What you did to Pete was just as bad as anything else. You rode side by side with that man."

Just hearing Pete's name was enough to send a wave of fire through Nick's blood. "Pete was a lying, no-good asshole who I wish was here right now so I could shoot him again!"

Red didn't give a reply to that. In fact, Nick couldn't hear any more sound coming from inside the barn, apart from the pounding of his heart within his chest. In that moment, he knew that he'd made a big mistake by talking too much and getting too worked up.

All of that talking and all of that bluster had been a trick to give Red and the others time to circle around him for the kill. Nick was certain of that because he'd learned that trick from Red himself.

Gritting his teeth, Nick took a breath and thought about where the others were hiding. He and the rest of the Vigilance Committee had been inside that barn plenty of times and Nick knew every corner of it like the back of his hand. After a few more seconds, Nick swallowed hard and pushed himself once more toward the door.

The first place Nick aimed was for a dark corner no more than ten yards from where he was standing. Although he couldn't see anything but shadows, he sent one of his bullets there anyway. He heard a pained grunt and saw one of the masked men fall over from where he'd been hiding in the darkness.

Shots were going off all around him again

and one of them caught Nick in the hip, twisting him around like a top. He spotted the man who had fallen from the shadows still unconscious on the ground. Just to be safe, Nick sent his second bullet through the man's skull before landing on the floor next to him. A few of the shots intended for him hissed through the air just over his head and body. Some or all of them might have struck home if Nick hadn't been falling straight down at the time.

The moment Nick's back hit the floor, he rolled to one side and looked for the first target he could find. But the pain was being piled onto him so much that Nick thought he might pass out from what felt like hot pokers being shoved and twisted into his flesh. Soon his head started to swim and the world tilted around him.

Knowing full well what was coming, Nick vowed to make the best out of the moments before darkness overtook him. One of the masked men stepped into view and Nick sent his third shot in that direction. Even as he pulled the trigger, he knew he'd missed, so he pulled the trigger again.

The man in Nick's sights flinched and then snapped his head back as though he'd been kicked in the face by a mule. His body remained bent over backward and a red mist hung in the air at what had been his face level. The body dropped over and hit the ground the way only lifeless things do.

Underneath Nick's body, the barn's floor was rattling with the impacts of hurried footsteps. They came from every direction, without even slowing down as Nick fired toward the heaviest steps. In a matter of seconds, the footsteps had stopped. Nick's breaths were coming in labored gasps as his vision alternated between a muddled blur and crystal clarity.

When he blinked away the haze, Nick saw the barn's door less than a step away. Then his salvation disappeared as Red's face stared down at him. The gun felt like it was weighted down and roped to the floor, just as he'd been moments ago. Even so, Nick managed to lift the gun and point it at a spot directly between Red's eyes. He started to pull the trigger when a beefy hand came from nowhere and wrested the pistol away from him.

After that, Nick was dragged from the clean air promised by the barn's door and back down into the smoke-filled, blood-drenched embrace of hell.

Red was shaking his head as he reached out and accepted the pistol that was handed to him by one of the masked men. "Goddamn, Nicky. If I believed in demons, I'd swear that you were one of 'em." Holding up the gun, Red pulled the trigger to drop the hammer on a spent round. "But even a demon's got to come up short sometimes. That was a hell of a fight, kid. I didn't think you had it in you."

There was genuine admiration in Red's voice. The surviving masked men gathered around Nick and took careful aim at the young man's head. Shad was still crying and swearing somewhere beyond the Committee's circle.

"Hold up now," Red ordered. He looked directly into Nick's eyes and didn't look away. "Maybe Nicky's right."

"What?" Owen asked as he stumbled out from the corner where he'd been hiding.

"The Vigilance Committee has worked all this time because the folks around here believe in what we're doing. They want law and order and we give it to them. Don't tell me that none of you have heard folks saying that we've been getting a little too quick on the trigger lately."

There was a heavy silence as the masked men glanced around at one another. Since none of them could dispute Red's statement, they focused angrily back at Nick.

"We ain't letting him go," one of those

men declared. "He just killed three men."

"Four," Red corrected. "But he was defending himself."

"What the hell are you getting at?"

Red turned toward the masked man who'd just asked that question and grinned. "I'm saying that we need to deal in justice. At least, we need to be seen that way. How many times have our skins been saved by the folks around these parts hiding us or turning deaf, blind, and stupid the moment some other lawman pokes his nose around here looking for Committee members?"

"Plenty." Owen replied.

Red nodded. "That's right. And they do that because they see us as protectors who are up to the job. We gun down one of our own and it makes us look weak."

Nick was pale and growing paler by the second. The fight was still in him, but his body clearly was no longer up to the task.

"Nicky here's got one more job as a member of this Committee," Red declared. "He needs to remind the lawless out there that Virginia City ain't the place for them to be. He needs to tell the law-abiding folks out there that we back up our word in ways the law never could." Reaching for the side of his right boot, Red drew a knife from the scabbard tied there.

The blade came out like a snake's tongue, swift and flickering in the light.

"That kid needs to die for what he's done," Will Culligan said. "Plain and simple. We ain't never worked another way."

"Oh, he'll die," Red assured him as well as all the other masked Committee members gathered around him. "It'll just be the kind of death that serves as an example. He'll make it out of this barn and probably out of town. Hell, this one's lucky enough to possibly even make it farther than that. But he's a dead man, no matter how far he gets. And all the others that get a look at him will know he came from Virginia City. They can figure out the rest for themselves."

There was still plenty of anger in the eyes peering out from behind those burlap sacks. Some of it was directed at Nick and some was directed at Red. Once they saw Red reach down with that knife, they all fell back into line with their leader.

Nick's first reaction was to pull his arm away as desperation flooded through his body to give him another burst of strength.

"Hold him down," Red ordered to nobody in particular.

Will Culligan was the man who slammed his boot down to drive Nick's wrist against the floor. Another one kicked Nick in the jaw as the kid started to turn toward that boot. When he landed, another foot pinned his other wrist in a similar fashion.

Red reached down slowly, the way a vicious boy would reach for a wounded animal. "You're real good with a gun, Nick. From what I hear, you and Skinner and the rest of that gang you rode with got around enough to be known in more than a few places. I'm anxious to hear what kind of things they'll be saying about you when they see you after we're done here tonight.

"If Skinner's still alive, he might come for a little payback," Red said as he dug the tip of his blade into the side of Nick's left little finger. With a twist of his hand, he carved out a sizable chunk of meat that dropped wetly to the floor. "Nah, I don't think you'll see Skinner anytime soon. He cleared out of here in a rush. When the rest of the gunmen in these parts see you, they'll probably do the same."

Hearing the name of the killer who had once been his partner was enough to fill Nick's head with memories that struck deeper than any bullet. His struggles were pointless against the hands and feet holding him to the floor, but he kept struggling all the same. Finally, it seemed that every man in that barn who was still able was doing their part to keep Nick pinned to the floor.

Every man, that is, except for Red.

Red was too busy with his own work as he started dipping his blade into the fresh notch that had been cut into Nick's finger.

"I'll make you pay," Nick snarled as he felt the knife chew into his hand. "For everything you done. I promise I'll make you pay."

"A dead man's promise ain't worth shit, kid." Red focused on his gruesome task. "Go ahead and scream if you want," he said as he started carving out more flesh to make the gouge even deeper. "Nobody'll blame you."

With that, Red stuck the knife into the gouge he'd just made and pushed until the tip of the blade emerged from the other side of Nick's little finger. He twisted once, flipping the top half of that finger off so it could dangle from one last, stubborn flap of skin.

"This little piggy went to market," Red whispered. With one snap of his wrist, he sliced the flap of skin and sent the upper half of Nick's little finger to the floor.

Where he'd been numb to a good portion of the pain in his body, Nick was now alive with the terrible sensations. His eyes opened wide and his breath caught in his throat. Before he knew what to think about losing his finger, he felt Red's blade slicing into the tips of the fingers on his right hand.

"You should take this as a compliment, boy," Red snarled. Rather than cut as efficiently as he had on Nick's left hand, he worked slowly and deliberately now. The blade in his hand was moving in short, twitching motions as Red whittled away at the fingers on Nick's right hand. "You see, although I want you to send my message, I also can't take the chance of you coming back gunning for me."

Red's knife peeled away another few layers of skin. It snagged on the side of a fingernail, but soon cut through that as well.

The Committee members were no longer laughing. They'd seen some blood in their time and had spilled plenty of it on their own. This, however, was something different. This was more gruesome than any of the men could have conceived. Going by the look on Red's face, it was something he'd been cooking up for some time.

"Hope you find yourself a new profession, Nicky," Red continued as he admired the way he'd whittled Nick's middle finger far enough down to expose a bit of bone. "Because I don't think you'll be using a gun anytime in this life."

Red moved on to Nick's ring finger. This

time he started whittling at the joint just above the knuckle.

Nick's world was pain.

His mind was full of it.

It filled him up the way water filled the lungs of a drowning man.

His pain was so extreme that he felt as if his soul had been pulled from his body to float up where those poor men had been hung from the rafters. In the years to come, Nick was uncertain if he'd actually been able to stay conscious throughout the whole ordeal or if some of it had been a nightmare.

Then again, no nightmare ever hurt that badly.

The cutting went on until Red's blade was slippery with blood. When his grip was threatened, Red wiped the blade on his shirt, cleaned his hand off, and went on. It was hard to tell what parts of Nick's hands were coated in blood and parts had been robbed of their flesh.

Finally, with sweat dripping from his brow, Red got up and examined what he'd done. He looked at the knife in his hand and nodded. He looked at Nick and shook his head.

"I bet you wish you could do things differently now, don't you?" Red asked between labored breaths. "Now you'll just have to think about the mistakes you made and how you should have fixed them when you had the chance."

When he spoke, Nick could barely find the strength to push his voice out of his mouth without keeling over. "Kill . . . me."

Red shook his head. "I don't kill my own Committee members," he said.

"Then . . . this isn't . . . over."

Still shaking his head, Red dropped his knife into its sheath and drew his pistol. He lowered his foot down on to Nick's wrist and took aim. "Your days as a bad man are over, all right. I promise you that."

The next thing Nick heard was a quick series of *pops.*

Each *pop* was a shot from Red's gun.

Each bullet blew off the mutilated remains of Nick's middle and ring fingers like bottles being shot off a fence.

# EIGHTEEN

*Ellis Station, Missouri*
*1883*

The wagon rumbled into town without anyone taking much notice. Those that did look in its direction saw nothing more than a rickety collection of boards and nails pulled by a pair of tired horses. As for the two people sitting in the wagon's seat, they didn't look in much better shape than the horses. All of them kept their heads low and their eyes facing forward.

"I don't believe this," Nick grunted.

Catherine looked over to him and asked, "What's wrong?"

"This isn't a few towns over from where my father is. This is the place. They must have changed the name."

"Those railroad tracks looked fairly new."

"That must be it, then." He shook his head and soaked it all in. "Christ, it's been a long time since I've been here."

"Looks pretty different, huh?"

"I only came through here once in the last ten years. Maybe longer. And the reason my father chewed my hide so badly was because I was drunk the whole time I was here. Since then, I've been to a hundred towns just like this one. They all tend to mix together after a while."

The farther he rode into town, however, the clearer Nick's memory became. Soon he found himself recognizing the occasional store. Although plenty of street names had changed, he was able to navigate them without too much difficulty.

"Does your father still live here?" Catherine asked. "I mean, are you sure, since you haven't been here for so long?"

"I actually hope he isn't here. Things would be a whole lot easier that way."

"Well, maybe he's decided to move on. If Red meant to do any harm, surely he would have done it by now."

Nick shook his head slowly. "Red used to send out his scouts without lighting a fire under them. He liked to give his men plenty of time to lay back and see what happened. Even for a season or two, just waiting for whoever he was after to make a mistake and step in the wrong direction. He was real patient that way."

Catherine thought about the story that Nick had told her on their ride into town. It was hard for her to think of him as a hired gun working for a bunch of vigilantes. Then again, the more she heard about Nick's youth, the more grateful she was for not having been there to witness it.

"Did you ever go off scouting like that?" she asked.

Nick shook his head. "Nope. I wasn't patient enough for that. I was just the one who rode in to take care of business when Red knew where to find a target for me."

"Well, we're here. Now what do we do?"

"The first thing is to get these horses somewhere they can rest. Then," Nick added reluctantly, "I suppose we'll see about finding my father."

"From what you've told me, it sounds like he can handle himself."

"He can, but he won't be able to fight off Red or whoever else he's got working for him these days. I was hoping to keep him out of this, but that was back when I thought we were riding into someplace my father wouldn't be. Now that I'm here, I've just got to keep him close so I can make sure he stays alive."

Ellis Station moved at a pace befitting the oppressive humidity that bore down on it like an invisible shroud. The heat had gotten worse the farther into Missouri Nick and Catherine had gotten. Throughout the entire trip, both of them had been thinking ahead to when they would arrive. Now that they were here, they longed to be on the trail once again. At least that way there would be some air moving across their faces.

Nick steered the wagon without looking much at the road in front of him. He merely flicked the reins when appropriate and headed for a building leaning precariously to one side at the end of Mercantile Avenue. They didn't have to get close enough to read the sign posted outside that building to know it was a corral. The scent of sweating horses was more than enough to mark it as such.

After driving the wagon straight into the open stable, Nick had a quick conversation with a man dressed in dirty coveralls who came over to take the reins from him. From there, Nick unbuckled Rasa and Kazys from their harness and unloaded their things from the back of the wagon.

On their way out of the stable, Nick leaned over to Catherine and whispered, "Stay with me. Don't leave my sight until we get settled, you hear?"

Now that she was on her feet, Catherine

was anxious to stretch her legs even more. The rumbling in her belly made it difficult to slow herself to Nick's cautious pace. "Let me find a hotel," she pleaded. "Or at least a restaurant. I'll keep to the streets and stay put once I get there. I'll even keep to this street here," she added, sweeping her arm to indicate Mercantile Avenue. "How would that be?"

"Not good enough. Stick with me and follow my lead."

"It doesn't even look like there's more than three people out and about. Don't you think I can handle myself to find a place to eat?"

"I don't doubt you for a minute," Nick shot back. "It's just that I don't trust Red or any of the men he might have sent to leave alone anyone, lady or not. After what I told you, you should know that too. I was one of those men who came to terrorize ladies who thought they were safe, remember? That makes me plenty qualified to keep you in one piece. You don't know these men like I do."

Catherine recoiled slightly. The thought of him taking a hostage and putting so much fear into an innocent girl was still tough to swallow. But it was the intensity in Nick's voice right then and there that made her take notice. More than anything, it seemed that Nick needed her to stay in his sight more than Catherine needed to stretch her legs.

"All right," she said. "I'll come with you."

"Thank you. Now just stay where I can see you and let me do the talking. If you see anyone taking too much notice of us, let me know."

As if Catherine couldn't feel any more uncomfortable, she found herself being led straight into the undertaker's parlor within spitting distance of the stable. She watched the street and the few souls standing on either side of it as Nick pushed open the front door of the parlor.

"Hello?" came a voice from the rear corner of the parlor. "I'll be right with you."

The stout man wearing the dark suit turned his back on the display case he'd been cleaning. He smiled at the two people standing in his doorway, dropped the rag he'd been using, and made his way past a table where caskets were on display. "What can I do for you fine people today?"

Before Nick could say a word, the stout man jumped back as if he'd just stepped on a tack. "Is that you, Nicolas?"

Ignoring the mispronunciation of his name, Nick nodded and gave the man a halfhearted smile. Although his name was Nicolai, most folks had taken to calling him Nick. Only one called him Nicolas on a regular basis. Strangely enough, it sounded good to hear that name just then. "Yeah, Harold. It's me."

Harold Abernathy rushed forward and embraced Nick as though he meant to lift him off the ground. Although he eased up on the hug, he kept his hands on Nick's arms so he could hold him steady in front of him. "Let me get a look at you!" Harold's eyes roamed up and down over Nick as he shook his head. When he got to Nick's hands, he let out a quick breath.

"Oh my Lord, what's this?"

Pulling his hands away before Harold could see the gnarled remains of his fingers, Nick reached into his pocket to pull out the business card Catherine had kept for him. "I'm here about this," he said.

Nodding, Harold took the card and said, "I knew one of these would find you. I just knew it. With all the men who have been asking about you and pestering your father, I've got enough of these cards to paper a room."

"So my father is here?" Nick asked.

"Of course he is." Harold's eyes shifted over to where Catherine was standing. "And who's this?"

"Catherine Weaver, this is Harold Abernathy," Nick said quickly. "He's the man who is about to show me where my father is."

"Oh yes, yes. He'll be so happy to see you." Harold stopped and took a moment to think it over. "Well, he'll be surprised, anyway. Where did you meet this lovely lady?"

Nick shook his head to clear it out a bit. "We can talk later, Harold. How long ago did the name of the town change to Ellis Station?"

Harold fretted to himself and shook his head. "It seems so long ago, but the railroad came through here about six years ago . . . maybe ten. But then that bridge was blown up and your father swore you and your friends had something to do with it."

"What?"

"Oh yes. Anyway, the town's been Ellis Station ever since, even though the only station around here is for the stagecoach line."

"And how long have these men been asking about me?"

"They said they were lawmen, but didn't show any badges," Harold replied. "At least, those were the men who came most recently. They said they were after you for killing a lawman in cold blood. I didn't believe a word of it, but your father . . . let's just say that he still has his doubts about you. Either way, neither of us knew anything about where you might be. It's not true, is it? What those men accused you of?"

"Of course not," Nick said absently.

Harold placed a hand upon his chest as if he'd just been saved from a noose. "I knew it."

"Did any of them go by the name Red Parks?"

"I think I heard that name mentioned. At least the first one. Some of the men mentioned something about what would happen if Red heard about something or what he would do when he got here. Things might not be so bad, though. We haven't heard from them for at least a few days."

Nick had to fight back the impulse to take hold of the squat undertaker and shake the rest of the answers out of him. Instead of that, he looked over to Catherine and got a shrug in return.

"How many of them are there?" Nick asked in a strained voice. "And where can I find them?"

The undertaker rubbed his chin and glanced up as though the answer to that question was written on the ceiling. "I'd say at least three or four . . . maybe eight. But they didn't start causing trouble until the last week or two."

"Why didn't you try to let me know so much was going on? I would've gotten here faster if I knew about all this!"

"Nobody knew where to find you," Harold replied. "As far as I know, you haven't even been in this state since you were a kid. Besides, even if I did know where you were, I couldn't send you anything. Those men spend a lot of time watching the post office."

"Great," Nick said. "That's just great. At least I know for certain this is where Red's been the whole time."

Harold's eyes widened and he started losing the color in his face. "Oh dear Lord. You know who this Red person is? Is he one of the gunfighters your father talks about?"

Nick gave himself a moment to collect himself. "Yeah. Actually, he is one of the bad men my father talks about. Please tell me my father's all right."

"Oh, he's fine," Harold exclaimed. "In fact, he'll be so happy to see you. Whatever he says, you've got to know that he's happy to see you."

"Did any of those men try to hurt him?" Nick asked.

"They said some unkind things," Harold said. "But Stan kept his chin up and didn't give them anything to cling to. For the first time, that actually worked in his favor."

It took Nick a moment to get over the oddity of hearing his father called Stan. It hit him on the same nerve that used to twinge every time he heard someone call him Nick rather than his proper name of Nicolai. Ever since Stasys had brought his son to America, they'd both had to make plenty of adjustments. Dealing with their names being stripped down and picked apart was the least of them. The last time he'd spoken to Stasys, the older man's accent was still thick on every word that came out of his mouth. Nick's had faded to only a subtle curl on the occasional syllable.

"Where is he?" Nick asked.

In stark contrast to the reluctant tone in Nick's voice, Harold replied with genuine enthusiasm. "He's out back, working to replenish our stock." To Catherine's perplexed look, he added, "Of coffins, of course. He's building some coffins. There have been some unfortunate incidents where some local men were killed."

"Yeah," Nick said, thinking about all the similar incidents that had happened in

Virginia City. "I'm sure you'll be needing every one of those extra coffins."

# NINETEEN

The back door to the undertaker's parlor
swung open upon well-oiled hinges. Nick
rushed outside and found himself looking
out onto a plot of land that stretched out
for miles. Like plenty of other undertakers
he'd worked for, Harold Abernathy's place
wasn't far from the burial grounds. Nick
looked at the nearby stacks of lumber and
then out to the fields beyond them. Less
than twenty yards away was a shack built
on a patch of land that had been cleared off
and neatly tended.

"Where do you think your father is?"
Catherine asked as she emerged from the
parlor behind Nick.

Nick's gaze had already settled upon the
shack. "This whole place has his signature
written all over it, but I'd guess he's in
there."

Before he'd finished talking, Nick was

walking toward the shack. "Pa, are you in there?"

The moment Nick got to the door of the shack, he heard something moving inside. Just as he was about to take a look in there for himself, he heard the sound of something heavy slicing through the air.

Nick lunged backward while sweeping his arm out to push Catherine back. Suddenly the blade of a shovel dropped into the doorway and came all the way down until it took a chunk out of the ground where Nick had been standing moments ago.

Acting more on reflex than anything else, Nick took a step forward so he could hold the shovel down with his boot. His left hand held open the shack's door while his right hand drew the modified Schofield pistol from its holster.

"I tell you before," came a gravelly voice from inside the shack. "You leave me alone!"

Nick squinted into the shadows that filled a good portion of the shack. He was still sighting along the barrel of his pistol, but it seemed as if he'd already forgotten the gun was in his hand. "Pa, it's me."

Stasys was several inches shorter than Nick. His hair was a thick tussle of coarse silver strands shot through with patches of dark gray. The old man's face was rounded and tough. His eyes, on the other hand, looked like a perfect match to Nick's mixture of blue and gray.

Stasys's hands were thick and callused, wrapped around the shovel's handle in a way that made it plain there was no chance of it escaping his grasp. When he looked closer at the man standing in his doorway, he leaned forward and squinted. There was nothing about him that spoke of frailty. Instead, he simply looked as if he couldn't believe what he was seeing.

"It is you, *sunus*?" Stasys asked, using the word for *son* in his native tongue. His thick accent wrapped around every word he spoke.

"Yeah," Nick said with a bit of disbelief showing upon his own face. "It's me."

After Stasys glanced away from Nick's face, his squint turned into more of a scowl. "If you do not put that gun away, I will knock this shovel against your head!"

The old man's voice had risen, but his tone was more scolding than threatening. When Catherine heard him talk to Nick that way, she instinctively winced. When she saw Nick cower a bit like a kid about to get a whipping, she had to fight to hold back a giggle.

"Better," Stasys said when Nick had holstered the gun. "Now give me my shovel back."

Nick took his foot from where it had been holding the shovel against the ground. Still looking every bit the child obeying his parent, he stepped back and allowed Stasys to heft the shovel and step forward.

"So, after all this time, you finally decide to pay a visit?" Stasys asked.

"I heard there was some trouble here, Pa. I wanted to —"

"Oh, I see. There must be trouble for you to see me. Any other time, you are too good to come. You are too busy to care if I live or die."

Rolling his eyes, Nick let out a weary breath. "You know that's not true."

Stasys remained quiet as he looked Nick over from top to bottom. It was a quick glance, but he nodded at what he saw and took a step closer. Without a word, he opened his arms and wrapped them around his boy so he could clap him on the back. "It is still good to see you, *sunus.*"

" 'Soon-yuss'?" Catherine said slowly, mimicking the sound if not the proper pronunciation of what she heard.

"Yes," Stasys said as he held Nick at arm's length. "*Sunus.* My son." Looking over to Catherine, he put on a wide — if somewhat crooked — smile. "And who is this? Has my Nicolai finally found a wife?"

"Not exactly, Pa. This is Catherine Weaver."

Stasys pushed Nick aside so he could extend a hand to Catherine. "Is good to meet you, Catherine. You are a friend of Nicolai's?"

Shaking Stasys's hand, she nodded. "I've known him for a few years, yes."

"And he has gotten you into trouble too?"

"Well, not him exactly. He did get me out of a scrape or two, though."

"A scrape that he caused, no doubt," Stasys asked, tossing a sideways glance in Nick's direction. "I think I am in something like that myself."

"That's what I wanted to talk to you about, Pa. Have there been any men coming around asking for me?"

"There have always been men asking for you. Usually, they wear a badge."

Perhaps it was the scolding tone in his father's voice or the words themselves that put the shamed expression on Nick's face. Whatever the source might have been, that expression hung on him heavily.

For the first time since they'd arrived, Catherine heard Stasys's voice soften a bit as the older man reached out and took hold of Nick's chin. "I tell them nothing," he said lifting Nick's face upward again. "Like all the other times."

Nick rested his hand upon his father's wrist before patting it gently. "I know, Pa. But this isn't like the other times. These men are different."

At first, Stasys seemed to be enjoying the sight of his son so close to him. Then, as he caught sight of the hand resting upon his wrist, he twitched and pulled in a breath. "I tell you not to run with those kind," he said, snapping his hand back while clipping Nick under the chin. "But you never listen to me! And now you say these men are worse than the rest. How do you know about any of the ones that have come for you? You were never here! You leave and never look back again."

Catherine knew that wasn't true. When she saw that Nick was biting his tongue, she almost told the older man that fact herself. But then she got a look from Nick that kept her from doing that. It was a quick, frustrated glance, followed by a subtle shake of his head.

"Harold said that there were still men in town," Nick said. "Have they been around here recently?"

Stasys shrugged and held his shovel in both hands. "I'm working all day. Men come here and try to start trouble, so I chase them off."

"Has anyone been following you or watching you?"

"Watching me dig? Why would they do such a thing?"

"Has anyone followed you or tried to talk to you when you were alone?"

"I'm always alone, Nicolai. I get used to it a long time ago."

That one hurt.

Catherine could see a wince right below Nick's surface. After that, the muscles in his jaw tensed and he turned his head as though he'd been slapped across the face.

"All right, then," Nick said. "I'll do this on my own. Thanks for all the help, Pa."

Nick started to walk away. He didn't even reach for Catherine's hand or motion for her to follow. He simply turned his back on his father and walked in the opposite direction.

"Can we come by later?" Catherine asked.

Stasys's entire expression brightened when he shifted his eyes toward her. "My house is not much bigger than this shack," he said. "Maybe there is not enough room."

"Do you have a stove?"

"Yes."

"Then maybe I can cook something for

supper. It seems like you two still have some things to talk about."

That brought the scowl back onto Stasys's face, but he tried to keep it out of Catherine's sight. Pointing toward the open land behind the shack, he told her, "I live on other side of that hill."

When Catherine looked, she expected to see a fence, maybe some other houses or perhaps a few animals grazing in the fields. Instead, all she could see was tall grass and well-tended ground, studded with wood crosses and stone markers poking up from the earth at regular intervals.

"We'll find it," she said, trying to keep the smile on her face. When she looked in the direction that Nick had walked, she joked, "I guess first I'll have to find your son, though."

"That shouldn't be too hard," Stasys grumbled. "Just try the saloons."

Catherine didn't have to go too far to find Nick. All she needed to do was go through the undertaker's parlor and come out through the front door. Nick was standing with his back against the post that supported the awning of a building across the street. As soon as he saw her step outside, Nick straightened up and waited for her to come stand beside him.

"Sorry about walking off like that," he said.

She patted his arm and replied, "It's all right. Things look rough between you and your father."

"I shouldn't have let you out of my sight."

"Is that all?"

After a moment, Nick sighed. "I guess you weren't too far off the mark on that other matter. I haven't exactly been the apple of my father's eye since I left home."

"Well, he still cares for you. He may not approve of the things you've done, but he still loves you. He's still your father."

"Yeah, well, maybe part of the trouble I have is that I can see his point in what he says. It's been a long time since I've been much of a son to brag about. Hell, it's only been a few years since I've come out of hiding and I've been doing my level best to keep out of sight. Before that, I was doing my best to be known from one end of the country to the other as a bad man and a killer. I'm sure he's heard all about them days."

"Maybe, but now it's time for him to learn about the man you've become."

"I don't know about that, Catherine. It might be too late for that."

"Well, there's one way to find out for certain."

Nick's brow furrowed as he studied Catherine's face. What he saw made him scowl a bit more. "What did you do?"

"Nothing much. Just offered to cook up a nice dinner for us. All three of us."

"There's things I need to do," Nick said sharply. "I didn't come here to pay social calls."

"You've still got to eat, don't you?"

"Yeah, but —"

"And you still need to watch over me, right?"

Seeing where she was going with this, Nick let his head droop forward before nodding. "Yeah, Catherine. Of course I do."

"Then you'll have to come to your father's house for dinner because that's where I'll be tonight." Stepping around so she was in front of him, Catherine reached out to place her hands on Nick's chest. She walked her fingers up the buttons of his shirt until she reached his neck. "If you don't show up," she said while tapping his cheek, "I'll be very disappointed in you."

Nick found himself smiling and nodding before he could stop it. "All right," he said. "We'll go there for dinner. But promise me that . . ."

When Nick trailed off, Catherine looked up at him expectantly. "Promise you what?" she asked. Then she saw that Nick was no longer looking at her. Instead, he was gazing off at something past her completely. She started to turn to see what had caught his eye when she felt his finger catch hold of her chin.

"Promise me you'll do what I tell you," he said under his breath while gently moving her head so she remained looking at him.

"What is it, Nick? What's wrong?"

"Remember those men that are after me?"

"Yes."

"I think I just found one of them. Walk with me like there's nothing wrong and then go into that store down the street. Stay there where someone can see you and if anyone else comes around, you start screaming, you hear me?"

"Yes, but what are you going to do?"

"I don't care if they tell you to keep your mouth shut, you just start screaming. You hear me?"

Feeling the tension in Nick's hand, she forced herself to take a breath and nodded. "I hear you. If anyone comes after me, I start screaming."

"That's right. I won't be far, but if I don't come back for you in ten minutes, start kicking up a fuss and cry for the sheriff. I spotted his office on the way into town."

Nick forced a smile on to his face and draped his arm over her shoulder. He walked with easy steps and looked around as though he was simply taking in the sights. "If you hear shots, just come outside and take a look like everyone else. I'll come for you when it's safe."

Although she tried to mimic his easygoing nature, Catherine couldn't exactly match his confidence. The closer she got to the spot where they were to split up, the more she needed his support to keep her from stumbling. Only when he was certain that she could go on, Nick let go of her and pointed Catherine toward the store.

She stepped inside and didn't even hear what the girl behind the counter had to say. Catherine turned and looked back outside to see what Nick was doing.

He was nowhere to be found.

# TWENTY

Nick was keeping low and working his way down the cramped space between the store where he'd left Catherine and the building next to it. As soon as he felt the shadows close around him like a cool cloak, he broke into a run.

He hadn't recognized the man watching them from the far end of Mercantile Avenue, but he'd felt that one's eyes boring a hole through him, as surely as if there had been a drill pressed against his forehead. Once he saw for sure that he was being watched, Nick had no doubt about what to do.

As he moved, Nick pictured a map of the town in his mind. It had been a while since he'd been there, but it didn't take much to remember the familiar twists and turns of the alleys he'd haunted in his youth. In fact, he and Barrett had made a game of trying to ditch one another many times and he was still the best at spotting shortcuts and hiding places at a glance. Sometimes he felt more at home in alleys than on the streets.

Before he made it to the far end of this particular alley, Nick saw a shadow moving just ahead of him. He came to a quick stop and heard another set of footsteps trying to do the same. They missed the mark by a fraction of a second and Nick heard the telltale scuffle of boots. These boots, however, came from above rather than behind him.

Nick lunged forward. He might not have been able to see whoever was on the roof, but he could try to catch up to the man he'd spotted on the street when he'd been with Catherine. Surprisingly, he didn't have to chase the other man down one more step, since the fellow was standing there waiting for him. The face hadn't been familiar from thirty paces away, but it was a different story when that distance was cut down to three inches.

"Howdy, Nick," the man said. "Been a long time."

Nick was already grabbing hold of the other man's collar and his other hand was cocked back in preparation for a straight punch. "Hello, Will."

If Will Culligan was nervous about being

on the other end of Nick's raised fist, it didn't show. His face was creased by deep wrinkles, which looked like cracks on the bottom of a dry lakebed. His teeth peeked out from behind an expectant sneer and his cold eyes gazed on Nick the way a hunter studied a deer.

"Red knew you'd be by here eventually," Will said.

"Is that so?"

Will nodded. "You ask me, I'd say he got impatient."

"That's not like Red."

"No, it isn't. Then again, he's not the only one who would like to finish up with you. Maybe we all got a little impatient at the thought of this little reunion."

Before Nick could say another word, he felt something dig into his ribs. Just as that was registering in his mind, he heard the *click* of a hammer being thumbed back. The sound was only muffled by Will's jacket. Nick looked down just to make sure and quickly spotted the gun in the other man's hand.

"Maybe he wasn't the only one to get a little impatient, huh?" Will mused. "You still got the eye, kid, but you don't have what it takes to back it up. We all saw to that, didn't we?"

The bait was right there, dangling in front of Nick's face like a worm on a hook. Even though he knew only too well what damage could be done if that hook sank in, Nick still felt the urge to nip at the bait anyway. He managed to hold back, but it sure as hell wasn't easy.

Slowly, Nick relaxed his grip and stepped back from Will. The gun barrel was no longer digging into his ribs, but it was still aimed at him, as surely as there was still a sneer on Will's face.

"How many of you are here?" Nick asked.

"Enough. That's all that matters. And soon there'll be more. All you need to know right now is that, since you're in town and all, Red wants to have a word with you."

"All this just to talk to me? I suppose I should be real impressed."

"Don't flatter yourself. You're just a means to an end. Then again, Red ain't ever stayed after someone for so long as he's stayed after you. Most of us thought that he wouldn't much care when we heard that you'd made it out of Montana. But that ain't the case. Not by a mile."

"So I'm just supposed to let you all follow me and keep watch over my father before you get the courage to come after me?"

"Your father and that pretty brunette.

Don't forget her."

"Fuck you. Fuck you all."

Will smiled and winced dramatically. "Oh, Nick, what would your pappy say if he heard you talking like that? Perhaps I could ask him, since we'll be paying him a visit. Least-ways, we'll be calling on him soon enough if you don't stick around to take what you got coming to you."

Nick shook his head. His gun hand itched as if it had been stuffed into an ant hill and the only thing to scratch it was resting in the holster at his side. "You don't want to talk like that, Will. Take my word."

"Keep your threats to yourself, kid. Me and the rest of the boys have been in town long enough to know what your pappy eats for breakfast every morning. If you don't behave like a good boy, we will pay him that visit. It may not be tonight or even tomor-row, but we'll come calling and when we do, we'll tear that old man into so many pieces that you won't know what to bury or what to feed to the dogs."

Stepping back, Nick put a yard or so between himself and Will. Once there, he planted his feet and shifted his shoulders sideways to form a straight line that pointed to the man in front of him.

Recognizing the duelist's stance, Will

straightened up and asked, "What's on your mind, boy? You want to fight? Go ahead and make a move. I'll even let you touch that piece of shit gun of yours before I pull my trigger, just to be sporting."

Before he took another breath, Nick calmed himself and thought about the man he was facing. Will Culligan hadn't been the fastest on the draw, but that knowledge was several years old. Will was, however, a good student of Red Parks, which meant that he subscribed to plenty of Red's tactics.

Knowing that, Nick also knew that there was more going on than what he could see. Will would never press him like this unless he knew he could kill Nick on the spot. And though he had plenty of reason to be confident in his ability to outdraw Nick, Will was busting at the seams to roll those dice. That's when a very important bit of information sprang to Nick's mind that he'd almost forgot out of sheer anger.

Nodding slowly, Nick let his shoulders drop to where they belonged and pushed all the air from his lungs. "All right, Will. When does Red want to meet with me?"

After a moment, Will relaxed as well. His eyes showed surprise at first, which gave way to disappointment. "Meet him tomorrow morning at ten. There's a poker hall on

Third. Red'll be waiting there for a game."

Nick nodded again.

"You made a good decision, Nicky. I'm sure your pappy and that pretty lady friend of yours will thank you for it."

Turning on his heels, Nick put his back to Will and started walking down the alley.

He could feel the air wrapping around him like a clammy set of hands.

He could smell the heat soaking into the ground, along with the pungent stench of Will's sweaty shirt.

And now he could see the ace Will thought he'd had up his sleeve.

Nick's elbow was already brushing against the side of his holster. Lifting his hand as if he was only going to scratch his nose, he snapped his arm up in a quick blur of motion the instant his palm brushed against the tooled leather of his holster.

One finger caught under the modified Schofield's handle just fine, but the gnarled stubs of his wounded fingers were unable to finish the job. But this was the very reason his gun and holster were specially tooled the way they were.

The barrel may have looked as twisted and gnarled as the remains of his own fingers, but the groove in it fit perfectly against the ridges inside his holster. When he lifted the gun out, the handle twisted to one side so it fit snugly in his hand. From there, all Nick had to do was close his grip and lift the Schofield the rest of the way out. It wasn't much, but it was enough to compensate for a few of the milliseconds he'd lost because of his injuries.

All of this happened in the blink of an eye. Nick's arm, hand, gun, and holster all worked as a single being. The Schofield was brought up until it was pointing toward the fellow who had been perched on the rooftop and looking down into the alley. Nick shifted his aim slightly until he had the rifleman in his sights.

The man on the roof fired off a shot, but he'd been caught off his guard and the angle was too sharp for him to catch any of his target. Nick fired in that same heartbeat, sending one bullet to cross paths with the round sent by the rifleman.

While the rifle's round lodged itself into the wall behind Nick, the bullet from the Schofield took a healthy chunk of meat from the side of the rifleman's neck. The head that had been leaning out to watch Nick snapped back and sent a spray of blood into the air. Although none of that blood made it down to where Nick was standing, the rifleman's hat dropped to the ground at

Nick's feet.

Will had been watching this through eyes narrowed in disbelief. No more than two seconds had passed from the time Nick went to scratch his nose to the moment when the rifleman's hat fell to the dirt. When he looked back at Nick, Will was staring right down the Schofield's barrel.

"You were never stupid enough to face me man to man," Nick said. "Not even after what you did to me."

Will licked his lips and shifted on his feet. Although he still had his gun drawn, that didn't make his own position any more favorable.

Nick let a cruel smirk come onto his face. "Wanna try your luck against this piece of shit gun of mine, Will?"

"If I meant to kill you, I could have had Brad drop you in the street."

"Is that who was up there? That's a shame. I kind of liked Brad."

"You're a dead man, Nick," Will said solemnly.

Nick shrugged. "I've heard that plenty of times before, and from better men than you."

"Red's the one you need to fear. He's been waiting years to get his hands on you and I intend on being there when he does."

Feeling the tension work its way up along his back, Nick gritted his teeth and started walking toward Will.

As Nick drew closer to him, Will didn't make one move against him. There wasn't any murderous intent in his eyes or anything left of the smirk that had been on his face. Instead, there was only the expression of a man who was looking into the face of a ghost.

A ghost or perhaps a demon.

"You want to shoot me, then you'd better do it," Nick snarled. "Because the next time you threaten my family or anyone else who's with me, I'll kill you before the words get out of your mouth."

Slowly . . . carefully, Will lowered his gun. Even after the pistol was holstered, Nick's Schofield didn't so much as budge.

"Smart man," Nick said. "If there are any more men posted on the rooftops or anywhere else for that matter, call them off. If I see any more sharpshooters, I'll put a bullet in their stomach so the whole town hears them scream as they die."

"All right," Will said with a nod. "What should I say to Red?"

"Tell him I'll meet him for our game. Until then, him and his goddamn Committee had better watch their manners."

"I can't make any promises, but I'll tell him."

Standing toe to toe with Will, Nick couldn't help but feel something familiar creep up into the back of his mind. It reared like a snake that had been sleeping inside of him, sending a rattle all the way down to his gut. It had been a while, but Nick was no stranger to that feeling.

He felt something pour off of Will's skin, which made that snake rattle and hiss even more powerfully, just as it had when Nick had beaten down that shopkeeper back in Traders Crossing. Standing there, doing his best not to shake in his boots or worse, Will wasn't only scared, but weak. For the outlaw Nick had been, the kind of man he used to be, that weakness tasted like honey lapped up from between a woman's breasts.

"I'm not afraid of you," Will said quietly and calmly.

"Yeah?" Nick whispered. "Well, you should be."

With that, Nick walked out of the alley and didn't look back.

Will knew better than to make a move.

# Twenty-One

Catherine was standing out on the board-walk among a few others who'd ventured outside to check on the shots they'd heard. Nick strolled out of that alley as if he didn't see anyone but her and made a line straight for her. All of those gathered outside watched Nick suspiciously. Although a few of them pointed and started to whisper, nobody did much of anything else.

"Come on," Nick said as he took Catherine's hand. "We need to go."

Falling into step beside him, Catherine yanked her hand from Nick's grasp. "You can ask like I'm a real person, you know," she said with a definite edge in her voice. "You don't need to drag me around like I'm a child."

By the time Nick stopped, he was several yards from the front of the store where Catherine had been waiting for him. "You're right," he said. And when he looked at her again, his face was different. It was as though he'd started off looking at a fire with the glow of flames dancing over his features. That fire was out now and it allowed Catherine to get a little closer to him.

"There now," she said softly while slipping her arm around his. "That's better."

The two of them started walking as if they didn't have a care in the world. Behind them, more and more people started venturing out from where they'd been hiding. By the time Nick and Catherine had turned the corner, they could hear the activity behind them really picking up.

"Someone must have found the body," Nick said.

Rather than force Catherine to ask the questions that surely sprang to mind, Nick gave her a quick rundown of what had happened after he'd left her. She listened and nodded, taking it all in stride. When he was done, they were still walking and had gotten close enough to see the hotel at the end of Masonry Row.

"And you had a problem with this Will person?" she asked.

"Will Culligan was a member of the Vigilance Committee and yeah, I've got a big problem with him."

"And what about . . . who was the other one?"

"Brad. He was on the Committee too, but not part of the main group. That must have changed, though."

"At least there aren't any newer members to worry about."

"None that I've seen, anyway," Nick said. "Red's not stupid. He'd know that I would recognize anyone from the old days. He's got to have some others keeping an eye on me. That's the only way he would have been able to keep track of me at all."

Catherine glanced over her shoulder at the commotion going on behind them. They were no longer able to see the people scurrying back and forth from the alley where Nick and Will had met up, but there was more than enough to be heard. Voices called out for one thing or another, but most of them were using the word *sheriff*.

"Sounds like you might want to find the law around here before they come looking for you," Catherine said.

"That was my intention, but first I want to see about getting us a room."

"Shouldn't we take care of business before —"

"I want to get you someplace safe," Nick cut in. "And I also want to make sure you stay safe. Once we get you situated, I can leave you for more than a minute or two."

"I'm starting to feel like a closely tended child again."

Nick was already walking into the hotel and holding the door open for her. "Then I might have to see about changing that once I get you alone in that room."

Stopping just outside the door, Catherine smacked Nick's arm loud enough for the sound to rattle around inside the hotel lobby. Despite the solid smack, Catherine was still unable to keep herself from grinning at Nick's proposition.

When he spoke to the man behind the front desk of the hotel, Nick had a very specific list of demands where the room was concerned. Although the clerk nodded and appeared to be flustered by the picky customer, he managed to come up with a room to meet Nick's needs. He pulled a key from the pegboard behind him and handed it over. Nick paid for three days in advance.

"Enjoy your stay," the clerk said with a refreshed smile. "Let me know if there's anything you need."

Nick had already snatched up the key and was headed for the stairs leading to the second floor. Catherine moved along in front of him and they made it to the room

308

before the ink of Nick's signature could dry on the register.

Once inside the little room, Catherine looked around and quickly lost the eager smile that had grown on to her face. "This is dreary," she said.

"Yeah," Nick replied. "Just the way I like it."

Catherine was right about the room. It had as much personality as a broom closet and even less light. Situated in the middle of the top floor, their room had only one window, which was a square no bigger than Nick's head. To make matters worse, the window was covered by a yellowed piece of linen that might have been white several lifetimes ago.

The only furnishings in the room were the bed and a dresser with a mirror frame fixed to the top. At the moment, the only glass in that frame was a few jagged pieces that hung precariously in place. The rest of the space within the frame was slowly being filled by the web of a particularly enterprising spider.

"I can't stay here, Nick," Catherine said. "Already, I feel like I'm about to climb out of my skin. How did you find a room like this anyhow?"

"Most hotels have at least one room like this. They usually go for less than half the regular rate."

"Less than half, huh? Imagine that."

"This'll do just fine for now. I'm going to go fetch the rest of our things while you settle in."

"So do I have to wait in here?"

"I'll be right back."

Catherine looked around as though she was in the middle of a swamp. After a lengthy series of pats and pounds on the mattress to clear the bed of dust, she sat down and folded her hands upon her lap. Nick found her in that exact spot when he returned carrying the bags containing their clothes and personal things.

"Did you sit like that the whole time?" he asked.

"No. I had to move my feet once to let a rat go by."

Nick chuckled and dropped the bags to the floor. He then reached down and pulled Catherine's rifle from the bedroll strapped to his own bag. "Here you go," he said, handing the rifle to her. "This should discourage any more rodents from bothering you."

She accepted the rifle with both hands, although she didn't seem happy about it.

"I know you can use that," he said. "Hopefully you won't have to."

"But . . ."

Taking the rifle from her, Nick propped the gun against the bed and pointed at the small square window. "That window may not be great for light, but it's too small for anyone to crawl through. This furniture," he said, waving to the clunky pieces around them, "is heavy enough to block that door, which is the only way in or out. Do you think you can push that dresser against the door in a pinch?"

"I guess, but —"

"Then that's what you do whenever I have to leave you alone in here. And if someone pushes their way in, you shoot them with that rifle. Understand?"

Catherine let out a flustered breath and jumped to her feet. "I understand what you're saying, Nick, but there's law in this town. Why don't I go to them?"

"Because we don't know if we can trust them. I want to handle this on my own. It'll be quicker."

"That sounds like a vigilante talking." The moment she said those words, Catherine regretted it. Even so, she wasn't about to take them back.

"Actually," Nick said after a quiet moment, "you're right. Maybe I am still trying to shake some bad habits, but crooked lawmen nearly got both of us killed a few years ago in Jessup. Red has a nasty habit of getting the law to see things his way, whether they're crooked or not, and I won't risk putting you in that sort of danger if I can help it. With my father here as well, that just makes me want to cinch this up and be done with it as fast as I can."

Taking a moment to reach out and hold Catherine's hands, Nick looked straight into her eyes and spoke in a softer tone. "I know this seems like too much to bear, but this is the way it's got to be. It might not even come to you picking up that rifle, but if it does, I want you to be ready.

"The men that are after me will keep coming until they're stopped. They'll come after me and anyone I care for. Even someone they think I care for might be in danger. With you, though . . ." Nick paused so he could pull up the strength to get his next words out. "Even a blind man could see how much I care for you. My best bet is to keep you close. When that's not possible, I need to keep you prepared so that we'll both make it through to the other side of this."

For a moment, Catherine didn't say a word. Instead, she looked up into Nick's eyes and saw more in that mix of blue and gray than she'd ever seen before. Before she could put her finger on what captivated her so much, she felt his hands on her cheeks and his lips against her mouth.

The kiss was gentle at first, but lingered too long for that gentleness to last. Since neither of them wanted to break away, their passion grew hotter until Catherine's arms were wrapped around Nick and holding him desperately close. Their breaths mingled as they tasted the other's lips.

Soon their bodies were pressed so close together that their hearts seemed to beat right up against each other. That rhythm drove them to even greater intensity until they both started to feel their knees grow weak beneath them.

Nick was the one to pull back first. And though the disappointment on Catherine's face was painful to see, he held her at arm's length.

"Please listen to what I tell you," he whispered. "Once this is over, things will be different."

"You mean we won't be in a rat-infested closet that smells like the inside of a shoe?"

Nick smiled and nodded. "Yeah. I know plenty of less defensible rooms that have a much better view."

Some of the fear returned to Catherine's eyes, but it was tempered with a greater amount of strength. "I'll listen to you, Nick, but you've got to take a moment and listen to me." When she saw Nick immediately start to nod so he could talk again, she stopped him by taking hold of his face and once more looking him straight in the eyes.

"This is important," she insisted.

Blinking as if he was clearing away the stray thoughts running through his head, Nick nodded once again. This time he returned her stare earnestly.

"The only reason I'm doing any of this is to see it through," she said. "I'm tired of the shooting, the running, and all the time I've spent being afraid. None of that's worth a thing unless there truly is something at the end of it. We're not in this world forever and time is the most precious thing there is. I'll keep fighting so long as you swear to me that it won't take up all of our time together."

"It won't," Nick said. "I promise."

"What about you?"

He brushed his hand against her face and added, "I'm sorry I got you into all of this, but everything I'm doing is to make sure you get through it. A man can't stop all the death around him, but he needs to do whatever he can when the chance presents itself. This is a chance to settle some old accounts and put an end to a whole lot of bloodshed. When it's done, I'll get you out of here and take you someplace you can enjoy."

Catherine gave him a scolding look, which caused Nick to nod and add, "Someplace *we* can enjoy."

"You swear?"

"I do."

She smiled at him and gave him another kiss. Although their lips only met for a short amount of time, they knew it was a moment they would both remember for years to come.

# TWENTY-TWO

"I still think this is a bad idea," Nick grumbled.

He and Catherine were walking down Mercantile Avenue. The sun had already slipped below the horizon and the few lamps scattered here and there had been lit to give the street a dim, flickering glow. Most of that light was pooled around those lamps like water that had spilled from a leaky pail to illuminate sections of the crooked boardwalk and not much else.

The night was thick with humidity and alive with the chatter of cicadas, mosquitoes, and the occasional human voice. Fireflies bobbled here and there, giving the illusion that some of the stars twinkling overhead had dropped close enough to be touched.

Although Catherine took all of this in with a smile on her face and a bounce in her step, Nick didn't seem as impressed.

"Oh, that's enough of that kind of talk,"

she scolded. "It's too nice of a night for it."

"We didn't just come here to pay a visit to my father," Nick said. "There's more I could be doing than having supper."

Catherine's response to that was simply, "You need to eat, don't you?" She gave him a moment to respond, but got nothing but silence for her troubles.

"The problem with you two," she continued, "is that both you and your father are too bullheaded to admit that you made some mistakes."

"That's not true."

"Isn't it? Then why don't you want to meet him for supper? I know you like my cooking and I know that you've faced worse than an old man armed with a shovel."

Nick rolled his eyes and stuffed his hands into his pockets.

Wearing a little smirk, Catherine said, "Besides, you told me that you got those other men to lay low until tomorrow."

Nick grunted in the affirmative.

"And so that means tonight should be just fine for our supper."

Although he wasn't about to admit it, Nick knew that she was right. He also knew that there was no way for him to talk her out of this supper apart from knocking her over the head and dragging her back to the room. After the way she'd taken to her instruction with the rifle, Nick wasn't too anxious to make a move like that against her.

Sensing victory, Catherine reached up and pinched Nick's cheek. "You wouldn't have let me step foot out of that room if you didn't think it was safe."

"Are you sure you wouldn't rather eat somewhere else?" Nick offered. "I mean, there's plenty of restaurants in town and you don't have to cook in one of those."

"I own a restaurant, remember? I like to cook. We're already here, so just stop complaining and put a smile on your face. No matter how gruff he is, I can tell that your father wants to see you."

"See me in jail, maybe."

The sound of Catherine's hand smacking against Nick's shoulder echoed past the undertaker's parlor and down the street. After that, they stepped down from the boardwalk and headed around the backside of Mercantile Avenue.

In the daylight the hill behind the undertaker's had seemed desolate and imposing. In the darkness it was enough to send a chill through Catherine's blood, despite the sticky heat clinging to the air. Nick walked without breaking stride or showing the slightest change in his expression. As the wind howled around his head and whistled over the grave markers sticking up from the ground, he barely even took notice.

"We should have brought a lantern," Catherine said. "This is a scary walk."

"I grew up on hills like these. Pa always kept them tended so I would have room to run and play."

"You used to run and play in cemeteries?"

Nick nodded. "Ever since I could remember. I was taught to pay the markers respect and not dig anything up, but those were just the rules I lived by. Every kid has rules."

"Mine were to come home before dark and not wander past the creek that flowed at the edge of our property," Catherine pointed out. "There wasn't anything in there about digging up graves."

"You weren't raised by a gravedigger."

"Good point."

Thanks to Catherine's quickening pace, she and Nick made it to the top of the hill in record time. Once the graves were behind them, they could see the open stretch of land that was empty apart from the single house and neat fence surrounding it. Now the moonlight cast a cool, pale glow on the ground to make Stasys's house look like it was frozen in a fading picture.

The air had cooled a bit and the cicadas played their droning song in a constant, soothing wave of sound. Catherine took in the sight and looked over to Nick. "It looks nice," she said. "Peaceful."

"Yeah. Pa always lived like this. He said it was to be close to his work, but I knew better. He liked being apart from other folks. Telling them about nights like this would only fill them up with noisy neighbors. At least, that's the way he always saw it."

Catherine's hand slipped into Nick's, where it was immediately enclosed. Together, they walked toward the cabin and knocked on the door. A smell drifted out through the wooden slats that brought a fond smile to Nick's face and furrowed Catherine's brow.

As soon as the door swung open, Catherine jabbed an accusing finger at the old man on the other side. "You started cooking without me!"

Stasys shrugged and waved her off. "Just some potatoes the way Nicolai used to like. I leave the rest to you."

"If I come in there and see anything else cooking, there's going to be hell to pay." With that threat still hanging in the air, Catherine stepped inside and gave Stasys a hug.

Nick stayed outside for as long as he could before he got an expectant look from his father. Then, like a boy being dragged in by his ear, he walked inside.

"Whatever it is you're cooking, it smells great," Catherine said.

Stasys shuffled over to the stove, where a pot was steaming. "It was my wife's recipe. She make for me and then I learn to make for Nicolai. He always like it."

Nick shook his head and whispered to Catherine, "My friends used to call me Spud because I always smelled like potatoes."

"Your friends?" Stasys snapped. "Fah! Those were thieves. They were not friends."

After a subtle pause, Nick added, "They still called me Spud."

Catherine fought back a smirk as she went over to the kitchen and started rummaging through the food in Stasys's cabinets. "I think there's enough here for me to work with. Seeing as how Stasys set things off on such a good foot, I only hope I can keep up."

"You'll do fine," Stasys said while lowering himself onto a chair. After kicking out the chair in front of him, he said, "Sit down, Nicolai."

Nick jumped as the chair next to him leapt

away from the table. He eased himself down and sat in front of his father. At first, he felt like he was about to get his hide chewed for disobeying his father. Then he took another look at the old man and was reminded that things weren't the way they'd been when he'd left home.

They weren't even close.

Stasys had always been the strongest man Nick had ever known. He'd been the one to carry Nick across the ocean and into a new country. He'd been the only man who could comfort him after the death of his mother on that same boat. He'd also been the man to head out across the strange, vast expanse of America and settle somewhere Nick could be raised properly.

Nick hated the ocean, so they lived far away from it.

Nick picked up the language like it was second nature and had taught his father how to communicate to the people they met.

They'd worked as a team and as a family, right up until that team had been split in two.

Now Nick felt as if every mile he'd covered in the last several years had been walked upon aching feet. He was all too familiar with the changes he'd made to himself. Now he was getting a good look at the changes that had been wrought upon his father.

Stasys hadn't stood up straight for more than a few seconds since he'd seen him earlier that day. The old man's eyes were clouded and tired. The calluses on his hands had become thick and leathery. Even his voice seemed stretched to the point of tearing. He studied Nick in much the same way that he himself was being studied. Eventually, his eyes drifted back down to the hands folded on the table in front of Nick.

"There was shooting today," Stasys said.

"Yeah, Pa. There was."

"Did you come here to kill a man? If you did, then maybe you should leave before the sheriff comes to put you into jail."

"That's not why I came, Pa."

Stasys squinted and fixed his son with a stare that could have started a fire. "You're lying to me. After all the times you lie to me, I get good at knowing when you do it."

Nick shook his head, but it was more at something he was thinking. "I came here because there's trouble. You already know about it."

"You mean those men who were asking for you?"

"Yeah. That's the trouble I mean."

Now it was Stasys who seemed to be mulling something over inside his head. The similarities between his and Nick's expression were almost frightening. Suddenly the shadow on his face broke and he placed both hands flat upon the table. "Why come back now? These aren't the first to come looking for you. Others come and they go. Some try to talk to me, but I tell them I don't know where you are and they go. Most of the time, I say you are dead. Sometimes I wonder if that's not best."

Nick's head snapped up and his eyes flared with anger. "How the hell can you say that to me? I know I'm not the best son there is, but Jesus Christ, Pa!"

"I didn't raise you to be a criminal! I didn't raise you to be a gunfighter! If you want to be these things, then I will end up putting you in the ground. I brought you here to have a good life, not to be buried."

"I did have a good life."

"Don't say that to me," Stasys growled. "My son is a wanted man and he tells me he has a good life. You ran off with your friends, become a criminal, and never look back. I am your father! How can I sleep at night knowing I raised a bloodthirsty animal?"

Nick leaned back and ran his knuckles over the stubble on his chin. He could feel himself trembling and fought to keep it from being seen by the man across from him.

"Look at you," Stasys said in a low shaky voice. "I try not to believe what I hear about you, but why should I not believe? My son is a killer."

"No," Nick said in a surprisingly calm tone, "not anymore."

That caught Stasys off his guard. "What do you mean?"

"I've killed men. I even killed a man today. But what I do now is only what needs to be done."

"You can look at these men and see they deserve to die?"

"No. All I need to do is look at what they do. That's more than enough to decide it. The men I go up against nowadays deserve a visit from me. If they don't live to see the next day, then it's because of what they've done or the moves they've made. Trust me, Pa. The world's a better place without some people in it."

Nodding, Stasys ran his fingertip over the sanded top of his table. Like everything else inside the cabin, it was clean and perfectly maintained. Although there was no dust to be pushed around by the old man's finger, Stasys looked down as if he could see the designs he was making.

"It is a hard thing for a father to hear," the old man said. "That his son kills. All I ever wanted was to look into your eyes and ask if you have truly done these things. And if you did, what could possibly be the reason?"

"There's not enough time to list all the reasons for what I've done," Nick said. "Some of those reasons don't even make sense anymore. Just know that I learned a hard lesson and I'm not the same boy who turned his back on you all those years ago."

Stasys straightened up in his seat and nodded solemnly. "You are no longer a boy. You are a man. A man doesn't need to explain everything he does."

After a few moments, Stasys shrank back down into his chair. The stoop returned to his back and more of his weight seemed to be supported by his hands pressed against the tabletop. "Your mother, she did not want to come to America. She wanted to go somewhere else, maybe not so far. I wanted a change for my family. I wanted to provide more than I could get where we were. For that change, we needed to come here.

"The trip to this country killed your mother. For that, I can never forgive myself." Seeing Nick lean in to offer a comforting word, Stasys raised his hand and put

Nick back in his place with a stern glare. Once he saw Nick retreat, the old man continued. "I could have made a better decision, but I did not know there was a reason for it until your mother was already dead. You were always a wild one, Nicolai. Wild and strong, just like this country where you grew up.

"You make mistakes and you will pay for them the rest of your life, just like I pay for mine. All that matters is that you see what mistakes you make and put them to use. Put them to rest, but never put them out of your mind."

Nick reached out to place his own hands flat upon the table. "I'm trying, Pa."

"I know that now." Although Stasys started to pat his son's hand, he stopped short. "You have been through so much, Nicolai. I have heard things about . . . what has been done to you. The man who is in town asking for you told me that . . . well . . . I don't know if I can trust what he told me."

Finally, Stasys lowered his hand onto Nick's and held it there. "Tell me what happened, *sunus*. Tell me so I can know the truth in my heart while others tell their lies."

Nick looked up and saw Catherine slicing vegetables into another stewpot. Although

327

her hands were busy preparing supper, her eyes were looking intently in his direction. When he looked back to his father, Nick started telling him about the night he'd been taken apart by the Vigilance Committee.

Nick talked all through the meal. Stasys listened quietly, wincing only occasionally. Catherine did her best to make sure her presence was felt, but not intruding on the conversation. There was plenty she wanted to say to Nick, but it was plain to see that there was much more going on between father and son than between Nick and herself.

As the tale had gotten more and more violent, Stasys pushed his bowl away before he'd even eaten half of the stew within. He kept his hands folded neatly and his eyes fixed upon his son.

Nick's voice never wavered and his face never twitched. He recounted what had happened with such a smooth tone that one might have thought he was talking about someone else. When he was finished, he looked down at his stew for the first time, picked up a spoon, and started eating.

"That's it?" Stasys asked.

Nick let out an uncomfortable laugh and nodded. "That's plenty for me, Pa."

"No. I mean what happened after you left Montana?"

"I rode for a while until I was far enough away from the Committee and then found a place to heal. There was some trouble along the way, but I was able to handle it."

Leaning forward a bit, Stasys glared into his son's eyes with an intensity that could never be matched by any of the meanest gunfighters in the country. "I know when you are not telling me everything, *spurgas.* Just like when you were little."

Hearing his childhood nickname made Nick feel like he was a child being called to answer for a broken window. What weighed on him even more was the fact that the old man was right.

"All right," Nick sighed. "Here's the rest of it."

# TWENTY-THREE

*Virginia City, Montana*
*1866*

It had been almost two months since the wounds were inflicted, but Nick still felt the pain as if it was still being inflicted upon him. His fingers had been stitched and the blood cleaned from his skin, but he could not see those things for the blessings they were. His thoughts wouldn't linger on the kind folks who'd taken him in and brought him from the brink of death. He couldn't even think about how lucky he was to be alive at all.

The pain was foremost in his mind.

It drove him away from those kind folks who'd taken him in.

It made each thought turn toward one direction.

Each twitch became geared to one specific purpose.

Revenge.

He was hungry for it.

So hungry, in fact, that he'd pushed aside all reason until making his way back to Virginia City somehow became a good idea within his rattled mind.

Nick's hands had been wrapped in bandages that had soaked through with blood several miles ago and were now hanging off his wrists in tatters. Most of the ride back into Montana had been made on a horse, but that animal was nowhere to be seen. Instead, Nick had taken what supplies he could carry and moved along on foot.

His pockets were stuffed with jerked venison and an empty canteen was slung around his neck to knock against his aching ribs. A shotgun was strapped across his back and was smeared with the blood from the times he'd held it throughout his journey. His face was a sunken mockery of what it had once been. When he stopped to kneel down beside a stream, Nick barely even recognized the man reflected in that water.

For a moment, he stared down at the demon reflected in that water. He took in the dark circles under his eyes as well as the paleness in his skin. Then he held out his hands and looked down at the mutilated remains of his fingers.

The ends of his fingers were stitched up

by thread that looped through his flesh like worms twisting through a dead man's innards. The knots at the ends of the stitches had been tied with care, but Nick didn't see any of that. All he saw was the gnarled flesh and crusted blood that was caked on like mud. All he could feel was the dull pain slice up through to his elbows when he flexed his hands.

The pain reminded him of what Red Parks had taken from him.

Nick's days of wielding a gun were over.

His days of functioning normally were over.

His days of being a whole man were over.

"All of it's over," Nick grunted to his reflection. He dipped one hand into the stream to try and scoop up some water, but pulled it out as the cold lanced through his wounds like a branding iron. Gritting his teeth, he fumbled with his canteen to fill it and take a drink.

Rather than dwell on how he could have let himself be tricked into thinking his friends were alive or even if they'd deserved to be saved, Nick focused on the man at the core of his fury. Instead of fighting to make due with what he now had, Nick could only think of exacting retribution on those who'd taken from him.

The other Committee members would get what they had coming, but Red Parks was to be first in line. Red liked to strut around like he was untouchable, but Nick knew better. If there was one thing that he'd picked up from Barrett, it was the ability to seek out an enemy's weaknesses.

Finding those weaknesses meant the difference between life and death. That was the key to planning any good robbery or getting out of any fight. It separated the killers from the men who strutted their way into a pine box.

Red was a man. He could be hurt. And while Nick had been healing, he'd been thinking of a way to hurt Red Parks.

Nick hadn't touched a drop of liquor since before he'd lost his hands. Sometimes he would feel lightheaded enough just trying to make a fist or change his bandages. Now he felt something close to giddiness creeping up on him as he shifted his eyes away from the water and set his sights upon a little house in the distance.

Although it was considered part of Virginia City, the house was a good mile from the town itself. Like several other houses built by the more prosperous locals, this one sat on its own plot of land with a few head of cattle penned up next to a small barn stocked with horses.

Of course, there weren't any horses in that barn at the moment. They were being used by Red and other members of the Committee who were in town making their rounds.

Nick couldn't even recall what the Committee did with their time anymore. His brain wouldn't allow such trivial thoughts to pass through it. All he could feel was pain. All he could hear were the shots and screams from that barn echoing through his head in a constant, maddening flow.

When he staggered toward the house, Nick felt like he was in a dream. He didn't remember climbing the fence surrounding Red's property or walking up to the house's back door. In fact, none of it was clear until he saw another pale, slender face staring back at him.

Unlike the face that Nick had studied in the water, however, this face didn't belong to him. It belonged to someone he'd heard mentioned several times, but had only met once. He couldn't remember her name right at that moment, but he knew this was the Chinese woman that Owen had bragged so many times about bringing across the ocean just so she could cater to his every need.

"Who are you?" she asked breathlessly. "What do you want?"

As if he'd been snapped from a delirium, Nick blinked and looked around. He was standing inside the house with his hands wrapped around the shotgun that he'd dragged all the way from another state. He knew what he wanted, but the words stuck in his throat.

"If you're looking for Owen or Red, they're not here," she said.

Hearing those names snapped everything into something close to focus.

"You're Owen's wife," Nick said in a voice that barely seemed recognizable to his own ears.

She squinted and stepped back. "I live here. I clean and cook. Who are you?" Her voice had become stronger and more defiant.

Nick lunged for her and grabbed hold of the woman's arm. Her frame was just slender enough for her to evade his first grab with relative ease. That only served to fan the flames within Nick's heart and he took hold of her hard enough to make her wince in pain.

"Get out of this house," she said.

Gripping his shotgun in his other hand, Nick pointed its barrel at her face. That simple movement made his hands feel like they were on fire. The pain washed over him until his eyesight began to blur and turn red around the edges. "Where are they?" he snarled.

"Who are you talking about?"

"Red and Owen! Tell me where they are and don't fucking lie to me!"

Just then, the woman's eyes darted to a window next to the door as the sound of approaching horses drifted through the air. The hooves pounded against the dirt just outside the house and came to a stop amid a few whinnies.

She opened her mouth and let out a scream that pierced Nick's skull like a saber. The familiar voices that followed, however, were much more welcome.

"Wait there and I'll be right back," Owen shouted from outside.

"Owen!" the Chinese woman shouted. "In here!"

Nick put his back to a wall and held on to the woman while keeping his shotgun pointed at her head. When the door flew open, Owen took one step inside and immediately stopped. Nick greeted him with wild eyes and a crazy smile. "Surprised to see me, Owen?" he asked.

Owen took in the situation quickly and nodded. "I thought you'd have the sense to stay out of Montana, Nicky."

Nick shook his head. "You can't do what you did to me and get away with it. You and Red and the rest of that damn Committee killed my friends. You took my hands. You took away my whole fucking life!"

"So, you can't be a hot shit gunslinger any more," Owen replied with a shrug. "You made it here and you're holding that gun well enough. I'd say you bounced back pretty well. Besides, all your friends ain't dead. Some of them left town when they were asked."

"I can't believe a word of what you say. They were more than my friends. We were brothers."

"You were a gang. Jesus Christ, Nicky, get your thoughts straight. You ain't right in the head. Hand over that gun and I'll let you —"

Nick had heard more than enough. He shifted the shotgun away from the woman and took a shot at Owen. His finger clamped down painfully on the trigger, pulling his aim to one side while sending a thunderous roar through the room. When he saw Owen jerk back amid a mist of blood, Nick let out a strained laugh. He barely even felt it when the woman tore loose of his grasp so she could run into another room.

"Mei Li!" Owen shouted. "Go fetch my

brother!"

Nick had one more barrel left in his shotgun and he fired it at Owen. The second shot was pulled even more off target, however, and didn't even draw blood.

Grabbing hold of his left arm, Owen felt the skin that had been shredded by Nick's first shot. Although the wound was wet with blood and stung like hell, it wasn't anything too serious.

"Come back here, you cowardly bitch!" Owen shouted to Mei Li's back. "Go tell my brother to come in here!" Turning his attention back to Nick, he shook his head and lumbered forward. "Wherever you were these last few weeks, you should'a stayed there," he grunted while balling up his right fist and taking a swing at Nick's jaw.

Nick dropped down low in a move that was far from graceful, but quick enough to dodge Owen's fist. The sudden movement forced the shotgun to slip out from between his bloody fingers before he could get a chance to reload it.

Seeing the pained expression on Nick's face, as well as the awkwardness in his steps, Owen charged at him like a shark that smelled blood in the water. He pounded his fist against Nick's back and then followed up with a swift knee to his ribs.

Although he let out a few pained, wheezing breaths, Nick could hardly even feel those blows when they landed. He was struggling to see through the fog that was filling his mind so he could try to find a way to live through the next few minutes. Once he cleared his thoughts enough, he forced himself to look up at the walls surrounding him and Owen.

In a matter of seconds, he found what he'd been after.

"What's the matter, kid?" Owen snarled as he straightened up and shrugged off his jacket. "You change your mind already? You want to leave when the party's just getting started?"

Owen slammed his foot into Nick's ribs again, feeling at least one of them crack on impact.

But Nick wouldn't be turned away from his objective. He absorbed another few kicks before finally making it to the wall where a lantern was hanging. He pulled himself on to his feet, turned around, and leaned back against the wall, as if that was the only thing holding him up. With trembling hands, he reached for the pistol tucked under his belt.

Owen watched the clumsy draw with amusement. He shook his head as he slapped the gun to the floor before Nick could even get half a grip on it. "You ain't about to draw a gun on me, kid. Red saw to it that you wouldn't draw on nobody no more. Now that I think about it, that was a real smart idea. At least this way I can have some fun with you before cracking open that ugly head of yours."

Now that Owen was busy gloating, Nick had the chance to reach up and pull the lantern from its hook. In one motion, he tore the lantern from the wall and knocked it against the side of Owen's head. The glass cracked, spilling its contents over Owen's head while splitting his scalp along a jagged line that ran all the way to the corner of one eye.

With kerosene trickling down his face, Owen lashed out with both fists as he reeled away from Nick. He pulled his gun from its holster and started firing in a wild spread that sent lead flying through the air to punch through the wall where Nick had been standing.

Nick dropped to the floor and fumbled for one of the matches laying on a nearby table. In his fevered dreams, he imagined the house engulfed in flames with Red and Owen flailing inside. When he found his matches and struck one against the wall behind him, Nick waited to see if Owen would give him more of a show.

"No! You'll kill us all!"

Those words came from over Nick's head amid a flurry of pounding footsteps.

Mei Li was running down the stairs, frantically waving her arms, as if trying to catch the attention of a rampaging bull. Nick glanced toward her moments before Owen managed to put a bullet within an inch of its target.

Hot lead whipped through Nick's sleeve and drilled into the wall. Although he wasn't hit, the shot had come close enough to force him to pull his arm back and tuck it in close to his body. Somewhere along the way, the match's flame was put out.

"Get my brother, you stupid whore!" Owen screamed as he rubbed furiously at his eyes.

Mei Li looked between Nick and Owen before finally making her decision. Without another word, she ran past both of them and bolted out the back door.

"Cowardly bitch," Owen grunted. When he turned to look once more at Nick, he saw the younger man rushing toward him with both arms outstretched.

Nick didn't know what he would do once he got his hands on Owen. He didn't have a weapon drawn and doubted he could make much use of one if he had. His vision was clouded over with a red haze and the pain in his body was like spurs digging into his sides. All he wanted was to inflict damage upon one of the men who'd damaged him. Beyond that, everything else was a blur.

Having been forced into a series of back-pedaling steps, Owen flailed and punched as best he could. His gun was empty, so he smashed it against Nick's shoulders and arms in a desperate effort to make him let go. But the more he tried to get free, the tighter Nick's grasp cinched in around him. Soon they were both smashing against the house's front door.

"You son of a bitch," Nick growled. "I'll kill you!"

Blinking away the kerosene, which still burned at his eyes, Owen reached for a rifle held up by two pegs over the door. He got one hand wrapped around it and was bringing it down to take aim when Nick saw what was about to happen.

When Nick reached up to keep the rifle from being pointed at him, the iron barrel pounded against the stitches in his fingers. He let out a wounded howl and stumbled back a step.

"In here!" Owen shouted.

Nick didn't know what Owen was saying

or who he was talking to. All he knew was how much he wanted his hands to close around Owen's neck.

"Get in here! It's Nicky!"

Nick didn't even recognize his own name when he heard it come from Owen's mouth. He did feel a dull pain as Owen used one foot to shove him back while getting a better grip on his rifle.

"No," Nick snarled as he lunged forward to grab the weapon in Owen's hands. He snarled again when he felt the rifle slide through his blood-slicked fingers. Rather than give up the rifle, Nick pushed it down Owen's legs, scraped his thumb against the trigger, and pulled it.

At that moment, Nick didn't much care if he or Owen caught the bullet. All he wanted was for Owen to suffer.

When a spark from the rifle's barrel touched against some of the kerosene that had dripped down Owen's leg, Nick got his wish.

The flame was small at first, but worked its way hungrily up the front of Owen's body.

Out of pure reflex, Nick leapt back from the growing fire as Owen started to furiously pat at his clothes. But rather than smother the flame, Owen fed it with the kerosene that was on his hands and arms. Before his screams could work their way out of his throat, Owen was sucking down a mouthful of fire.

Nick stumbled over his own two feet, but couldn't take his eyes off of Owen, who jumped and flailed his arms while more and more of him was wiped away by the blaze.

When he'd been getting his fingers stitched shut, laying in bed on the verge of sleep, or even sitting through a bout of stabbing pain, Nick couldn't have imagined a better death for Owen Parks. Now that it was happening, Nick could only feel the bile rising up to the back of his throat.

Owen turned toward the door and ran straight into it before managing to push it open. The moment the latch was jarred loose, Owen stumbled through and immediately dropped to his knees on the porch. His legs weren't strong enough to hold him up any more and he fell forward like a melting wax statue.

Every place Owen had touched was now on fire. The flames were spreading up the doorframe to feed upon everything from the walls themselves to anything hanging on them. Soon the fire worked its way down a coatrack and farther into the front room.

Nick was about to turn and run out the

back door when he saw movement out front. Beyond Owen, a group of riders had come up to the house and were dismounting in a rush. Red was one of them and the first to get to the front porch.

From where he was, Nick couldn't hear exactly what Owen said, but he could see Red listening intently while trying not to catch fire himself. In moments, Nick couldn't see anything more, since the entire inside of the house was filled with thick smoke and rolling flames. He ran out the back door and kept running until he reached the trees surrounding the house.

He kept running as the sound of the fire filled his ears with its consuming roar. The stanch of smoke and burnt flesh stuck to the back of his mouth and remained there even after Nick dropped to his knees and gave in to a series of convulsing retches.

Owen's screams were gone.

The house would soon be gone as well.

The only thing Nick could hear was Red's voice thundering over the roar of the flames.

"Burn in hell, Nicky!" Red shouted at the house. "I hope you can hear me, you son of a bitch! Burn slow and die in agony!"

Red and Shad and a few more of the Committee were all there, clustered in one place to watch the fire. Nick figured he could kill at least a few of them if he took advantage of the situation.

But Nick was already choking on the taste of death. The pain was still there and all he wanted was to go home.

# TWENTY-FOUR

*Ellis Station, Missouri*
*1883*

This time when Nick was finished talking, Stasys wasn't looking at him. Instead, the old man's eyes had lowered to his own hands still pressed flat on the table in front of him. The sorrow on his face was unmistakable.

Although there was plenty more to tell, Nick couldn't bring himself to say any more. Looking at the disappointment on his father's face, he wished he hadn't even said as much as he already had. "I made it out of there and stayed out this time. Looking back on it, surviving any of that mess was enough of a miracle to convince me that someone must have been looking over me."

Stasys bristled at that and pressed his hands flat upon the table. "There are no angels for outlaws, boy. You remember that."

"I told you, I thought I was doing good.

It's not like I can ever be a lawman. Besides, I thought I was buying freedom for my friends."

Shaking his head and pushing away from the table, Stasys began straightening up the kitchen.

Catherine sat down at the table beside Nick and reached out to pat his hand. The moment she touched him, she felt Nick violently pull his hand away.

"The past is over, Pa," Nick said angrily. "I know I've made mistakes, but I've been doing my damndest to make up for them."

"Why do you come back here then? Why can't you stay away so I don't have to worry about where you are or what you're doing? I hear things, Nicolai. I hear when people say you are a gunfighter and a killer. I hear about all you do and I am ashamed to say you are my son!"

"I came back here because . . . because there are still things that need to be taken care of," Nick explained. "There's still things I need to do before —"

"Before what?" Stasys snapped as he turned around and reared up to Nick as if he was going to knock his son to the floor. "Before you get yourself killed? Before you get shot or hung or . . . or worse?" When he'd said that last part, Stasys took hold of

Nick's hands and shook them like he was rubbing a dog's nose in its own mess.

Nick didn't have much to say to that. In fact, he let his arms drop as though he no longer had the strength to lift them. Staring into his father's eyes, he took a deep breath and let it out from behind clenched teeth.

Stasys took a step forward until he was nose to nose with his son. "You need to hear this, boy. You need to hear someone talk sense to you instead of listening to those criminals you called friends or whatever other crazy ideas have gotten into your head."

As Nick got ready to defend himself as well as explain his actions, he realized something that made him stop dead in his tracks. "Like you said, I don't have to explain what I've done, Pa."

"Maybe you do," Stasys shot back. "Maybe you are trying to get yourself hurt. Look what happens when you are on your own. You get yourself torn to pieces and nearly killed more times than I can count. Maybe you do need to answer for what happened!"

"You deserve to know what happened to me, just so you don't have to hear it from drunks talking in saloons or men trying to collect a bounty. Whether or not you believe me is up to you. I guess I always thought my word would mean more than anyone else's just because I'm your blood."

For the first time since Nick had arrived, his father's face softened a bit and there was no edge in his voice when he spoke.

"I did my best to raise you," Stasys said. "I make mistakes, but I try to fix them the best I can. When I hear what you have done with your life and I see the pain you have felt, it is . . . it is hard for me. I should have done better with you."

Nick didn't know what to say to that. His mind was still chewing on things that had been said way before that and his emotions were making it difficult to put the rest into perspective.

"You did just fine," Catherine said from where she was sitting. "Both of you did the best you could with what you had. Mistakes were made on both sides, but for God's sake, you're both only human."

She quickly felt both men's stares turn toward her as she got up and walked over to where Nick and Stasys were standing.

"I only just met you," she said to the older of the two men, "but I can already tell you love your son to pieces. It must be awfully hard to listen to the things you hear about him, even if only a few of them are true.

And you," she said while turning toward Nick, "I don't see how you can say what you just said to anyone and expect them to just listen and eat their supper."

Nick nodded and even let out a bit of a laugh. "I guess you're right."

"Then cut your father some slack and tell the man why you're here in the first place."

Looking toward Stasys, Nick let out a relieved breath and stood as though a weight had been lifted from his shoulders. "The man I told you about is here. Red's here and I came back to put the matters between us to rest before they get any worse. I'm trying to own up to my past so I can move on. I know you can understand that."

"You know I can understand?" Stasys asked. "How am I supposed to understand the way a wanted man thinks? I understand you were a fine boy and a beautiful child, but I will never understand how you can carry a gun and ride with the likes of that Barrett Cobb or those awful Cooley brothers."

"Jesus Christ," Nick grumbled. "All I wanted to know was where I could find Red Parks or any of the men that were stirring up trouble around here and I get nothing but a lecture. Fine, then. I'll just go look for him myself the hard way. It sure as hell beats putting up with this."

"Wait a moment," Catherine said, feeling the fragile truce she'd thought she'd built melting away. "All you two need to do is —"

"Save your breath," Stasys said with exasperation. "He won't listen. He won't even listen to his own father, so why should anyone else bother?"

As much as he wanted to shake the old man with his bare hands, Nick forced himself to walk past Stasys and head out the door. He didn't even bother looking to see if Catherine was behind him. All he wanted was to get out of there as quickly as possible.

"Let him go," Stasys said as Catherine started running after Nick.

Looking back and forth between both men, Catherine couldn't decide which one of them was more infuriating. Nick was too angry to think about what he was doing and though Stasys had listened intently to every word of Nick's story, his first instinct was still to scold Nick like a child.

Neither man could get himself to sit still long enough to get through to the other one and neither of them seemed inclined to even try. In the end, Catherine decided that she couldn't get through to either one of them just then, but she would have more of a chance with Nick if she didn't let him get too far away.

Before Catherine made it to the door, she was stopped by a firm grip on her arm. Stasys held on to her without bruising her, but also made it clear that she wasn't about to get away as easily as his son.

"The men he wants to see are here," Stasys said. "There are three of them that came first. I don't know how long they were in town, but they started making trouble about a month ago."

"I should bring Nick back here so you can —"

"No," Stasys said firmly. "I tell you and you can tell him." Rather than wait for Catherine to agree to that, Stasys merely went on. "The first three men watched and waited for Nicolai to show his face. I thought they would leave like the others had over the years, but they stayed. Not too long ago, the other one showed up. It was the man who did those terrible things to Nicolai."

"You mean Red Parks? You're sure he's here?"

Stasys nodded. "I see the man only a few times, but he has cruel eyes. He is a man capable of doing the things that . . ." Stasys's eyes wandered from Catherine's face until he could contain the anger he felt from the story he'd been told.

His next words seemed to be stuck in his throat as his teeth gritted in response to the cold rage in his belly. "This man is Red Parks," Stasys said. "I have heard some of his men talk to him in the same way Nicolai talked to him. They take orders from him, but they fear him also. The rest of the people in town don't fear him so much."

"Really?"

Stasys nodded. "The man named Red acts like a good man. He buys drinks in the saloon and donates to the church every Sunday, but he is not a good man."

"Has he done anything besides throw his weight around to you and Mr. Abernathy?" Catherine asked.

Stasys paused before answering. Finally, he just blurted out what he needed to say. "I have seen him speaking to the sheriff. Some people say that Red Parks has done more than any sheriff and could do better than the man we elected to wear that badge. I try to tell them that they don't want someone like this Red Parks to wear a badge, but nobody listens to me.

"I recognize the animal in Red's eyes

because I have seen the same thing in the eyes of my son and some of the men he called friends. But this one, this Red, he hides himself very well. He apologized for the way he treated me when he came here, but his men still do whatever they please."

"What about the law? Why haven't they done anything about these men?"

"Why would they?" Stasys replied. "My son is a wanted man. His friends are known killers and thieves." The old man's eyes dropped so they were no longer meeting Catherine's. His voice faltered a bit and the corner of one eye twitched as he said, "It is no crime to hunt down men like that. Most people see that as a service."

Catherine reached out and took hold of his hand. After stooping down a bit, she put herself back into Stasys's line of sight. The old man looked back up at her almost immediately. "Your son isn't the same as he was."

"Did you know him before?"

"No, but I know him now. He's not exactly a church mouse, but he's trying to do the right thing. He's trying to put his skills to good use." She smiled a little wider and added, "He tries to make a living as a Mourner or a gravedigger. He carves headstones and builds coffins. He does beautiful work. You'd be proud of it, sir."

Stasys returned her smile, but the sparkle in his eyes was like a sputtering flame trying to stay alive in a brisk wind. "I have only seen the work he's done with that gun he carries."

"Then give him a chance to redeem himself to you. That's a big reason why we came all this way, you know."

Reaching out with one hand, Stasys brushed his finger along Catherine's chin. "You are a pretty woman and if my son has someone like you at his side, that says a lot to me. But I still wonder why you would leave your home and come here with Nicolai."

"I came along because he asked me to," she said. "But I would have come along even if he hadn't. There's too little time in life to waste sitting alone and wishing for things to change. Some of the time I've spent with Nick has been wonderful and some of it has been terrifying. He's only been directly responsible for the wonderful parts. The time without him after that has just been a lot of sitting, waiting, and wishing. I don't want to waste one more minute doing any of those things. Not anymore."

Stasys kept his hand on her face as he studied her eyes. When she spoke to him, he took in every last syllable. Still, it seemed as though he was looking deeper than just her eyes. He gazed into them in a searching sort of way and when he found the answer to his unspoken question, he blinked and nodded.

"You're right," he told her. "Nobody's life should be wasted with hopes and dreams when they could just as well be chasing after them. I know this well enough, since I should have told this to my own wife. She was like you in some ways. Even though there were bad times, she tried to make the best of every second she had."

"Everyone has bad times," Catherine said. "Perhaps you should keep that in mind the next time you talk to your son."

Stasys not only smiled at her, but he laughed as well. "You are a smart woman, Catherine. Smarter than me, I think."

She shrugged and started to walk toward the door. "I should go see where Nick has gone off to. Next time we have supper together, I won't let it get spoiled the way it did tonight," she said sternly.

"All right."

Catherine was about to open the door and head outside when she noticed Stasys watching her. The old man was no longer studying her intently as he'd done before.

Instead, he seemed to have already come to terms with what he'd found in her eyes, as if he'd seen the same thing plenty of times before.

She wondered if she should say anything or even just wrap her arms around the old man to give him a hug.

"Take care of yourself," Stasys said. "And . . . thank you for taking care of my son. I think that he wouldn't have been changed like you say without meeting you."

There wasn't much that she could say to that. Catherine figured that she'd come up with something by the time she met up with the old man again. For the moment, however, she felt an urgency in her mind that made her want to hurry and catch up with Nick. After all he'd told her about wanting to keep an eye on her, being away from him this long made her feel out of sorts.

She waved and walked to the door. When she took a quick look at Stasys before leaving the cabin, she found the old man already fussing with the supper plates and cleaning up the table.

Outside, Catherine walked into darkness so thick that she practically felt it brushing against her face. It took a moment for her eyes to adjust. When they did, she noticed a solitary figure standing less than ten paces from the cabin's front door. She recognized the silhouette and started walking straight toward it.

Catherine stopped and studied him for a moment. Nick wasn't moving. He stood like a rock formation overlooking the nearby cemetery. Keeping her steps as quiet as possible, she worked her way to his side and slipped her arms around his waist from behind.

"You never told me you went back to Montana," she said while leaning her head against the back of his shoulder.

She could barely feel Nick's chest moving beneath her arms. When he spoke, it was in a voice that drifted only a short way on the humid wind before fading away completely. "I've never told anyone the whole story like that. Honestly, I don't even like to think about it."

"I can't blame you for that."

"But I can never get away from it," he continued. "I know men who were wounded in the war far worse than I was and they move on with their lives. Thinking back to that last night in Virginia City, I wonder if it wouldn't have been better if I had burned up in that fire. It would have saved a whole lot of people a whole lot of trouble."

"Don't talk like that. You've done plenty

of good."

"That's a nice change of pace after having my father look at me like I was a pile of trash."

"He didn't do anything of the sort. The two of you just have trouble seeing eye to eye."

"He's got good reason to hate me, Catherine. After all he did to give me a better life, after all the sacrifices that were made to get us here, it hardly seems fair for me to do what I've done. In plenty of ways, it seems like I deserve what's coming."

"If that's the case, then you must have brought me along to make sure I went down in blazes right beside you." She squeezed him a little tighter and said, "I know that's not the case, Nick. And I'm certain your father knows it too."

Nick didn't respond to that. He didn't even grunt to acknowledge that he'd heard her.

"He does have a right to be a little upset, you know," she told him. "You can't expect him to just pick up like nothing happened."

There was still nothing from Nick. Not even a shrug.

"Didn't you come here to try and make amends?" she asked. "Doesn't that mean you need to put a little effort in that direction?"

Still nothing.

And despite the fact that she was trying to be nice and not make things any worse than they already were, Catherine felt her own frustration growing by the second.

"Look," she said after taking her arms from around him and taking half a step back. "I'm trying to help here, but if both of you are too stubborn to budge, then I don't know why you even bothered coming here tonight."

"You want to know why I bothered?" Nick asked. Lifting his arm to point into the cemetery in front of him, he said, "Take a look for yourself."

Catherine stepped around Nick and finally gazed off in the direction he'd been staring. Her eyes had become more adjusted to the murky darkness, but it didn't take much to spot the row of torches being carried by the riders in the distance. There were four of them that Catherine could see and they were on the opposite side of the cemetery. As if responding to a silent cue, the riders slowly started to move between the headstones.

"Who are they?" Catherine asked timidly.

"We're about to find out."

# TWENTY-FIVE

As the riders worked their way through the cemetery, they took up a formation that vaguely resembled a cross. One of the riders was at the front of the rest, with two others flanking him and slightly behind. Another trailed from a few yards back, keeping the other three in his sights.

Nick squinted into the shadows, but he already had a gut feeling of what he would see. As the riders drew closer, Nick felt his hand drift closer to the gun holstered at his side. The seconds ticked by like hours in his mind. All the while, Nick's mind was occupied with visions of another group of men who'd ridden in that formation. Unfortunately, whenever they'd approached a man like that, it was never to bear good news.

"Stay close to me, Catherine," Nick said.

"Are those the men you were telling me about?" she asked. "Should I go tell your father about —"

Nick snapped around so quickly that Catherine reflexively flinched. She'd never seen him look at her with that kind of fire in his eyes. It was enough to put a fear into her that felt like a cold metal stake through the middle of her belly.

"Don't mention my father," he whispered. "Don't mention his name. Don't even look back at that cabin. Whatever I say, you go along with it. Understand me?"

She nodded quickly and was more than a little grateful when Nick turned his burning glare back in the direction of the approaching riders.

The horses drew up to within five paces of them. They fanned out a bit, but kept their same basic formation with one man at the head of the group, two covering his flanks, and one lagging behind. In the darkness Nick could make out the rifle in the hands of the man at the back of the group of riders, as well as the shotguns carried by the men on both sides.

As for the man at the front of the group, Nick had picked out his face some time ago. It was a face that was very familiar to him since it had inhabited the darkest corner of his mind for many years.

"Well, well, well," the man at the front of the group of riders said. "Is that little Nicky

Graves?"

Nick didn't bother nodding or returning the cold smile the other man was giving him. His only response was: "Yeah, Red. It's me. I thought we weren't supposed to meet until tomorrow."

Red Parks sat in the saddle with a slightly stooped posture that leaned him to one side. On most other men, it would have made him look tired. But Red looked more like a bird of prey staring down at a field mouse with mild amusement that would get ugly as soon as he got hungry.

"Guess I couldn't resist," Red replied. "Especially after you shot up one of my men and all."

"Yeah. I guess not. It's so much easier to shoot me from a rooftop or set up an ambush in some poker hall."

"Or I could have set you on fire," Red said in a voice that was as sharp and grating as hail scraping against a windowpane. "You ever seen your own flesh and blood die, Nicky? Or what about watching them melt down into paste? When I thought you'd died in that house along with Owen and his wife, I was able to carry on a bit more. But looking back on it, I guess it wasn't too surprising to hear that you'd resurfaced. After that war you had with Skinner in Nebraska, you've become quite a famous man again. Too tough and too famous to die in some fire."

Nick nodded and pulled in a measured breath. "So I guess you always thought highly of me, huh, Red?"

"Nah. I wanted to make you suffer and then I wanted you to die. Why else would I put you through seven kinds of hell before booting your ass out of my town? And why would I put the gears in motion to bring me here the moment I heard you were alive?"

That started a ripple of laughter throughout the rest of the men gathered around Red. As Nick stared down each of those men in turn, that laughter was quickly snuffed out.

Although the laughter was gone, Red still managed to look mildly amused. His head was rounded and bald at the top. A thin layer of wiry hair formed a ring around the back of his scalp, joining one small ear to another. His eyes were black pits in the darkness, which seemed even darker when he smirked and his teeth caught a bit of the paltry light coming from the torches.

Red wasn't a big man, but his slender frame would never be mistaken as weak. Narrow shoulders pointed slightly forward and the dark jacket he wore hung off him like they were resting on the shoulders of a seamstress's dummy. But no amount of muscle would have made him look any more imposing.

His hands gripped the reins loosely without ever straying too far from the gun at his hip. Red's eyes never left Nick and Catherine. In the darkness he hardly even seemed to blink.

"I've been looking for you, kid," Red announced. "Ever since you stuck your head up after hiding all those years, I've been looking for you. Guess you were too busy licking your wounds to pay me a visit and finish what you started with Owen."

"I was told that you were killed in Jessup," Nick replied.

Red nodded. "Guess maybe I took a page from your book, kid. On that account, I guess we're even."

"Even?" Nick snarled. "You think we're even?"

Sensing the tension crackling through the air, the men around Red slowly brought their guns to bear. Even though the weapons were shifting in his direction, Nick hardly seemed to notice.

Shaking his head and holding out his hand to calm the other riders, Red smirked down at Nick and said, "You got what you deserved, kid. After you killed Pete, there were plenty who said you deserved a hell of a lot worse."

"You and your men killed my friends. They raped that poor girl until there wasn't any life left in her. You mutilated me for sport and I don't even want to think about all the other shit you pulled that nobody but your precious Committee even knows about! I may have committed my share of sins, but I owned up to them. You're still riding around like you own this world."

Red stuck out his lower lip. "Awww, ain't that just precious." He squinted at Nick a little harder, glanced at Catherine and then up toward the cabin. Suddenly Red's eyes widened and a thoughtful expression drifted across his face. "Is that what you're doing here? Are you trying to set things right?"

Nick glared back at Red with nothing but hate.

"He is!" Red shouted to the men around him. "This murdering, lying, thieving, no-good, backstabbing cocksucker is trying to set things right and he thinks that standing up for his pappy and whispering sweet nothings into some bitch's ear will —"

Red was cut short by the flutter of motion when Nick's arm darted to his holster and emerged with gun in hand.

All of the riders started to bring up their weapons, but thought better of it when they saw Nick's eyes flash in their direction.

Catherine took a step back, but couldn't move any farther. She tensed like a deer that couldn't decide whether or not to run. For the moment, she held her breath and waited to see what would happen.

The only one whose composure hadn't changed was Red. Even staring down the barrel of Nick's drawn gun didn't seem to affect him. Red even leaned forward to study the weapon that was threatening to deliver him from the world of the living.

"What's that you're holding there, Nicky?" Red asked. "Is that a gun that actually fits that sorry, mangled excuse for a hand you've got?"

"It sure is," Nick said with a sinister grin. "And I've got enough of a finger left to pull this trigger."

"You see?" Red asked as he looked directly into Catherine's frightened eyes. "You see why I needed to put him down? Can you imagine this one when he was still young and full of piss?" Shifting his eyes again, he added, "You've got a problem with your temper, Nicky. That's what always got you into trouble."

"And you've got a problem with being too fond of old habits." Seeing the question in Red's eyes, Nick nodded. "You hear from Shad lately? And what about them boys you had waiting for me in Jessup? How are they doing? When was the last time they even sent word to you?"

The smirk was still on Red's face, but the amusement in his eyes was long gone. "Last I heard from Shad, you weren't much more than a sorry drunk. Could you be drowning a guilty conscience, Nicky? I wouldn't be surprised, since I hear it was you that killed Barrett Cobb."

Red spotted the twitch in the corner of Nick's eye instantly. It sent an excited chill down his spine that made him shift a bit in his saddle. "Barrett was your best friend, wasn't he?"

Reflexively, Nick nodded.

"Skinner was one thing," Red mused. "That one was a bigger animal than you ever were, but Barrett only wanted the best for you. He was like your brother. I'll bet you'd shoot that old man in that cabin back there if it would bring Barrett back."

The fact that Red even mentioned that cabin spoke volumes to Nick.

"Barrett doesn't have anything to do with this," Nick quickly said. "You and I still have business to take care of."

Red nodded. "Yeah, we sure do. In fact, I'd say I'm the last bit of business there is that links you to Montana. At least, the only one that you know of."

"You're the only one in my sights right now, Red. That's all I care about."

"Then go ahead and shoot me."

The challenge echoed through the night like thunder. It rattled around, raising the hackles on the necks of everyone who heard it.

Completely ignoring the gun in Nick's hand, Red leaned forward a bit more in his saddle. "Pull that trigger to show that lady there just what kind of man you are, Nicky.

"Skinner was an animal. I knew it right up to the end when I showed him that shit hole of a town in Nebraska. For old times' sake, we agreed to let me be dead for a while, but that was the limit of his reasoning. Every moment of every day, Skinner knew what he was and was contented to be just that: an animal.

"Your friend Barrett Cobb knew what he was too. He was a manipulating son of a bitch who was smart enough to survive, even though he didn't have the skills with a shooting iron that you did. He struck the deal with me that landed you and the rest of that gang in the hands of my Committee. Did you know that?"

Nick gritted his teeth and thumbed back the hammer of his pistol.

"Yeah," Red said with a nod. "You must have found that out somewhere along the way. Did he confess before you killed him?"

"Shut your mouth."

"I guess maybe he did. What do you think, boys?" he asked to the men flanking him on either side. "What do you think ol' Nicky here will confess when he's at his end? Maybe he raped that Chinese bitch before murdering my brother."

"Shut . . . up."

"When this whole thing started, I thought of you as a partner," Red continued. "An equal, even. Then you became a message or maybe a . . . a piece of art," he said after taking a moment to consider it. "You know, kind of like a painting that hangs up for all to see. It doesn't have a choice of what it says to folks that look at it. Even if it could hang itself somewhere else, that still wouldn't change the message."

Red's voice lowered just enough to send another chill through Nick's veins. "Owen died like a sniveling, frightened little girl. With his last words, he begged me to kill him. By the time he passed on, I wished I'd had the guts to finish him off before he was reduced to crying like he did. All I needed to do was leave a little trail of cards to bring you here so you can find out what it's like to go through something like that."

Nick was barely even listening any longer. Something didn't fit. Red was trying too hard to get Nick to shoot. Either that or he was buying time for one of his other men to get the drop on him.

Red's voice dropped even lower until it was a whisper that slithered through the air. "If you thought I hurt you before, you're gonna have a whole new definition for pain when I'm done with you, your pappy, and that sweet little bitch at your side. Truth be told, I was happy to hear your name after I left Jessup. That meant I'd get a chance to kill two prize birds with one stone."

"The only dangerous one around here is you," Nick said. "Even a blind man could see that."

"Oh? What about that man you killed earlier?" Red asked. "Poor ol' Will didn't mean no harm and you went and put a gun to his head after killing a young man named Brad. Plenty of folks on the street saw what you did and they're scared to death of you. I'll bet they wish someone would step up and protect them from a monster like you."

Nick glared at Red without saying a word.

"And what about poor Shad?" Red asked. "He had a family, you know. So did one of those men you killed while you were kidnapping that poor lady out of her own home in Jessup."

Catherine took a quick step forward. Shuddering at the way the men on either side of Red shifted their aim in her direction, she forced herself to speak out before it was too late. "I'm that woman," she said. "And those men tried to kill us! I'll say that to God himself if it ever came to that."

"Really?" Red asked. "Maybe you should tell that to the town you left behind because it seems they've somehow gotten the idea that you were stolen away by a dangerous outlaw who killed several men on his way across the state line."

"Those are damn lies."

Red shrugged and replied, "That's not what the law in Jessup thinks. And before too much longer, the law right here will start thinking along those same lines. I give it about five or ten minutes before my good friend Sheriff Bristow comes to ask for my help in apprehending this dangerous fugitive."

"You're crazy," Nick said.

"Is that a fact?" Red asked as the men on

either side of him climbed down from their horses. "Well, we'll just see who folks believe once they see you covered in your lady's blood."

It happened in the blink of an eye. After those words were spat out of Red's mouth, the men who'd been riding beside him lifted their guns to put both Nick and Catherine in their sights. A shot blasted through the air, but it didn't come from either of those men. Instead, Nick was the one who'd pulled his trigger first and his quick shot clipped one of the other men's arms.

"Out of the way!" Nick shouted as he reached out to shove Catherine to the ground.

Catherine was one step ahead of him and dropped so she almost disappeared within the grass. The other shotgunner managed to take his shot and the storm of lead raged over her, scratching at her back like a hundred burning talons. She winced and pressed her face against the damp earth, praying that the stinging she felt was only in her imagination.

All of this took place in two beats of Nick's racing heart. Pointing the modified Schofield as if he was pointing his finger at the shotgunner who was still on his feet, Nick squeezed his trigger and felt the

374

weapon buck against his palm. Just as that bullet drilled a hole through the other man's skull, Nick took another shot that hit the man squarely in the chest.

The combination of those two shots not only killed the shotgunner instantly, but knocked him flat on to his back so he didn't have a chance to take one last shot at Catherine.

Red was already riding away with the fourth member of his group beside him. Gritting his teeth against the rage that clenched around his chest like a fist, Nick ran forward and took aim at Red's back.

Just as he was pulling his trigger, Nick felt something hit the back of his left shin. The next thing he saw was the black starry sky as he toppled over. Nick hit the ground hard. The impact knocked the wind from his lungs and rattled his eyeballs in their sockets. Before he could focus on the blurry shape coming at him, he felt knuckles slam into the side of his face.

"Son of a bitch," grunted the man that Nick had shot in the arm a few seconds before. The man lunged forward and slammed his fist into Nick's wrist with every ounce of strength he had.

The Schofield slipped from Nick's mangled hand to hit the ground with a solid *thump* that might as well have come from a hundred miles away.

Blood seeped into the man's shirt and glistened like wet tar in the moonlight. His face was twisted into a pained grimace as he propped himself up while taking another swing at Nick's jaw. The punch landed a little higher than intended, but managed to snap Nick's head back.

Rather than try to duck away from the punch, Nick rolled with it and twisted his entire body around in that same direction. Using his own momentum as well as the power of the punch that smashed into his jaw, Nick rolled over his side and onto his belly. He came to a stop a few feet from where he'd started with both arms tucked in close to his body and his ribs pressing down against the Schofield that had been knocked from his hand.

The gunman was already moving on, grinning hungrily when he spotted Catherine on all fours and watching from a couple paces away.

"Don't worry, darlin'," the gunman said. "I still got plenty left for you."

Catherine wanted to get up and start running. She also wanted to get up and try to help Nick. The only problem was that she was too frightened to move. When she did try to act on her impulses, she felt pain in her back and panic at the knowledge that it would take more than she had to put down the wounded gunman who was now coming straight for her.

The gunman struggled to his feet and hefted his shotgun in one hand while his wounded arm dangled at his side. Once his hand was settled around the grip, he brought it up and thrust his chest forward as both arms splayed to the sides and a gunshot echoed through the air.

Catherine watched in confusion at the other man's sudden, jerking motions. Then she realized that the last shot had come from behind the gunman.

Still wobbling on his feet, the man with the shotgun dropped to his knees to reveal Nick crouching behind him. The Schofield was smoking in Nick's fist, leaving a wispy trail as Nick rose to his feet.

"Don't do it," Nick growled.

The other man was starting to shake as more blood poured from the wound in his shoulder and pain from the bullet's passing truly sank in. His eyes jumped from Catherine to Nick and back again. Finally, they settled on Catherine as he made the most important decision he would ever make.

That shotgun jumped up as if it had a life

of its own. It shifted about half an inch in Catherine's direction before Nick pulled his trigger.

The Schofield barked once more. That sound was joined by the slap of lead against flesh as the man with the shotgun was pulled to the ground by the force of Nick's bullet. This time, when he hit the ground, the man didn't budge.

He didn't curse or make one more move to defend himself. He lay crumpled in the dirt with the side of his face pressed against the earth and his body twisted in a way that no living thing could tolerate.

Catherine was still frozen in her spot as the dead man's eyes remained fixed upon her.

"Come on," Nick said as he pulled her to her feet. "Stay low and do what I say." Seeing her wince in pain, Nick felt the wetness on her back. He looked at the hand that had touched her and saw it was spattered with blood. "Are you hit?"

Now that she was on her feet, Catherine was moving easier. "Just a scratch. Doesn't feel too bad."

"Looks more like a bunch of scratches," Nick said as he examined her back through the portion of her dress that had been shredded. "None of them look too deep, though."

"I'm fine, Nick. We need to check on your father."

Nick had seen plenty of wounds in his time and knew that Catherine's were nothing to get worked up about. Still, seeing her blood spilt made him want to get his hands on Red even more. Nick reloaded the Schofield and ran toward his father's cabin.

There was still a warm light flickering inside the modest home, but there was also a horse standing outside of it that hadn't been there before.

# TWENTY-SIX

Nick rushed to the front of the cabin. About halfway there, he noticed the front door was slightly ajar and swinging on its hinges. His father had never left the door open in all the years he'd known him. That alone was enough to make Nick rush even faster toward the cabin while completely ignoring the reflex in his mind that told him to take a less conspicuous approach.

"Pa!" Nick shouted as he got closer to the front door. "Are you all right?"

The moment Nick stepped into the cabin, he spotted movement from the corner of his eye. Although he'd ignored one set of instincts, Nick wasn't about to ignore the one that now filled his mind like a screeching bird. Ducking down while taking a step back, he was just quick enough to avoid the meaty fist that had been coming straight toward his already bruised face.

That fist sliced through the air and

pounded against the doorframe, rattling the entire cabin around the spot where Nick had been standing. The fist belonged to a man who Nick had spotted on the streets of Ellis Station. If Nick knew back then that he would cross paths with Deacon like this, he would have shot him back then and been done with it.

Unfortunately, it was much too late for that.

Deacon was bearing down on him again, already too close for Nick to take a shot at him. The big man snarled viscerally as he leaned in to put all of his weight behind his next punch. This time, however, Deacon's swing came in too low and too fast for Nick to do anything but brace himself for the impact.

The punch landed on Nick's chest, thumping solidly like a battering ram against a castle's gate. Nick could feel the hit echo through him and, for a moment, thought he could push past it and answer with a punch of his own.

But then the force of the punch worked its way through him to turn his legs into limp noodles. The next thing he knew, Nick was sliding against the wall on his way to the floor. He tried to pull in a breath, but that only ignited the pain that had been

waiting to explode just beneath his breast-
bone. What little air he did manage to get
was then forced out of him in a hacking,
groaning wheeze.

Deacon smirked as he looked down at
Nick, causing the blood trickling from his
forehead to curve a little in its path down
his face.

As Nick forced himself to breathe one
more time, he noticed the blood as well as
the split in Deacon's skin. The next thing
he noticed was the way Deacon's eyes suddenly darted to one side as a worried
expression jumped on to his face.

The sound was a solid *slap,* mixed with
something vaguely metallic. Whatever it was
that made the sound also knocked Deacon
away from Nick.

"I tell you to leave and I meant it!" Stasys
shouted as he hefted the shovel he'd just
used to rattle Deacon down to the marrow
in his bones.

Nick struggled to his feet, hoping to get
all the way up before his father saw him
slumped against the doorframe.

Deacon had regained his footing and
positioned himself so his back was to a wall
and both men were in his sights. Swiping at
the blood on his face, Deacon winced as
fresh pain jolted from the spot where Stasys

had hit him with the flat of his shovel.

For a few seconds, all three men stared at each other. Nick and Stasys shot each other reaffirming glances to let the other know they were doing all right. Deacon watched them both with frustration brewing in his eyes. After his hand brushed past the empty holster around his waist, the black man reached for his boot and pulled out a bone-handled knife that had been hidden there.

The blade glinted in the light of the few lanterns within the cabin and made a glittering trail back toward Deacon's ear. With his arm cocked, Deacon was about to snap it forward when Nick took quick aim with his Schofield and fired.

For a moment, Deacon didn't move. He appeared to be just as ready to throw his knife as he'd been a moment ago. But instead of sending the blade spinning through the air, he let it sip from his fingers. Wobbling backward, he tripped over one of the chairs near the dining table.

Nick stood over the man and waited until he heard the last breath seep out of Deacon's lungs. Squatting down, he holstered the Schofield and patted the man's pockets.

"You killed him," Stasys whispered.

"I didn't have any choice, Pa."

Although Stasys nodded, he wasn't able

to change the expression on his face. He seemed equally frightened when he looked at Deacon as he did when he glanced over to Nick.

"Do you know this man?" Nick asked, doing his best to keep himself from meeting his father's eyes.

"I have seen him in town. He and two others came to threaten Mr. Abernathy."

"Mr. Abernathy? What did they want with an undertaker?"

"They were looking for me," Stasys replied. "They wanted to make sure I was the man they were after and that I could tell them about you. I tell you before, they weren't the first to come looking for someone who might be your father."

"Maybe not, but they'll be the last."

Those words were like a splash of cold water in the older man's face. "What? I won't have you killing more men just to protect me."

Nick looked over at his father and shifted his eyes toward the shovel in Stasys's hands. "Looks like you did a fine job of that for yourself."

Glancing down at his own hands, Stasys lowered the shovel so he could place the blade against the floor and lean upon the handle. "He came in right through the front door. I saw him coming because I was watching you and those other men. This shovel was the first thing I could grab before he came stomping in here. I hit him and made him drop his gun. That would have been enough if you hadn't come stomping in as well."

"Yeah, whatever. We can argue about this later. We need to get out of here."

"But why are they still after me?" Stasys asked. "Those men already know where to find you."

"Red wants to make it look like I hurt you." Suddenly Nick's head snapped toward the window as he recalled the rest of what Red had said. Without another word, Nick bolted for the door. He snatched up the gun Deacon had dropped along the way.

Catherine was huddled outside and when she saw who was coming out to join her, she pointed to the solitary figure on horseback. "Nick, that one just rode up."

Nick wasn't paying attention to her. He was too focused on the torch in that figure's hand. He didn't have to wait for more than a second before that figure hauled off and tossed that torch through the air toward the cabin.

The fire crackled as it fed off the wind rushing past it. Turning once as it reached the top of its arc, the torch started falling toward the cabin's roof. Without taking his eye from the flame, Nick tossed Deacon's .32 to his other hand so he could draw the Schofield, which better fit in his wounded hand. He pulled the trigger once and hit the torch on its way down, knocking it toward the dirt road that led to the front door.

By this time, Catherine had caught her breath. She watched as the rider who'd tossed the torch dug his heels into the sides of his horse and raced off in the other direction. "Was there someone in there with your father?" she asked.

"Yeah. There was. I should have just let the old man take care of it for himself."

"That's some fine way to talk," Stasys said as he came outside with his hands still clasped around the shovel. "Are you all right?" he asked Catherine.

She nodded. "A little rattled, but I should be more used to this sort of thing."

"If my son knew better, he would give you a proper home instead of putting you in a shooting gallery."

Nick shook his head, knowing better than to snap at the bait again. And before he could say anything at all, the smell of burning wood slipped into the air around Nick's head. Turning on his heels, Nick brought himself around and instantly spotted the other riders bolting over the hill.

The sound of popping and crackling could be heard as flames licked around one corner so they could finally be seen from the group gathered in front of the modest home. Nick's first impulse was to grab hold of his father's arm the moment Stasys made a move toward his house.

"It's too late, Pa," Nick said.

"But that is my home!"

Although his father was still struggling to get back into the cabin, Nick felt the resistance lessen as the flames grew higher and higher. Finally, half of the cabin was consumed and smoke started flowing out through the doors, windows, and even the cracks in the walls.

"I'm sorry," Nick said. He wished he could say more, but he knew there simply weren't any words to fix what had just been done.

The old man started to run back to his house, but even he could see it was too late to stop the spreading flames. He looked at Nick and then glanced out at the spot where the first torch was still smoking in the dirt. Finally, he let out a snorting breath and turned his back on his burning home. "I won't hide somewhere — if that's what you want. These men came into my home and then they —"

"You're coming with me, Pa," Nick interrupted.

"What did you say?"

"I said you're coming with me. It's the only way I can make sure that you're safe. When he sees you're alive, Red will just be waiting for you or Catherine to be alone so he can send a bunch of men after you."

"Maybe he would come for me himself," Stasys huffed. "Then I would put another dent in my shovel."

"If he came for you himself, you'd wind up a whole lot worse. I know that for damn sure."

"So what do we do? I have my life here. I won't be run out of town for doing nothing."

Nick met his father's eyes and said, "You get used to it before too long. Take it from the mouth of a common criminal himself." Once again holding up the .32, he added, "And take this with you. It might come in handy."

The muscles in Stasys's jaw tensed as he straightened up indignantly. "I will not! How many times must I tell you that guns are no good, Nicolai?"

"Pa, for the love of God, will you just take the damn thing?"

"No."

Suddenly a hand reached between the two men and snatched the gun away from Nick. Catherine took hold of the .32, flipped open the cylinder to check how many live rounds were in there, and then snapped it shut again. "As much as I'd like to listen to you two bicker, we need to get moving. Red mentioned something about talking to the sheriff. Why don't we get there first and tell the law what really happened here? If Stasys wants to stay there, I'm sure the law will protect him."

"Fine," Stasys grumbled.

"All right, then. It's settled." Looking back to his father, Nick said, "You got lucky once, but that shovel's not going to protect you if things get too rough."

"Since I will not carry a gun, my boy will have to protect me."

Nick flinched when he heard that, more out of surprise than anything else. Stasys's voice hadn't been emotional or affectionate, but it was completely honest in the sudden faith he was showing to his son.

"Do you have a horse nearby, Pa?"

"Just the nag that pulls the cart."

"Well, make sure that nag is clear of the

fire. If things get too bad, I want you to head back here as fast as you can, saddle up that nag, and get the hell out of here. We'll meet up again at Trader's Crossing."

"You mean the place where you and those no-good friends of yours robbed that store?"

Nick rolled his eyes. "Yeah. That's the place."

# TWENTY-SEVEN

The sheriff's office was within spitting distance of Ellis Station's bigger saloons. It made it easier for the law to respond to the fights and complaints that inevitably came from that part of town and it also allowed Sheriff Bristow to keep an eye on some of the larger trouble spots without having to leave the comfort of his desk.

Of course, neither of those things meant much to Nick as he hurried to get to the modest little building across the street from those saloons. Since this was the busiest part of town, it made things rather difficult for him in his current situation.

"There is the sheriff's office," Stasys said from the shadows of the alley where Nick had brought them. "Why do we stop here?"

"Because of him," Nick replied, stabbing a finger out to point to a man with stringy blond hair and painfully reddened skin.

"Who is that?" Catherine asked.

Nick studied the man in the distance and whispered, "I don't know for certain, but he's not joining in on any of the revelry and he's obviously not moving from that spot. He's also got a gun."

"You noticed all that just since we got here?"

Nick looked over to Catherine and winked. "Years of practice."

But Stasys didn't seem impressed. Instead, he stood in his spot with his arms folded sternly across his chest. "I still don't know why we stop."

"Because they're waiting for us," Nick explained. "After what happened at your place, there's bound to be some commotion." Squinting at the street and the constant flow of people walking from one saloon to another, he asked, "Why isn't there any commotion?"

"Maybe they didn't hear the shots," Catherine offered.

"Could be. The cabin is a ways from here." Although the flames had already consumed that cabin and were dying off, Nick decided not to dump salt on his father's wounds by pointing that out. "Still, I don't like the look of that one standing across the street. You two wait here and come to me when I signal you. Pa, keep an eye on her for me."

Stasys nodded and just missed the quick glance that Nick gave to Catherine, which told her that she was the one he wanted to be on guard duty. She nodded just to get him on his way, patting the gun tucked into one of the pockets of her skirt.

"Now comes the fun part," Nick said with a grin. And without another word or even a sound to mark his steps, he disappeared from the alley.

Stasys shook his head and let out a short, disapproving grunt. "He was always too good at sneaking around."

Concentrating on trying to spot where Nick had gone, Catherine said, "It sure comes in handy sometimes."

"Not for a man in a respectable job, it doesn't."

Catherine shook her head, knowing there wasn't anything she could say that would get Stasys to ease up on his son.

Now that she had a chance to observe the blond man across the street for a little bit, she could see what Nick had been talking about. People were going about their business as anyone might expect for a saloon district after dark, but that armed man didn't budge. Nobody on the street made eye contact with him. In fact, they seemed to go out of their way to avoid him.

There was no badge on his chest and no nonsense in his eyes as he gazed through everything else in his search of something — or someone — very specific. Catherine had to hand it to Nick. He sure had a good eye for spotting trouble.

Before she could get too nervous about the blond man's gaze lingering in her direction, the man was gone.

She hadn't seen much more than a flicker of motion as a shadow sprang to life behind the man across the street. There was a brief glimpse of one arm snaking around the man's throat and a hand clamping down over his mouth. After that, he twitched, started to go for his gun, and then was hauled back into the darkness.

Catherine had to blink a few times to make sure that she could trust her eyes. There wasn't even a trace of the man. For anyone just passing by that spot, that man hadn't even existed.

"Nicolai was like a rat," Stasys said. "No, no, no," he whispered while shaking his head. "A mouse. When we would go somewhere, he would always look for ways to sneak around and get places quicker than anyone else who just uses the streets. Yes," he added with a satisfied smile. "Like a mouse."

By the time Catherine got a look at the old man's face, she spotted Nick making his way back down the alley and coming up behind them.

"He was one of Red's men," Nick whispered.

Not surprised to have Nick creep up on him, Stasys asked, "How do you know?"

"I asked him." To Catherine, he said, "I know a back way to the sheriff's office and there isn't anyone else lurking there. Let's get moving before Red notices that his lookout isn't where he's supposed to be."

The three of them walked quickly through a series of alleys and crossed the street at a spot well away from the more populated spots. Another few twists and turns in the dark and they were soon coming up to the little building that housed the office of Sheriff Bristow.

They were approaching a side door to the sheriff's office when they heard what sounded like someone screaming at them from a few streets away.

"Don't mind him," Nick said as he nodded toward a lump squirming behind a stack of empty crates. "He's just got an aching head."

That lump was actually the man who'd

been standing lookout in the spot no more than ten paces from where he was now resting. His jacket had been tossed over him and he squirmed just enough to show that his shirt had been stripped off and torn so it could be used to tie his ankles and wrists together. Another wad of material was stuffed into his mouth.

"Here, Pa," Nick said as he handed over a pistol. "Since our lookout won't be needing it anymore, maybe you should take it."

Stasys refused with a stern, tight-lipped glare.

"Fine," Nick said as he started knocking on the side door. "Suit yourself."

The sound of knuckles rapping against the door rattled within the space between buildings. It also echoed on the other side of the door without generating so much as a footstep in reply. Nick's eyes narrowed and began darting back and forth between the door and the two people standing next to him.

He knocked again, louder this time, but with the same results.

"Maybe he is out," Stasys offered. "Perhaps he is looking at all the dead bodies left on what is left of my doorstep."

Nick shook his head. "There should be someone here. Even a deputy or someone to watch the office."

"There might not be a lot of deputies," Catherine offered. "With all the shooting and the fire, maybe the sheriff brought all his men along with him to check on it."

"That might be so," Nick said. "But in that case, he would have probably locked his doors."

Sure enough, the door had opened less than an inch after the last set of knocks. It wasn't much, but it was more than enough to prove that the door hadn't been latched or even pulled shut all the way. For a home or barn, it might not have been noteworthy. For a sheriff's office that contained weapons and a jail cell, it was downright strange.

"Take this, Pa," Nick said as he handed over the lookout's gun. This time Stasys took the weapon without a fuss.

Nick pushed open the door slowly. The hinges were well oiled and barely made a sound as they moved. Keeping one hand on the door and the other hand on his gun, Nick took a step inside and looked around.

The office was a mess. What few chairs there were had been tossed about and broken. A few desks were scattered about the room after having obviously been shoved from their normal spots. Gun cabinets had been broken and emptied. Everything that wasn't nailed down was either ripped up or tossed onto the floor.

Nick took all of this in quickly. He got all the way into the office and was about to check on his father and Catherine when he heard something drop in the next room. Holding his gun at hip level, Nick walked to the back of the office where a jail cell had been sectioned off by a small dividing wall. The stench of death became more overpowering as Nick got closer to the cell. By the time he reached the bars, the place smelled more like a slaughterhouse.

The cell was large enough to hold four or five men and two rickety cots. Almost twice that amount of men lay inside the cell. Some leaned against the cots with their arms and legs splayed out to the sides as if they'd lost all control of them. Others were piled up on the floor or propped against the back wall. Blood pooled onto the floor, leaking from several gunshot wounds. Most of those wounds were in the men's heads and chests. Even though the men's eyes were open, they were clouded and lifeless. The skin of their hands and faces had already become waxy and bruised.

"Aw Jesus," Nick said under his breath as he spotted the badges pinned to some of the men's chests.

All of the men were of solid build with wide shoulders and muscled arms. Their faces ranged from lean to squared off at the jaw and not one of them could have been more than twenty-five years old. Faces tilted up at awkward angles and hands lay stuck to the floor with thick, pasty blood. The deputies had been good men, according to what little Nick had heard about them. As for the rest, they were probably just in the wrong place at the wrong time.

The cell's door was locked and the keys weren't anywhere in sight. They might have been somewhere in the other room or possibly in a desk drawer, but Nick knew that finding those keys wouldn't make a bit of difference. Those men were dead and, by the looks of it, they'd been dead for a while now.

In fact, now that he was staring through the bars and examining the grisly scene in front of him, it appeared as though the bodies had been occupying their spots on the floor since well before Nick had come along. He straightened up and shifted on the balls of his feet to examine the rest of the room.

The cell took up most of the space behind that dividing wall. There was, however, a small room at the end that Nick had overlooked. It was just a square nook facing the cell, intended to seat one man on a stool to watch over the prisoners. This one man, as opposed to the ones in the cell, was alive and kicking. He was also looking at Nick over the top of the shotgun pressed against his shoulder.

"Red sends his regards," the man said.

With the image of those dead bodies still fresh in his mind and the smell of all that blood thick in his nostrils, Nick wasn't about to make a mistake and wind up on the floor in that cell. He didn't take the time to utter one word before dropping to one knee and squeezing his trigger.

The shotgun went off. Its thunder enveloped the blast from Nick's Schofield and sent a payload of lead through the empty space Nick had been occupying before seeking lower ground. Nick's luck held, since the shotgun had been loaded with larger rounds intended to do more damage in a smaller area, as opposed to smaller buckshot, which spreads out over a larger space. The grape-sized bullets burned through the air and clanged off the iron bars at Nick's back.

The man in the alcove was lucky as well. If Nick's shot hadn't punched into the frame of the narrow room's entrance, it would have drilled a messy hole through the man's side.

Still, some men were luckier than others.

"You had your shot," Nick said as he aimed his Schofield at a spot directly between the man's eyes. "Since I've got five left and I'm not about to let you reload, you might as well toss that weapon."

The man did as he was told and leaned out of the alcove to pitch the shotgun so it skidded across the floor and out of Nick's reach. He kept his body turned sideways so he could lean against the alcove's entrance. That was also a good way to keep his shoulder holster out of Nick's sight.

Nick squared his shoulders and put his back to the cell. He took a moment to study the little room where the man was standing. Then he took a second glance at the man himself. "Warren Wheatley? Is that you?"

The man nodded once.

"It's been a while," Nick said.

The thin mustache on Warren's face was sculpted with a generous amount of wax. Another patch of hair sprouted just beneath his bottom lip like a bit of grease that had been smeared on with the tip of one finger. His eyes started to twitch as Nick drew closer. Reflexively, Warren eased back into the alcove. "It has been a while. I think the last time I saw you was in the Dakotas."

"It sure was. When I saw you there, I knew Red was keeping an eye on me. Since I doubt you've joined up with the law, I'd say you're still working with that bastard."

"He pays well," Warren said with a shrug.

"I'll bet he does," Nick said disgustedly. "But he must also be getting crazy in his old age. Killing lawmen is a quick way to the end of a short rope. It's not his style."

Warren shook his head. "No. It's yours." With that, he snapped his hand up and out to grab hold of a rope that was hanging along the inside of the alcove's wall.

Nick couldn't see the rope from where he was standing. He also couldn't see the hole in the ceiling where the rope led up and out of the room. And he sure as hell couldn't see what the rope was attached to, but did hear the bell start clanging almost loud enough to wake the men stretched out in the nearby jail cell.

As Nick lunged forward, his mind raced to figure out what had happened. It didn't take long for him to guess that the bell was designed as an alarm to be triggered by the guard in case one of the prisoners acted up too badly. That only left one question in his mind once he'd grabbed hold of Warren's shirt and pulled him out of the alcove.

"Why kill these men and put them in here?" Nick snarled.

Warren smirked and replied, "You'll find out soon enough."

Jamming the barrel of his pistol under Warren's chin, Nick pushed hard enough to force Warren's head back to its limit. "Why pull that alarm?"

"It's to let folks know about what you did."

"You were the one sitting with the bodies when I got here."

"And who's to say anyone will believe you, Graves? After all, you're a wanted fugitive with a bounty notice in this very office. That's plenty reason to want these deputies dead. Me, Red, and the rest of us have been doing our best to help around here. We've been warning the good folks about vermin like you."

Nick's eyes widened as he put all the pieces together. "Red's crazy. He can't think this will work."

Warren looked up, traced the bell cord hanging down from the ceiling, and stared at the wooden planks overhead as if he could see the clapper that was still clanging against polished brass. "You hear that? Those are the sounds of your very own jury coming to see what kind of man you truly are." As Nick's barrel pressed up even harder against his chin, Warren spoke in a torrent of words that flooded out of him.

"It's too late to stop this now," Warren sputtered. "You can start running or you can wait for Red and the others to finish you off, but it's all over for you! Your reckoning is coming for you."

Nick tightened his grip on Warren's shirt and threw him toward the cell. Warren's feet almost didn't touch the floor before he bounced against the iron bars hard enough to rattle them in their mountings. Already, the sounds of shouting and frenzied movement were making their way into the office from the streets outside.

As soon as Warren got his footing, he pushed himself back a few more steps from Nick and reached for the gun holstered under his left shoulder.

Without taking his eyes from Warren's face, Nick slapped the man's hand away from that shoulder holster as if he was swatting a fly. He used that same hand to grab a fistful of Warren's hair and shove his face against the bars.

"You want a reckoning?" Nick asked. "Then you sit in that cell with the men you killed and watch them rot for a little while."

"Red's gonna kill you, you murdering —"

Nick cut him short by yanking Warren's head back and then slamming it into the bars. "Shut up and unlock that door."

Warren fumbled in his pockets a bit before producing a single key that was the size of a man's finger. His hands were trembling as he tried fitting the key into the lock, but he eventually got it open.

Making sure to knock Warren into the bars a few more times along the way, Nick eventually got him through the door and shoved him into the cell. He then pulled the door shut and twisted the key that Warren had left in the lock.

Warren was slipping on blood by his second step into the cell. His arms started flailing and his legs both went in opposite directions as his heel found a particularly thick crimson puddle. He fell over onto his side, which brought Warren face to waxen face with several of the dead lawmen.

Holding the jail key in front of him, Nick said, "I wasn't completely sure you'd killed those deputies. Or even locked them in there. Not until you took this out of your pocket, that is."

Warren shook his head and crawled as close to the bars as he could. "That won't matter. Everything you do from here on will just put another nail in your coffin. Red'll be running this town before sunup."

But Nick had already turned his back on the cell and was rushing toward the side door. The closer he got to the door, the more noises he could hear from the streets. To add to the chaos, Warren was screaming from his cell.

"Before sunup!" Warren shouted. "You hear me, you murdering son of a bitch?"

Catherine was peeking through the door, but hadn't come into the office. She was holding her gun at the ready and watching the alley.

"What happened in there?" she asked the moment Nick was close enough to hear her. "There was an alarm and now people just started shouting about some deputies getting killed. I think someone found the bodies by that cabin."

Nick stepped out of the sheriff's office. "They already know about the deputies?"

Stasys's eyes snapped over toward Nick and he looked over his son from head to toe. "What happened? Were you hurt?"

"Not me," Nick said, stepping out to get a look down the alley. "It's the sheriff's men. They're dead."

"All of them?"

Nick was already rushing to the opening of the alley and studying the street as he replied, "Looked like all of them. Plus there were some others killed for good measure."

"Oh my God," Catherine said.

Stasys crossed himself and backed away from the door.

All the sounds of revelry were gone. The pianos had stopped playing. The singers had stopped singing and the drunks had stopped screaming at each other. All of the activity going on now had a serious edge to it and more of the attention was getting focused upon the sheriff's office.

Nick had his back pressed up against the building neighboring the sheriff's office so he could watch the street that passed in front of it. The saloon district was growing more and more crowded by the second. A mess of people moved to and fro like fish caught up in a powerful current. All the while, those people talked about murdered lawmen and a killer on the loose.

When he felt something brush against his back, Nick twisted around and almost shoved his gun barrel into Catherine's ribs.

"What's going on, Nick?" she asked. "What happened in there?"

"The deputies were dead when I got there. One of Red's men was waiting for me."

"Was he one of the ones who came to my

house?" Stasys asked.

"No, but he was definitely one of Red's. I crossed paths with him a while back in the Dakotas. Near as I can figure, Red Parks has been gathering up men and trying to make his presence known in towns from here to Wyoming. It must not have taken long after I was run out of Montana that the folks there got sick of Red's ways. I don't know if they found out about all he'd done, but it was only a matter of time before they saw how much blood he was spilling and stopped letting him run roughshod anywhere he pleased.

"Up until a few years ago, I thought that Red had finally been strung up or gotten himself shot. Then I heard he'd started pulling some men together and was headed into Jessup." Locking eyes with Catherine, he said, "That's what I was doing there when we met the first time. I was after Red and meant to put him in the ground before he finished whatever he wanted to do. It seemed that Skinner had gotten to him first, so I figured that business was finally done."

"Who is this Skinner person?" Stasys asked.

"One of the men I used to ride with." Before his father could say another word, Nick added, "Skinner and plenty of others had scores to settle with Red, so I didn't have any trouble believing that Red was laying in that grave outside of Jessup.

"Once the scouts started showing up and I noticed the men keeping watch over me again, I knew Red had to be alive. All those men acted the same and hunted the same. They were all trained by Red . . . just like I was."

Catherine was pressed up against Nick as if he was the only thing from keeping her from being swept away by the madness growing in the streets. Behind her, Stasys paced and occasionally took a look at the chaos for himself before muttering in his native tongue.

The growing crowd had parted a bit and started moving toward the sheriff's office. In their wake, there was one man who didn't seem half as worked up as everyone else around him. That man had the lean profile and sharp eyes of someone with a purpose. Those things alone made him stand out from the crowd that was screaming and waving their fists out of blind anger and confusion.

"The gravedigger's son killed those deputies!" the man across the street shouted toward the crowd. "I saw him do it! He even killed another innocent man who went in there to help!"

Hearing that, the crowd started moving toward the sheriff's office with a few armed men stepping to the front. They took hesitant steps toward the office and retreated. A few of them looked back to the man Nick had spotted.

"We ain't seen any bodies," someone said.

The man stepped forward, allowing Nick to see his stringy blond hair and the reddened sunburnt skin of his face and neck.

"That's Bo," Stasys whispered. "He was one of the men threatening Mr. Abernathy."

"You heard the alarm!" Bo shouted. "That means someone busted out of the jail or that one of them deputies needs help. I already been in there! I saw them all piled in that cell. Someone go in there and see for yourselves if you don't believe me!"

Two men separated from the crowd, drew their guns, and approached the door to the sheriff's office. If their eyes hadn't been focused so intently on that door, they would have easily spotted Nick and Catherine watching from the shadows.

Stepping back into the alley, Nick said, "Catherine, you need to take my father back to the room and barricade yourself in like I showed you."

"What room?" Stasys asked.

"It's at the hotel on Masonry Row."

The old man shook his head. "I have a better place, where we won't need to barricade anything. Nobody will know where to look."

Nick looked over to his father for a moment before realization shone in his eyes. "You mean your bank vault?"

Stasys smiled and nodded. "Ask John Allen. He will tell you where it is."

"Good enough. I'll come and find you when this is over." As he spoke, Nick shoved Catherine and Stasys down the alley and away from the growing noise of the crowd. "If I'm not back by morning, then get out of town as soon as you can without being spotted." Before his father could protest, Nick added, "If things don't get straightened out here and now, this place won't be fit to live in."

Although Catherine moved along, she struggled to get a good look at Nick's face. "What's going on, Nick? What bank vault are you talking about? What the hell is happening? Where am I going?"

"Pa will explain the vault to you along the way." Pausing for a moment, Nick took hold of Catherine's face and leaned in to kiss her.

Their lips met and locked together in a

way that made everything else going on around them melt away. With their hearts pounding and the blood racing through their veins, the heat that passed between them was enough to set off a spark. Then, all too quickly, their kiss was over.

"Please, Catherine," Nick said. "Just go with him and wait for me to get you. I need to pay Red one last visit."

There was so much more that Catherine wanted to say, but Nick had already rushed back to the opening of the alley. Besides, with the fire of that last kiss still burning on her lips, she probably couldn't have strung together enough words to make a complete sentence.

"Come now," Stasys said as he pulled her away from Nick and the screaming confusion of the crowd. "Those people are shouting for blood. We must get away from them."

"But Nick is —"

"He can handle himself," the old man said resignedly.

# Twenty-Eight

Nick could feel the rage within that crowd. It grew like a storm brewing overhead and he knew all too well that it was only going to get worse. Even as he heard the footsteps moving around inside the sheriff's office and the raised voices as the locals found the grisly mess inside the jail cell, Nick kept his eyes focused on Bo, who was still across the street.

Squirming in his boots, Bo was so anxious to get moving that he could barely stand it. Nick could have read that on him from a mile away. As soon as the locals came rushing out of the sheriff's office, all of that anxiousness and rage boiled over.

"They're in there!" one of the locals said. "Not just deputies, but Dave Winslow and a few of the workers from the Saunders Hotel! I saw 'em with my own eyes! There's even a fella still alive who saw it all happen!"

"Who did it?" Bo shouted.

"He says Nick Graves did it. He says the killer's still right here in town!"

"Everybody stay put," Bo said. "I'll find Sheriff Bristow!"

More and more people were gathering outside the sheriff's office. For the moment, they were still shocked and confused by what they were hearing. More of the locals ventured into the office a few at a time. Every so often, angry shouts or screams came from inside.

Nick was no longer in the alley. The moment Bo took off running down the street, Nick had taken off after him. He moved like just another one of the shadows, following Bo as he dashed across two more streets as if the devil himself was chasing him. Every now and then, Bo would toss a glance over his shoulder, but any of the people he saw were on their way to the brewing mob in front of the sheriff's office.

Nick had no trouble at all following Bo straight to the Saunders Hotel.

Bo jumped up the few steps leading to the front door and rushed inside. He was in such a hurry that he didn't even bother shutting the door behind him.

"They found them," Bo said breathlessly as he made it into the dining room, which now substituted as a meeting area for half a dozen armed men.

Red Parks stood at the head of the table. Instead of place settings or bowls of food, the table was covered with tools of Red's trade. There were rifles, shotguns, boxes of ammunition, and even a few knives. Along the edge of the table, there were ten burlap hoods with square holes cut out of them right where a man's eyes would be. There were also lengths of rope by each hood, laid out like forks beside a plate.

"They found the bodies?" Red asked.

Bo nodded. "They're at the sheriff's office right now, hollering and raising hell."

"They'll get plenty of hell. What about Graves?"

"I didn't see him, but Warren pulled the alarm, so he must have been there."

Red didn't look pleased about that, but he nodded to assure his men. "We'll find him." Sucking in a deep breath, Red took the masks and tossed one to each man. "Once those locals get a look at what we done to the poor souls in that cell, they'll be begging for someone to set things right."

"And that's where we come in," said one of the others as he caught his mask and pulled it over his head.

"That's right," Red answered. "Hell, there

sure ain't anyone else left to fit the bill. Tonight marks the first ride of the Ellis Station Vigilance Committee. By this time in a month or two, we'll be the only law this town will ever need. A few months after that and we can take our pick of which town to take next.

"You men that have been with me for a while will be glad to know the glory days are coming back. And for those of you who have just joined up, you'll find out what real power is. Once this Committee takes its proper place here, we'll have more say of what goes on than any sheriff, mayor, or marshal ever could."

Red pulled his mask over his face and tied one of the lengths of rope around his neck to secure the burlap good and tight. His eyes burned from behind the square holes in the rough fabric like a demon peering out from the gates of Hades. "After tonight," he said in a muffled voice, "this Committee will make the laws and enforce them without ever having to abide by them. And God help anyone who gets in our way."

" 'Anyone who gets in your way'?" came a voice from the hotel's entrance. "I guess that would be me."

The men all turned in the direction of that voice. Some of them wore their masks and others were in the process of putting them on. Every last one of them, however, looked at Nick Graves with murder in their eyes.

Nick stood in the doorway to the dining room, returning each of the other men's stares as he slowly looked around the room. His holster was laying across his belly and both arms hung motionless at his sides.

"I'm surprised you didn't turn tail and run, Nicky," Red said. "After playing dead for so many years, I'd have thought that's what you're best at."

"If you wanted to call me out for what happened to Owen, you didn't need to go through so much trouble."

For a moment, Red stared at Nick as if he didn't have the first notion of what he was talking about. Then Red nodded and said, "That's just icing on the cake. You'll get what you got coming, but once you're dead, I'll be ready to lead my Committee again. And to get my Committee rolling, I need to set us up as a real bunch of heroes. You were a godsend in that regard, kid. Not only are you a wanted man with one hell of an impressive past, but you were the one wanted man who I knew I could draw to a specific spot at a specific time. After that," Red said as he opened his arms proudly, "I work my magic. Soon I'll be right back up to where we used to be. Remember those days, Nicky? Remember when we ruled that town without answering to anyone else?"

"I remember riding with a bunch of murdering bastards who were worse than any gang of outlaws I've ever heard of."

Red shook his head. "You know better than that. You were there. Don't tell me you wouldn't like to go back to the way it was. Well, while you've been playing dead and killing your friends, I've been coming up with ways to make things even better than how they were. All I need is someone to get that ball rolling. That's you, my friend."

"Where's the sheriff?" Nick asked.

"The sheriff? He's passed out in a gutter after you bushwhacked him earlier tonight." Shaking his head, Red grinned beneath his burlap mask. "Hell of a thing you did to all them poor folks down in that jail cell. Did you get a look at your handiwork?"

"Yeah."

"Then you can imagine how much folks will appreciate us bringing you in. Sheriff Bristow may be a pain-in-the-ass lawman, but he'll vouch for me once I bring in the man who killed his deputies. Once he's put me in the good graces of this town, I won't need him around.

"Thanks to my own little rumormonger,

damn near everyone in town thinks the killer of those poor deputies is you, so I'll make you an offer. You come along with us nice and quiet and we won't even bother hunting down your pappy and that lady of yours. Going against us is pointless by now. I'm an hour from having this town eating from my hand and after that, my little Committee will be as well known as the Pinkertons. Can't you imagine that?"

"You want me to go along so you can hang me?" Nick asked. "And then do to Catherine what was done to Missy Weyland?"

"She'll go free. Your future won't be so good, but I promise you both her and your pappy will go free."

Silence rolled through the room like a cloud of smoke. Red and Nick locked eyes and the rest of the gunmen waited to see what would come of it. Finally, Nick's voice slithered up from the back of his throat.

"A dead man's promise ain't worth shit, Red. You taught me that."

Red slammed the table with an open hand and said, "All right, then. If none of you men are up to killing this son of a bitch, then you got no place on my Committee!"

None of the men seemed overly eager to follow up on that, so Red drew his gun and got the fire burning.

Nick's hand flashed to his holster and he hooked his fingers under the grip of his gun. The special modifications to the barrel and holster twisted the weapon into the palm of his hand so he could lift it out and slip a finger around the trigger. The practiced motion happened in a fraction of a second. As Nick aimed and fired, he turned to the side and started walking into the room.

Red's gun barked once and sent a round through the air where Nick had been standing a heartbeat ago. The rest of the men around the table filled their hands with guns from their holsters or from the selection spread out in front of them. The quickest among them fired before they even had Nick in their sights, filling the air with black gritty smoke without doing much else.

From his spot next to the doorframe, Nick picked out the closest armed man he could see. He pointed the Schofield and squeezed the trigger, carving a hole through that man's chest.

Bo had picked up a shotgun from the table and thumbed back both hammers. His breathing became frantic as more and more shots crackled through the room. Another man to his right was knocked over as the back of his head exploded onto the wall behind him. When Bo looked toward the front of the room, he saw Nick getting to his feet as if he had all the time in the world.

Letting out a scream from the bottom of his lungs, Bo pulled both of the shotgun's triggers. He saw Nick lunge away from the doorway, but it was too late to shift his aim. The shotgun belched its smoky cargo with a thundering roar, turning a sizable chunk of the doorframe into sawdust and splinters.

Nick extended one hand to stop himself abruptly and bumped one shoulder against a wall. From there, he bent his elbow and took a shot at Bo, delivering a chunk of lead into the man's gut. He could tell right away that Bo still had some fight in him, so Nick shot another hole into Bo's chest to drain it right out.

As Bo dropped, the rest of the men were firing wildly and fighting to see through the thick smoke that now filled the air. That smoke brought tears to their eyes and coated the backs of their throats with a foul-tasting grit.

By the time the man closest to Bo had swiped at his eyes with the back of his hand, he saw a tall figure walking straight toward him.

"Over here!" the man shouted as he fired a few more wild shots from his pistol. "He's right over here!"

Nick had one bullet left. Just to make sure he didn't waste it, he jammed the Schofield's barrel under the screaming man's ribs and pulled the trigger. There was a muffled *thump* and a spray of blood as the bullet lifted the man off his feet and tore its way out through his back.

Without missing a beat, Nick calmly took the gun from the dead Committee member and pushed the body aside. The pistol felt odd in his hand, but that only served to remind Nick about what had been taken from him so many years ago. He tightened his grip around the gun and felt it shift to one side due to his wounded fingers resting uncomfortably on the handle.

The sounds of coughing and frenzied breathing mixed with the deafening roar of gunfire. With every one of his senses focused upon his surroundings, Nick could even pick out the sound of one man pulling his trigger out of sheer panic, causing the hammer to drop again and again on to empty bullet casings. One of the remaining men was simply praying in a continuous, trembling voice.

After compensating for the awkward feel of the gun in his hand, Nick extended his arm and sent the praying man to deliver his words to the Almighty in person.

As Nick walked around the table, he saw one of the remaining men was on his knees, fumbling to reload his weapon. Staring the man straight in the eyes, Nick stood like the Reaper himself as he waited for the man to shove a few rounds into his gun and hurriedly close the cylinder.

With a shaking hand, the kneeling man was able to lift his newly reloaded pistol and take aim before Nick fired a shot that tunneled through his neck.

Shifting the gun a bit, Nick pulled his trigger again and put the man down properly.

One more figure stood at Red's side. Instead of trying to use the gun that fit so terribly in his wounded hand, Nick bent his elbow and then snapped his arm out like a whip. The borrowed pistol left Nick's hand and flew across the room to catch the other man on the left temple. Nick had been aiming for the man's forehead, but the results wound up being just as good. As he crumpled over, he seemed grateful to be out of the fight.

Nick took hold of his modified Schofield and emptied the shells from its cylinder. As he slowly walked toward the head of the table, he slipped fresh rounds into their chambers.

Red stood where he'd been before the

room had filled with the stench of blood, smoke, and the piss that now ran down the twitching legs of several new Committee members. Red's hands were flat against the top of the table and his arms were the only things propping him up. Breathing was getting harder and harder for him and each time he exhaled, pink foam dribbled out of his mouth.

Red's hand was on top of his gun, but he seemed to have forgotten about the weapon. All he wanted just then was to quench his thirst for a full breath.

Shaking his head once more, Red looked up at Nick just as the modified Schofield's barrel snapped shut. "Wh . . . what . . . what . . . ?"

"I got you with the first shot," Nick said quietly. "Through the lungs, by the look of it. Might have clipped your heart as well."

Red looked down, wheezing as he spotted the dark crimson stain that had spread well across the front of his shirt.

"Oth . . . other men will come looking," Red spat out. "I've got . . . I've got friends, lawmen, and pl . . . plenty more that owe me. They'll hear about th . . . this and come to make sure you pay. You and anyone you f . . . fucking care about will pay."

With his left hand, Nick reached out and

gently pushed Red back. That was all it took for Red to drop to the floor and slump against the legs of a chair. Pink foam coated his chin and his eyes were barely able to focus on Nick's face. He tried to talk, but the drop to the floor robbed him of every bit of steam that he had left.

Nick sighted along the Schofield's barrel and pulled the trigger.

## Twenty-Nine

When Nick made it back to the sheriff's office, it looked as though most of the town was gathered outside of it and screaming for blood.

The only reason the group hadn't charged into the streets on their own to look for Nick was that they had someone there to stop them. That someone stood in front of his office, shouting at the top of his lungs to keep everyone in line.

"We can't get anything done this way," Sheriff Bristow hollered. "I need you all to quiet down so I can hear what happened from someone who knows!"

"There's a man inside who saw everything," someone from the crowd said.

"Then I need to talk to him without having everyone run off to do something stupid. I don't know if Nick Graves truly did this, but whoever did is a dangerous man. The last thing I need is another body to hand over to Harold Abernathy."

"I didn't do any of it," Nick said as he stepped out with both arms held high.

Everyone wheeled around as whispers rippled through the crowd. In a matter of seconds, those whispers changed into shouts.

"String him up!"

"He's a damn murderer!"

Sheriff Bristow's eyes were blackened and smoldered under a bloody forehead. His thick, drooping mustache nearly covered his whole mouth. When he stepped forward, his hands went reflexively toward the double-rig holster strapped around his waist. Although the crowd still grumbled and spat hateful words at Nick, they parted like the Red Sea to let Sheriff Bristow walk through them.

"I spent a good part of the night knocked out behind a feed store after taking a shot on the back of the head from the butt of a pistol," Sheriff Bristow snarled. "Several folks told me I've got you to thank for that, so I wouldn't suggest this as the time to try anything funny."

Nodding, Nick said, "I understand, Sheriff, but I'm not the one who hit you. I'm also not the one who killed any of those men in there."

"There's a man in there who says otherwise. He's been screaming it since I stepped in to see what happened."

"Did you let him out?"

"He's out of the cage, but I got someone keeping an eye on him."

"Good," Nick said. "Because he's the man you're after. Well, one of them, anyhow."

"And why should I believe you?"

"Because there's no way I could have gotten the drop on all those men and gunned them down before they got to me. See for yourself." Saying that, Nick moved his hands so the sheriff could get a better look at them.

When he spotted the gnarled remains of Nick's fingers, Bristow winced. "Good Lord. What the hell happened to you?"

"Mining accident," Nick lied. Most of the folks who met him gave that as their first guess to the source of his wounds. Those words served their purpose well enough now and seemed to answer Sheriff Bristow's question to his satisfaction.

"I see you still carry a gun."

"You're free to examine it, but I don't think it's got enough to it to knock out a man like yourself."

The sheriff took the gun from Nick's holster and looked at it as if he was examining a gutted skunk. To the unknowing eye, the pistol looked like it belonged in a trash heap. The barrel appeared to have been melted down after being dropped into an open forge. The handle, although specifically carved for Nick's hand, looked like a dog had gnawed on it and spit it out. Bristow opened the cylinder and emptied the bullets onto the ground.

"I didn't get a real good look at who hit me," Bristow said, "but I saw a pistol being swung at my head and it sure as hell wasn't this one." He started to walk away from Nick and stopped after four paces. "As for the rest of it . . ." Bristow tossed the gun toward Nick with a snap of his wrist.

Although Nick reflexively grabbed for the Schofield, he closed his hand around the grip just enough for the weapon to slip through what was left of his fingers and drop to the ground with a dull *thump.* Embarrassed, he bent to pick up the gun and slip it clumsily back into its holster.

"No offence, mister," Sheriff Bristow said, "but I wouldn't have deputies working for me that could be killed by a man with half a gun hand." Turning to the crowd, Bristow asked, "What about the rest of you? Do you still want me to hang this man on account of some rumors and quick accusations?"

Nobody spoke up. In fact, the people in the crowd who knew Nick's father looked ashamed to be standing there.

Bristow turned to Nick. "You look like you've been in a fight. Care to explain that to me?"

"I was nearly killed by some men at the Saunders Hotel. They burned down my father's house to force me to take the fall for all of this. They started fighting among themselves, so I snuck out."

"Hell, with all the screaming that's been going on around here, I could have missed the Second Coming. Was anyone hurt?"

"There was an awful lot of shooting," Nick replied with a nod. "I don't know about my father."

Sheriff Bristow looked over his shoulder at the crowd. Although there were still plenty of people outside the office, the more boisterous among them had already gone back to their saloons. "I'll need to sort through this mess, but you're free to go. I'd appreciate your help in letting me know where to find those men who did this."

"Of course, sheriff. I can tell you right where to look. But first, there's some personal business I need to tend to."

It was bordering on that time of night where

it started to feel more like morning. The sun wasn't in the sky just yet, but its presence was near enough to be felt and some of the chill was starting to fade from the air. The humidity formed a mist that rolled over the cemetery in a way that kept most folks away from the cross-studded field out of fear of the ghosts that surely had to be there.

Nick only had to look around once to know he wasn't being followed. Apart from the cabin in the distance, there wasn't anywhere for anyone to hide. Actually, he knew that wasn't exactly the case.

After a few minutes of wandering up and down the rows, Nick came to a stop in front of one particular headstone. There was a name inscribed on it: JOHN ALLEN. Like all the other stones in the cemetery, the letters were carved in Stasys's distinctive style. Bending at the knees, Nick ran his fingers along the edge of the grave until he found the spot he'd been looking for.

Digging his hand through the thin layer of dirt and sod, he kept going until his fingers curled beneath the wooden panel beneath it. He pulled the panel up and to the side. It came away much quicker once he got some help from the two sets of hands emerging from underground.

Catherine poked her head up first, gasping for air. "Get me out of here. Right now!"

Extending his hand to her, Nick pulled Catherine out and lifted her from the hole in the ground. "Pa never did trust banks. He said that his money was safer in a hole in the ground."

"But you were the one who called it our own bank vault," Stasys said as he climbed out of the hole and moved the panel back into place. "I trust it is safe to show my face again?"

"Actually, Pa, I need to talk to you about that."

"What is it, *sunus*?"

"I told the sheriff that you were killed and that I needed to take your body up north to be buried."

Stasys's eyes widened and he nearly stumbled back over the marker in front of his trap door. "What? Why would you lie like that?"

"Red's gone and so are most of his men, but those are just the ones here. There are more of them. Knowing Red, he even told somebody that you were here and that you were my father."

"You say that like I am already gone."

Nick shrugged and looked his father in the eyes. "That's how it's got to be, Pa. We all need to move on and put this place behind us. You can start up somewhere else and have a good life. Take another name and nobody will be the wiser. I just . . . I just can't leave you unprotected."

Although he wanted to fight about it, Stasys grumbled and ran his hands over the top of his head. "I will go on one condition."

"Name it, Pa, but just be quick about it."

"I know you don't like to see the ocean after losing your mother on the trip to this country, but I have always loved the sea. Now that you don't need me to wait for you to show up again, I want to go to California to start this new life of mine."

"Wait for me? What do you mean?"

Stasys stepped up so he stood toe to toe with Nick. Looking up into his son's eyes, he took Nick's face in his hands and said, "I waited here because I wanted you to be able to find me when you decide to come home. We needed to have this time so we could put the past behind us. I would have preferred a quieter talk, but what can I do?"

Nick smiled at his father. It wasn't an amused smile or the expression he might wear when rolling his eyes or biting his tongue. It was a smile that reflected true joy which blossomed from the bottom of his heart. He hadn't felt that way toward his father since before he'd run off as a hot tempered kid with a stolen pistol wedged under his belt.

"You pick a spot on the coast," Nick said, "and I'll take you there. That is," he added while looking to Catherine, "if that's all right with you."

"After being stuck in that hole," Catherine said, "I'd agree to live in a swamp."

# EPILOGUE

Warren Wheatley hung from a gallows in the center of town. As a known associate of Red Parks, the closest he ever got to riding in Ellis Station's ill-fated Committee was the hood which covered his face and was held tight by the rope around his neck.

Things weren't quite back to normal, but folks were doing their best after all the blood had been cleaned up and the last guilty man had been put in his place. As for the other men found guilty in the shootings from two weeks ago, their places were in freshly dug holes in the field outside of town.

Just outside of that field, Nick Graves pulled back on his reins and brought the cart to a stop. Catherine sat beside him, wearing a hat she'd bought specifically for the trip to California. Climbing down from the back of the cart, Stasys lugged a heavy

435

bundle wrapped in a canvas sheet with him.

"Let me help you with that, Pa," Nick said as he set the brake and jumped down.

Swatting his son away as soon as he was close enough to do so, Stasys hefted the bundle over one shoulder and carried it around the cart. "You should worry about those horses, instead. They should eat better since they have a long trip ahead of them." He paused in front of the horses and scratched their ears. The animals waggled their heads and snuffed his hand appreciatively. "What are their names?"

Nick smirked and said, "Rasa and Kazys."

"Those are names from the old country."

"I know, Pa," Nick said proudly.

As his mouth twisted into a disgusted frown, Stasys said, "That is terrible! I know people with those names. You don't give people's names to animals. Fah!"

Nick let his smile fade away and bit his tongue while following behind his father, who carried his bundle to the freshly dug hole where Harold Abernathy was waiting.

The stout undertaker greeted Stasys with open arms poking out from rolled-up sleeves. His jacket was draped over one of the other tombstones. Other than that, he wore his normal attire of black pants, black vest and white shirt.

"Sorry I could not dig this grave, Mister Abernathy," Stasys said.

The undertaker waved off those words and then wiped some sweat from his brow. "I needed the exercise. Besides, under the circumstances, it wouldn't have been appropriate. You are supposed to be the one in that coffin, after all."

"About that," Nick said. "Is there anyone actually under there?"

Harold nodded. "Oh, yes. It's the man I found burned up inside Stan's house. He wasn't exactly the right size but, well, let's just say he wasn't too recognizable."

"Good enough. Let's get going."

Stasys shooed Nick aside as he removed the canvas to reveal a simple wooden cross with words on the front that had taken most of the last week for him to carve. The cross read: STASYS GRAVES — LOVING FATHER.

With about as much ceremony as he would spend on driving a fence post into the ground, Stasys planted the marker into the spot over what was supposed to be his own grave. He then took the shovel from Harold Abernathy and knocked the marker a little deeper with a few solid taps.

"There," Stasys said. "Now I am officially dead."

"I'll miss you, Stan," the undertaker said.

"Good luck in California."

As the other two shook hands, Nick examined the letters that his father had so carefully carved into the cross. All this time, Stasys wouldn't let Nick see what he was engraving. "I thought there would be more," he said.

Stasys walked over and put a hand on Nick's shoulder. "More? What, more?"

"I don't know, maybe something about *motina.*"

"Your mother will hear plenty from me when I see her again. Remember, *sunus,* what we write on these markers are for the living, not the dead."

When he stood up, Nick felt his father take hold of him by the arms and turn him around so he could face him head-on. "No matter how much trouble you give me," Stasys said. "No matter what I say or what I do, I will always be your *tevai.*"

Hearing the word for father spoken in their native language brought a whole new smile to Nick's face.

"I know, Pa."

Leaning in, Stasys glanced toward Catherine and added, "Now maybe someday you can make me a grandpoppa."

"Don't push it, old man."

Stasys smirked and waved one last time to

438

Harold Abernathy before climbing back onto the wagon.

Catherine sat waiting for Nick on the driver's seat. She was anxious to get to California, but he was even more anxious just to get close enough to brush his fingers against her cheek.

Although he was still a mourner by trade and would always take pride in practicing his crafts, Nick was more than happy to climb into the seat next to Catherine, snap the reins and put that cemetery behind him.

The past was the past and the dead would always be there to haunt him.

For Nick Graves, it was time to stop mourning and start living.